AF112849

INGRID DARLING

Nicole I. Burgess

INGRID DARLING

Copyright © 2025 by NBM Publishing, LLC
Third Edition, 2025

All rights reserved. No part of this book may be reproduced or used in any manner without written permission of the copyright owner except for the use of quotations in a book review.

Published by NBM Publishing
Chapel Hill, North Carolina
www.nbmbooks.com

This is a work of fiction. Names, characters, places, and incidents are either the product of the author's imagination or are used fictitiously. Any resemblance to actual persons, living or dead, events, or locales is entirely coincidental.

First edition published 2011
Second edition 2023
Third edition 2025

ISBN: 9798994453919

Cover design by NBM Publishing

To my friends and family, you are the inspiration for my art and the color on my canvas.

INGRID DARLING

Prologue

2 Days after Thanksgiving, 2009

I sat in the window seat, staring through the oval glass as clouds passed slowly by. I thought about how amazing planes were; how a single flight could take you from one time zone to another. Time was a funny thing in that it was only limited to what it was perceived to be. One minute could seem to last a lifetime, while one lifetime could seem to last a minute. I gazed down at the closed book resting on my thigh. I studied the cover, thinking about how Karl seemed to know me better than I knew myself and giving me this book was his way of telling me that I was still on my journey.

"The Alchemist," the woman to my left said, also looking at the book in my lap.

I smiled and nodded, glancing at her face. Tired eyes smiled back at me.

"Is it as intriguing as you make it seem?" She asked.

I returned my gaze to the book.

"It's perfect," I said.

"Well, that's an interesting response," she said. "What is it about?"

She pushed the wire frame glasses up the bridge of her nose and waited patiently for me to respond.

"It's about a young man who is on a journey to find an alchemist who can help him turn metal into gold, but what he learns along his path is that what is material will always be material, and what matters most is knowing who you are and following your heart."

The woman raised her eyebrows, the corners of her mouth dropping slightly.

"It sounds like a spiritual journey," she said.

I nodded.

"It sort of is."

"That reminds me of a passage from my favorite book," she said, facing away from me and resting her head back against her seat.

"What is that?" I asked.

"Even a mind that knows the path can be dragged from the path, the senses are so unruly. But he who controls the senses and recollects the mind and fixes it on me, I call him illumined."

"What book is that from?"

"Bhagavad-Gita," she said. "There are many paths one can take to get to that place. I imagine you are on your own journey?" She asked, closing her eyes.

I looked back to the book in my lap and thought about my past. Memories of the past four years flashed through my mind, washing over me like a flood of emotion. Each memory seemed to be its own path, with twists and turns, happy and sad, like a long road to self-discovery. But it hadn't ended for me yet. I was still on my journey.

"Yeah..." I said. "I guess I am."

I glanced out the window, looking at the clouds again. They reminded me of situations in life that seem to hover over us, clouding our judgment and blocking us from seeing who we really are. My vision had been cloudy for four years. I had spent four years of my life following others, trying to find satisfaction in material things, instead of finding treasure within myself.

    I sat in contemplation for several minutes. The woman had fallen asleep by now and I could hear a faint snore escape her breath every few seconds. I smiled and thought back to the message in the book; that you can't find love until you first find yourself.

    Sudden turbulence interrupted my thoughts and jolted the woman awake. She gripped the armrest waiting for it to pass. After a few rocks and bumps she seemed not to care anymore and fell back asleep. The fasten seat belt sign lit up and as I clicked mine closed, one more thought flashed through my mind:

    I wonder if James ever read that email.

INGRID DARLING

One

No one ever remembers the beginning. No one pays attention to the journey. Most people get so caught up in their own lives that they forget about how it began and why it's happening. I remember how my journey began.
It started in Raleigh, four years ago in the stairwell of Larks apartment. As always, it began with a choice. I could knock on the door and spend the next 24 hours on a feral binge with someone I was unsure of calling a true friend or I could go home and spend Thanksgiving Eve with my parents. As I stood there contemplating my decision, my focus turned towards the stars. Surely they would tell me what to do, I told myself. I stood for five minutes, vainly searching for an answer from above, and when it never came, I decided to knock on Lark's door.

Lark opened the door with a huge grin on her face. She was wearing jeans that were too tight for her plump frame and a dark blue tunic. Her hair looked like it had been dipped in motor oil, pulled into a side ponytail and resting on her shoulder.

"Ingrid! Come in!" She exclaimed.

The tacky outfit distracted me from listening to her rant about her day at work and the argument she'd had with her boss. She quickly mentioned that we would be walking to another apartment to meet up with some other people before continuing to rage about her job. I followed her out of her place and down towards the parking lot. I glanced at my car, feeling the sudden urge to jump in it and haul ass to my parents' house, but I turned my focus back to Lark as she described the crowd at the next

INGRID DARLING

apartment.

"They are not my friends," she emphasized for the ensuing ten minutes while explaining how she'd met them.

I didn't know why she cared so much about my opinion. I wasn't going to pass judgment on the people she chose to hang out with. As we neared the next apartment complex she continued to babble on about her boss as I trailed closely behind, still contemplating an escape. When we finally reached the apartment, she knocked on the door, leaning her body close to mine and suddenly lowering her voice.

"Remember Ingrid, these people are not my friends so don't tell anyone we're going to hang out with them" She whispered.

But when the door opened I would have guessed otherwise. A tall lanky guy appeared in the entrance wearing faded jeans and a plaid shirt. Oversized glasses sat at the edge of his nose. He smiled and opened his mouth to greet us, but Lark's shriek of excitement stopped him.

"Jonah!" She hollered, jumping to give him a hug.

Not her friends, huh? I thought, noting the similar reaction she had to me just ten minutes earlier.

She introduced me to Jonah who already seemed to know who I was. I guessed she'd played me up in some Jesus like way as she usually did, convincing people that I could possibly turn water into wine if I really wanted to. It always unnerved me that she idolized me in such a way. Idolatry only leads to disappointment.

She and I both grew up in North Carolina. Our parents were lawyers at the same firm and our families occasionally vacationed together. We went to the same private school from

INGRID DARLING

kindergarten through 12th grade, where she was two years ahead of me. We were strong academic students and had very active social lives. But after her tenth grade year, Lark started acting out. Her first boyfriend, whom she continued to refer to as the "love of her life" broke her heart, and though it had been several years, she was still struggling with the break up. She always said that relationships were the hardest to get over because attraction eventually became attachment and attachment was always the means to an end. Her attachment to her ex left her vying for attention from something else, and by the time we got to college, her attention turned to drugs. We had gone down different paths, but for some reason we continued to end up in the same room.

This room was small and cramped. And though there were only seven of us, Lark dragged me around the apartment introducing me to everyone so I wouldn't feel uncomfortable. Several minutes later I ended up in the armchair in the corner of the room, opposite the door. I made small talk with two people around me, not caring much about what was being said, as the conversation lacked stimulation. Lark sat on the couch smoking a cigarette, talking above everyone as if to remind us of her presence in the room. After a while I began to feel bored. The conversations became uninteresting and the people dull. Lark must have sensed my boredom because she whispered something to Jonah who disappeared for several minutes. When he returned, he took a seat beside Lark on the couch and the two busied themselves on the table in front of them.

A moment later she turned to face me, stuck out her hand and opened it. She was holding a red straw that looked as though it had been cut in half.

INGRID DARLING

"You wanna try?" She asked, grinning.

Her big eyes were heavily lined with black eyeliner. The dark blue eye shadow made her look more trashy than attractive, like she should have been on the corner selling her body instead of sitting in a dark room selling a soul.

My stomach tensed. I glanced around the room at the others, standing around the room chatting idly or loudly slurping their beer. It wasn't the peer pressure, because I had wanted to try it for some time. And even though I had prided myself in having gone years without "doing that", I wanted to see how different it really was. Most of my friends had done it, and though that was probably not the best reasoning, I was curious. Logic told me no. I'd even had a few opportunities to try, but I never took advantage. Once in high school, I opened the bathroom door at a party, only to check my hair and makeup, to find my friend and her boyfriend kneeling beside the sink cutting lines with their American Express cards. I was offered but said no:

"That's not really my cup of tea", I said, shutting the bathroom door behind me as I walked out.

I later discovered that my friend had a real lust for dust. She always came to class wiping her nose and leaving for the bathroom every fifteen minutes. Everyone in our class noticed how skinny she had gotten, but her addiction wasn't obvious considering how every girl at my high school had an eating disorder, so she was lucky to keep her secret and was private about her passions.

I had a few more opportunities at college, but every time I was offered, I declined. I liked my dignity and I didn't want to delve too far into the realm of the unknown. I didn't mind Mary Jane, who gave me the occasional high.

INGRID DARLING

I always thought: *what do I need Snow White for? I don't need seven dwarfs to keep me company.*

But here I would find myself, faced with six dwarfs and seven red straws. I looked down at Lark's outstretched hand. Her eyes were big and glassy.

"It's not that bad, you just saw me do it. Go ahead, indulge, Darling." She purred.

I looked at the straw she was holding. The decision reminded me of a movie I'd seen a few years ago: the red pill or the blue pill? I asked myself if I should stick to what I was used to, or if I should see how far Wonderland really went. I looked around the room, catching a glimpse of a cat that I hadn't noticed earlier. I watched it claw at the armrest on the other side of the couch. The sound of its nails digging into the fabric drowned out the chatter from the six other people in the room. I could feel them watching me, with drunken expressions on their sweaty faces, waiting for my decision, like six dwarfs waiting for me to join them so we could all hide in the woods with Snow White. I looked down at the table. There were three small white lines on a square mirror. I took a deep breath and had one more thought:

What is my mother going to think?

"Alright, let me see that straw."

I grabbed the straw from Lark's hand and held it up to my nose. Leaning over the table, I placed the end of the straw at the tip of the line. I inhaled across the line of cocaine and did the same for the other two, wiping my nose when I was done. I gripped the straw and smiled, sitting back in the armchair. The powder burned the inside of my nostril, dripping down the back of my throat, it was bitter. Several people in the room applauded me then continued to converse about college life. Lark pulled out a small plastic bag, filled to brim with cocaine, and passed it and the square mirror to Jonah.

"See, I told you it wasn't that bad." She said, wiping her nose.

Her pupils were dilated, huge.

"You're right. I don't know why I was so scared." I said, wiping my nose again.

I felt my nostril open wider, as if growing to inhale the damp air or another line of cocaine. A rush of exhilaration swept over my body and gave me a feeling of weightlessness. I wanted more. I wanted this feeling to last. Five lines later I found myself in the bathroom, fixing my hair and reapplying lip gloss. I blew a kiss to the mirror and walked out of the bathroom and into the kitchen. Lark, Jonah and the four others were standing in a circle, each holding a shot glass full of tequila. She handed me one and we toasted to the night. We were all ready to go out, all ready to party like the next day would never come.

Two

The next day came. And every day after that seemed to be the best party I'd ever been to. Thanksgiving break was over and I returned to my apartment near campus. I partied hard with my friends who did cocaine. Days flew by and nights thumped wildly until dawn. I was having so much fun and I didn't want it to end. I wanted to try everything and experience all that the world could offer. My college classes became less and less appealing, and then I stopped going altogether. Instead I would sleep all day, resting from the long night before, hoping my body would recover from the excessive drug intake so I could do it all over again the next night. My priorities were shifting. I was oblivious to the effect cocaine was having on my life.

Lark and I moved in together. It was probably not the best idea considering the fact that she and I each had a growing cocaine addiction. She started dating her dealer who would spend weeks at a time at our apartment. The three of us would stay up until sunrise, sometimes never sleeping, doing line after line, indulging in our lusts. I got a job at a pharmacy and would spend my after hours at a bar downtown, talking with Jonah who had been promoted to bar manager. We would occasionally hang out on the weekends at his apartment with Lark and her boyfriend, and the four of us would do lines until the sun came up. This continued for a few months. It was fun, carefree. I was enjoying myself and not thinking much about the consequences.

INGRID DARLING

In winter of 2005 Jonah moved into a house near downtown Raleigh. By the time February came, I was practically his roommate. We watched a lot of basketball and hockey in his newly constructed den which had been converted into a bar. The night the Hurricane's played in the Stanley Cup, he decided to throw a small party, so I hurried home to change after work then drove straight over to his house.

I parked my car in his gravel driveway and walked up the wooden steps to the front door. As I opened the front door, Jonah's cat dashed out, startling me. I made my way through the house towards the den, and my eye suddenly caught on a plaque above the doorway to the kitchen that I had never noticed before.

KNOW THYSELF

Is what it said. The words sent a familiar chill down my spine as I continued through the house. I rounded the corner and entered the den, and found four faces staring intently at the hockey game on the screen. Jonah and Lark stood behind the bar, Lark bent over the bar counter, inhaling a line of cocaine. She licked her fingers and groaned when the referee called a foul on a player. Shawn, her drug dealing boyfriend, sat on a bar stool in the corner of the room, an oversized sweatshirt covering his large frame. I walked in and sat my purse on an empty bar stool.

"Ingrid, you finally made it." Jonah said, giving me a high five over the bar.

Lark did another line, lifted her face and bounded around the bar towards me, wrapping me in a huge hug.

"I'm so glad you're here! How was work?" She exclaimed,

wiping her nose and pulling me to the other side of the room.

Shawn turned and greeted me then quickly turned his attention back to the game. Jonah passed me a beer from the box on the back counter.

"Awful." I said, opening the beer and taking a sip, I sat on a bar stool and focused on the TV.

We drank beer and talked, watching the hockey game. When the home team won, Jonah opened a bottle of champagne to celebrate. Lark pulled out a small bag and placed it on the counter, cutting two lines for each of us. We each took our lines, dancing and laughing around the bar. Shawn muted the TV and turned up the music on the stereo and I immediately recognized the Jimi Hendrix song that was playing. I pointed up to the ceiling and smiled at Jonah who was standing behind his bar, arms crossed over his chest.

He laughed and wiped his nose.

"Hendrix, good stuff."

Shawn swiveled in his bar stool towards Jonah.

"Oh yeah, great guitar player. And the guy was so far out. He thought the world's ills were because the planet's axis was off, like not perpendicular, so he was gonna straighten it out with music." He said, opening another beer and taking a sip.

I nodded in agreement. The cocaine was dripping down the back of my throat, opening my nostrils.

"He was just so all over the place with his guitar. He was in his own class." Jonah said pulling out a small bag from his pocket and pouring the contents onto the bar.

Mushrooms spread across the countertop.

I shifted uncomfortably in my bar stool, realizing that the

night had just taken a different turn. Lark hoisted herself onto the bar. It shook when she plopped down onto the counter. Jonah set five glasses atop the bar and filled them equally with champagne, topping each glass off with a fistful of mushrooms.

"The first time Hendrix performed he was on LSD, and that just shows how mind altering substances really bring out your creative talent." Shawn said, reaching over and taking a glass from the counter.

"It can, but you gotta be careful." Jonah said.

He handed me a glass. I glanced inside of it, only seeing the mushroom particles floating around in the drink.

"Yeah, because clearly too much mind alteration equals death, like all the forever 27's." Lark said, swirling the glass in her hand.

"I guess we have a few more years." Jonah said, winking at her.

We all laughed, toasted each other and drank the shots until our glasses were empty. My face cringed as I swallowed, it was sour and lumpy.

Ten minutes later the four of us found ourselves walking down Jonah's street towards the excitement of downtown Raleigh. Then the hallucinogen set it. A police car sat in the middle of the road patrolling the crowded streets. I stared at the car, mesmerized by the blue and red lights flashing from its hood throughout the street, rippling like a psychedelic rainbow. The colors were marvelous and seemed to form exquisite patterns in the sky, painting auras of euphoric bliss that hovered over the people crowding the street. I laughed with my friends as we skipped down

INGRID DARLING

the street.

    We ended up at Jonah's bar which was packed. Intoxicated, exuberant people were singing loudly to the music that blared through the speakers. I could hardly move in the crowd. I laughed at the sight around me, unable to stop because for a moment everyone looked animated. It was as if I had been suddenly thrown into a really bad sci-fi comedy. I felt like an extra in an alien movie or something of the sort as what appeared to be large heads, bulging eyes and skinny bodies danced around the room. I didn't understand what I was seeing, why these people appeared odd, why I couldn't understand what they were saying; the babble. It seemed as though I had stepped out of the human realm and was observing a pack of beavers or elephants or something. And I asked myself how it was that people could appear to be animals, unless the perception we have of ourselves is just an illusion in the first place.

    Perhaps I would have delved deeper into that thought, but Lark grabbed my arm, breaking my concentration, and dragged me through the crowd, towards the bar. However, as she pulled me, I had a moment of clarity:

There is something more to this world than it appears to offer, something beyond what the naked eye can see and perhaps our senses are barriers to that grander reality.

    It seemed like everything around me in the bar, at that moment, was different than what it had been every other time I had been there. I knew what people looked like, I knew what people sounded like, but this was different because nothing normal seemed to make sense. I felt foreign listening to people speak my own language and the feeling was surreal.

    A tall man bumped into me, spilling the pint of beer in his

hand down the front of my dress. But I didn't care, I suddenly felt very compassionate, like I was complete with everyone else around me. And despite my inability to understand anyone at the moment, I felt like we were all one being, dancing together around the room.

Though my head was floating in a hallucinogenic state and I seemed to have lucidity amidst the chaotic scene and altered mind state. Yet as much as everything seemed to be clear at that moment, I realized that I was locked in tunnel vision and I was still unsure about myself.

The tall man who had spilled his drink apologized and asked me who I was. I told him "Ingrid Darling", but shook my head and turned away, thinking that other than my name, I didn't really know the answer to his question.

As I turned around, I looked towards Lark who was no longer holding my hand and was nowhere in sight. I realized that not only had I lost my friends in the bar, but I had lost myself as well.

INGRID DARLING

Three

I woke up the next morning to the sound of my alarm. I sat up and looked at the clock: 7:30. I rubbed my eyes and moaned. I didn't want to go to work. The last thing I remembered from the night before was lying in the middle of the street by Jonah's house, staring up at the sky. Stars poked through a blanket of blackness, shining brightly, offering a glimpse of a different world, a different existence, somewhere in a far away galaxy. Everything that had happened was now a blur, a memory faded in the reality of the present. Every moment I'd experienced the night before was gone, like a dream and I was now awake. And for the most part, everything seemed to go back to normal.

But it wasn't normal. Every day I wanted to duplicate the feeling I'd had that night. Every day I did more cocaine or tripped mushrooms, hoping for a good high. Shawn was now living with Lark and I, something that only fueled my addiction to the high, to the feeling of seventh heaven. But it wasn't heaven, it was hell. My insides burned from the drugs, and I desperately tried to mask the pain with the pleasure of a high. I don't know why I was coddling the need for a different state of mind so much, perhaps I was unhappy, perhaps I was depressed. All I knew is that I had let my desires and cravings come to a point of ruling my life.

Then we got evicted. I don't know how it happened. Somewhere between January and March Lark hadn't paid her half of the rent and our apartment complex decided to kick us out. I didn't have anywhere to go. I didn't show up to court either, so deciding on the fate of the eviction was clear. Then I found out there was a warning out on my credit, making it even more difficult to find a new residence. Lark moved in with Shawn and his brother and invited me, but I didn't want to impose. Nor did I want a reason to continue to binge, in vain, on drugs.

  I decided to ask Jonah if I could stay at his place until I found a new apartment. He agreed. I packed my shoes and threw them into the trunk of my car and stored my bins of clothes in his den. I didn't really care about my lack of residence because it made me feel more alive. I was living the aesthetic life, despite all of the clothes that traveled with me. My mom wanted me to find a place of my own, but I was reluctant to search anywhere. I was content so long as I had a warm house to sleep in. Lark would come over to Jonah's house occasionally. She didn't really have an apartment of her own either, so she would spend the night on the couch the nights I would sleep upstairs on the daybed in Jonah's guest room. I was always content to have her around when she wasn't with her boyfriend. Though it wasn't often, I continued to do drugs when she came around. She fueled my habit and I didn't realize how much I was spiraling out of control. Often my days would get mixed up with my nights. I had no grasp on reality. I was on a wild rollercoaster ride and my life was becoming that which I'd dreaded. I was a slave to my passions. I thought about what my parents had taught me about power when I was younger. How power tends to grab a hold of people and won't let them go. It takes a strong person to let go of that power and see it just as desire. I allowed myself to succumb, I needed to change my ways quickly before it was too late.

  I did. After much consideration and deliberation with my parents, I decided to take a job offer in New York City. It was for a small Real Estate law firm. I would be one of two paralegals in an office near Central Park. The lawyer was a friend of my dad's, so I would be taken care of. The job paid well so I moved to Manhattan in August.

Though I was far from home and my friends, I was in love with my new apartment, which was also around the corner from Central Park. It had vaulted ceilings and hardwood floors and the kitchen had a window that looked out onto the street. I decorated it quickly. I didn't like my living space to be bare, which was in stark contrast to how I'd been living the past few months. I don't think my mother was quite content with my hobo ways.

"I raised a lady, not a vagabond", she would say.

It always made me laugh. She was so proper and the thought of her daughter being a homeless bag lady made her cringe. She was happy now that I had an apartment of my own, even if it was eight hours away.

The first few weeks were fun. I'd become friends with my neighbors and would invite them over for dinner then we'd drink wine and talk about interesting things. But when my work load picked up, I was forced me to spend evenings at the office and spent less and less time with my new friends. We eventually faded back to casual acquaintances, waving to each other on the street or having a brief conversation in the stairwell if time permitted. Work consumed my life and I had become a lonely New Yorker.

I wasn't doing cocaine much anymore. I had been trying to savor the last of my huge baggie, which I'd bought from Lark's boyfriend before my move, for a fun night out. But I only had a little left and I never went out. I was too busy with work. I didn't care either. I was sick of doing it anyway, the satisfaction was gone, I had to snort too much to get high, and it was giving me sinus headaches. The stinging pain between my eyes lasted all day and wasn't worth the 30 minute high, so I stuffed the baggie in a drawer and eventually forgot about it.

    I began to spend my weekends at a coffee shop reading, or touring the city. I'd been to New York plenty of times before deciding to live there, having visited family when I was younger and having gone on field trips to the Statue of Liberty and the Metropolitan Museum. I loved to visit the Ancient Egyptian section and the exhibitions in the Contemporary Art section.

    That was where I met Theresa.

    She was standing with her mom in front of a Dali painting. I overheard her discussing the painting with her mother. *Metamorphosis of a Narcissus* is what it was called. She was saying that it was this piece that Dali showed to Sigmund Freud during their only encounter to prove that he was one of Freud's most zealous pupils. Fascinated by her knowledge of Dali, who nonetheless was my favorite artist, I struck up a conversation with her about his life, art, and genius. We became close friends after that, meeting every weekend for coffee and eventually became roommates once I'd discovered that my fabulous apartment had a rodent problem. She and I moved a few blocks uptown, so she could be closer to Columbia, where she was finishing her undergrad. The move didn't bother me as I was happy to have someone to spend my evenings with. She and I talked about everything and nothing, laughing about our past relationships and current ones. She was dating a musician named Darryl and the three of us would drink wine and discuss life. Theresa and Darryl were avid pot smokers and thought that people could use a little marijuana to help them relax from the anxieties of life. I smoked with them often, but was always conscious of the priority I'd given drugs in my life before. I had become content, but something still didn't feel right, like I was missing a part of me, like I wasn't quite complete.

INGRID DARLING

Four

October, 2006

"Human beings are aware that something is wrong with their condition; they feel at odds with themselves and others, out of touch with their inner nature and disoriented. Conflict and lack of simplicity seem to characterize our existence. Yet we are constantly seeking to unite the multiplicity of phenomena and reduce them to some ordered whole."

"Who said that?" I asked, taking a bite of the long celery stalk in my hand.

Emerald's voice lowered then rose on the other end of the line, like she dropped the phone or changed the volume level.

"Karen Armstrong. I just finished reading her book, *A History of God*. It was really...historical." She said bluntly.

I laughed. Emerald had a way of making me smile at the most inconspicuous things.

She and I went to college in North Carolina together, met as pot-luck roommates and instantly became friends. She was from a small town outside of Charlotte and grew up on a farm so she had a deep sense of self and was very comfortable with who she was. When I left school, she never asked me why, so I never had to confess that my absence from class was because I was high on cocaine all day. She respected my privacy and was always someone I could rely on for support. We remained close when I moved to

INGRID DARLING

Manhattan, and though I hadn't seen her in almost a year, she was still one of the only friends I could call when I had a serious problem. I called her the night Theresa and Darryl were in New Jersey for a show of his. I could always rely on Emerald to give me good advice, and I needed it now. I felt so empty despite my good job and good friends. Something was lacking, a void that I had previously tried to fill with drugs, but it hadn't helped, nothing did.

"I don't know what my deal is. I have a good job, it pays well. I have great friends. But something is missing and I don't understand why I'm feeling this way." I sighed, slumping back against the couch.

I sat cross legged, balancing the cordless phone between my ear and shoulder, peeling the skin from the celery stalk.

"Well, you're not the only one, babe. So many people out there are going through similar situations."

"I know, but why me? What am I going through that's making me feel so unfulfilled?"

"You know, the reason why we suffer is because we are trying to have a different experience than the one that is happening to us right now." She said. Her voice was calm and gentle.

"What do you mean?" I asked, taking another bite of my celery, it was bland.

"We are not allowing the current feeling, thought, or experience to happen in our body at that moment. We resist it so much and then by internally fighting with our current experience by wishing, hoping or praying that it will change, we are not honoring the universe as our most powerful teacher." She said.

I rested my head against the back of the couch and stared at the ceiling, silent. I understood what she meant. I had read somewhere that the greatness of man's power is the measure of his surrender. I needed to relax and let things happen, to stop worrying about unimportant things in my life, to go with the flow.

"You're right." I said. "I need to chill out and not try to be in control all the time."

"There you go babe. Because remember, you can't control life, you just have to put it on cruise control and make sure you stay between the lines."

I laughed and took another bite of my celery.

"I just wish I could allow myself to be happy. I'm finding myself sad for no reason at all sometimes. I'm not depressed, but I'm not perfectly content either." I said, between chews.

"Don't let your emotions get to you. Emotions are deceitful," she said. "One minute you can be happy and the next minute you can be sad. I mean you could be sitting on a bench and kill yourself and if you had waited, you probably would have been fine the next minute. You have to be patient. If you can be patient, then everything will work itself out."

"And patience is a virtue." I said, staring at the long green stalk.

"Exactly. You know what? I wish more people understood that. I wish more people understood that impatience and greediness only leads to addiction and guilt. My neighbor came to me the other day and asked me if I knew where he could get some cocaine, because he had had a bad day at work. Can you believe that?!" She said, with horrified exasperation.

I swallowed hard, hoping she wouldn't sense my hesitation. A piece of celery lodged itself in my throat. I coughed. I hadn't told Emerald about my year long cocaine binge, I was embarrassed about the fact that I relied on some drug to make me feel better throughout the day, to give me a rush at night, to take me out of my reality for the sake of indulgence. The truth was that I still wanted to do it. I'd lost the baggie with the last bit of coke I had left during the move uptown. I didn't need it in my life, but I wanted that feeling again, that excitement.

"Yeah, that's wild." I said, choking down the chunk of celery.

"I mean, that's the problem with how we view things in America. Americans are so used to instant gratification that they expect everything to go their way, and when it doesn't, they freak out and commit suicide. There is no patience in the American mindset, which is why so many people are strung out on drugs and alcohol."

"You're right." I said, tossing the remaining celery stalk onto the coffee table in front of me. I sighed and thought about how much fun I'd had with Lark, doing lines all night long, acting crazy at the bars and clubs. I didn't need that in my life anymore, besides, I was a serious working woman.

"Well I hope you feel better tonight, Ingrid. I have to finish cleaning my dishes. Give me a call anytime you want to chat. Have a good night."

"Alright thanks, Em. Have a good night too." I said, hanging up the phone.

I placed it on the coffee table next to the half eaten celery. I went to bed that night without eating dinner, I wasn't hungry. Tomorrow was Thursday which meant only one more day until the weekend.

The next day at work my cell phone rang at the office. I

usually had it on silent but I had forgotten to change the setting that morning. Mary, the other paralegal gave me a snide look and said I should be humiliated for even having my cell phone at work. I didn't mind her rude comments because she had wrinkles and smelled like a pipe. I just smiled and answered my phone.

"Darling!" A voice shrieked.

It was Lark.

"Hey girl, what's up?" I said, swiveling in my chair so Mary couldn't eavesdrop on my conversation.

"Get ready!" She exclaimed. "I'm coming to N-Y-C this weekend, and it's time to *partaaaay*!"

My heart skipped.

Finally, I thought, *someone to have some real fun with!*

INGRID DARLING

Five

Dying doesn't just happen in a moment, it takes an eternity. When you die, your soul leaves your body and goes into a different realm of existence. At the moment of death, you have the most vivid outer body experience like no other experience you've ever had in your life. It is euphoric. It is perfect, and you are perfect. At least it is in theory.

Lark arrived Friday afternoon just after I'd gotten off work. When I got to my apartment, she was standing outside my door, smoking a cigarette. She squealed and jumped on me when I got out of the cab, nearly knocking the briefcase out of my hand and burning my arm with the end of her cigarette. I flinched at the pain.

"I'm so glad you're here!" She cried.

"I tried to leave earlier but Mary, my insufferable coworker, wanted me to file some Condominium Declarations. I took a cab back hoping to get here before you. I hope you weren't waiting long." I said, rubbing my arm and fishing for my keys to unlock the door.

"Nah, not long." Lark said, tossing her cigarette to the ground.

She pulled a piece of gum from her pocket and stuffed it in her mouth, smacking loudly as we went inside and up the stairs. She had a small suitcase that thumped on each step behind her, echoing through the narrow corridor. Inside I showed her around the kitchen, living room and bathrooms. She would be sleeping in Theresa's room, who had conveniently gone to Chicago with Darryl and his band for the weekend, and was trusting enough to allow

INGRID DARLING

Lark to sleep in her bed while she was gone.

The evening went by quickly as we showered, and ordered a pizza from Lorenzo's, my new favorite pizza place. It was just a block away and had authentic Sicilian ingredients. I had taken my mom there during my move uptown and Lorenzo, the owner, had become smitten with her after she'd struck up a conversation with him about her travels through Italy. Every time I'd been in to order a pizza since, he always asked in his thick Italian accent, "how my ma was doing and when he'd get to see her again".

Tonight I called my order in. It was delivered forty-five minutes later by a thin man with dark hair. He said something in Italian to me as I signed the bill. I thought he was flirting, but once I brought the pizza into the kitchen I realized he was telling me that my robe was untied, revealing a breast to him unbeknownst to me. I was slightly embarrassed but it didn't matter, I couldn't do anything about it anymore.

Lark and I ate fast then dressed and went downtown to a lounge. Inside, it was crowded despite the early hour. We sat at a booth towards the back which had quilted seats and a sheer curtain that could be drawn around it. We ordered martinis and Lark gushed about her now ex-boyfriend who'd cheated on her with a woman in her 40's who was recently widowed and had developed a serious cocaine addiction. Lark moved out of his place and in with some guy she had just recently started dating. He too was a drug dealer, this time, heroin.

I listened, in awe, to Lark tell me that she'd tried it, that it wasn't much different from cocaine, just more mellow. I told her I could never stick a needle in my body for a high, that inhaling something was already more than I had told myself I would do. She said it was easy not to think about the needle, that the satisfaction of the high was greater than the pain of drawing the syringe. A lump formed in my throat at the thought of my friend doing heroin. I told her not to do it anymore, that it wasn't worth it. She laughed and pulled out a small plastic bag.

"I won't be doing that anymore," she said, reaching over me and drawing the curtain. "Besides, why would I disfigure my arm when I can just powder my nose?"

I laughed, nervously. I knew what was about to happen, I knew as soon as she called me to tell me she was coming to New York. I had wanted it then, I still wanted it, but something in me screamed no. My subconscious, maybe, but I wasn't listening. I should have listened, but I wasn't, and I didn't.

Lark opened a small flat mirror on the table and poured out a mound of white powder onto it. It sparkled in the dim light and there were no lumps. I proceeded to roll up the dollar bill I had in my purse and she cut six lines onto the mirror for us.

"I stole this from Shawn right after he cheated on me with that widow, it's the best shit. The closest to pure you can get without it coming right from the bean," she said as I leaned down over the mirror.

I inhaled the three lines and handed her the bill, wiping my nose. The sweetest cocaine I'd ever tasted dripped down the back of my throat. I licked my fingers and rubbed them on my teeth, a numbing sensation overwhelmed my mouth and my nostril flared to attention. The high hit me before Lark finished her last line.

"Whoa!" I gasped.

She wasn't kidding, it was very pure.

"I told you," she said, licking her finger and winking at me.

INGRID DARLING

"We're going to get into some *trouble* tonight!"

     My chest tightened then expanded, as if demanding me to stop, to listen to my gut, to go home and go to sleep. But I didn't. And I'll never forget that night.

     They say that when you die, you feel free, alive, almost as if you were being born, given the chance to live it all again. I'm not so sure about that.

     On Saturday morning at 4am, I died. It was a slow process. Three hours earlier, Lark and I, already having snorted eight lines each, decided to split an ecstasy pill, take three shots of tequila, and cap the night off with another ten lines. My dangerously dehydrated body now lay limply on the cold bathroom floor, gasping for breath with each passing minute. My face was numb and the air was thick, heavy. Sweat poured from my pores, melting the mascara down my cheeks. I'd tried to wash the makeup from my face but I couldn't stop shaking. I was freezing, but my skin was hot, feverish. I tried desperately to sit up against the wall, but my sense of place was displaced. Every deep breath left me trembling, frightened of what was happening to me.

     The color faded quickly from the fluorescent room and the sound of the heat pumping through the vents became quieter and quieter. I couldn't see anything but gray objects and my heart was thumping slower with each passing moment. My breathing became longer and I could feel the life draining from my body. I managed to prop myself against the tub and sat there, staring at the dark gray wall as it faded to black. Sweat drenched my hair and dried on my face, down my neck. My eyes were still open, but I couldn't see. I tried to call out to Lark, but she was on the other side of the apartment, locked in Theresa's room. She couldn't hear my weak cry. I wondered if she was feeling the same way, if she was as helpless as I was, dehydrated and shaking. I wanted to cry but there was no water left in my body, only drugs that I had shamefully taken out of gluttony, out of the desire for fun. Now I could only sob and heave, praying that I wasn't going to overdose, praying that I hadn't overdosed, hoping that I would wake up and be okay. My ears rung, there was a deafening silence. I couldn't breathe.

    I sat lifelessly along the edge of the tub and tile floor, nearing a convulsion. I fought the feeling, focusing on my heartbeat. It was slow, too slow. I was dying, and I knew it. I felt trapped in my own body, as if I had been diagnosed as a coma patient but still had a functioning brain and could hear everything but do nothing. Then a light came towards my body. It was small and bright in the black room and it grew in size and brightness as it came towards me. A blast of heat surged through my body. I wasn't breathing anymore, I was just there, still. The light engulfed the room and I could see only white, every object disappeared, there was only heat and blank space.

    They say that in your deepest depression, the moment you hit rock bottom, you experience a sort of grace like nothing you have felt before. Many people discover their true being, others say they find God. It is in this moment when you are fully aware of life and its beauty and you marvel in it, because it is now clear that everything you have ever done in your life has been for your own self discovery, to find the truth to your very existence.

    At that moment, it felt as though a presence had lifted me

from the floor and stood me on my feet. I could somehow walk again, as if nothing had happened. The light was gone and I was awake. I walked from the bathroom into my room across the hall and stood in front of the window. It was as if life had poured back into my body and I could feel warmth and see glowing light around everything in the room. I stared out the window onto the dark, empty street. A cat dashed by, disappearing in the shadows. I walked back into the bathroom and nearly fainted. Staring down at the floor, I saw my lifeless body slumped over the tub, dead.

I screamed, but there was no sound.

What is going on?!

My heart raced wildly in my chest. I bent down to look at myself. My face was expressionless and my skin was a pale gray. My body was comatose, heavy, and limp against the tub. I stood up and screamed. Again, there was no sound.

Am I in a horror movie? What the hell is going on!

I put my hands over my eyes, hoping to wake up from this nightmare. I didn't feel my face. I could feel nothing, there was no sensation in my body, I was just there.

The light returned. I moved my hands from my eyes and stared into the brightness. A soft voice echoed the room and rung in my ears.

"INGRID." It resounded.

"Yes?" My subconscious voice responded.

I stared blankly into the light. I was mystified and mesmerized, like a deer in headlights, I couldn't look away.

Who was calling my name? What is this?

But there was no response. Then the light faded away. It faded quickly, and I was surrounded by blackness once again. I didn't know what had happened.

Am I dead? I asked myself, confused.

An empty feeling rushed over my body and suddenly I realized that I was lying on the ground again. I was no longer standing next to myself. I was myself, lying on the cold bathroom floor.

Puzzled, I looked around the room. Objects began to take shape. I didn't understand what was happening or what had happened to me in those brief minutes.

Did I pass out or was that something else, like a sort of death? I thought. *Why did it only last for a few minutes? Perhaps it wasn't my time to go; maybe I'm not supposed to die today.*

A moment later I could feel my hands. A tingling sensation swept through my body and an exhale escaped my lungs. I felt my heart beat quicken its pace, it matched the drum of the heat pumping through the vents. My hearing had returned.

The bright bathroom lights were blinding and the room suddenly looked as it did earlier. I was mystified, confused yet idly relieved. I managed to stand up and crouch over the sink. I splashed my face with water and gazed into the mirror. Bloodshot, dilated eyes stared back at me.

Who am I and what am I doing?

My head pounded through my temples, screaming at me, punishing me. I wiped my face and stared into the mirror.

"I almost overdosed." I said aloud, staring at my sunken features. The color had returned to my face, but I still looked dead, hollow, like I was just a body and had no soul.

And for what, the sake of indulgence, to get a high?

I hated myself for doing what I did, for doing drugs in a

vain attempt to have a fun night. It was bullshit and dangerously unnecessary. So many people lose their lives in vanity, succumbing to their own vices. I didn't lose my life, and I didn't want to be a statistic.

    I slept until 1pm that day, rejuvenating all energy I had lost earlier in the morning. I didn't know what had happened to me or why but I didn't question it. Sometimes it's best not to know. I was fortunate and fortune only smiles once. I needed to change my priorities; I needed to change my life. I never touched cocaine again after that night.

Six

I woke up to find a note on Theresa's bed. Lark was gone.

Darling, Had to go back to NC. I'm on the red eye flight. Didn't want to wake you. Had fun last night. Will visit again soon.
Xoxo, Lark.

Her handwriting was sloppy, as if she were shaking when she wrote the note. I was relieved she was gone. She was a good friend, but I was always too tempted to make bad decisions with her. I hoped she got home safely and wondered why she had to leave so soon after she'd arrived. I didn't think much about it and spent the rest of the day drinking water and resting.

Theresa came back on Sunday afternoon. She looked tired from traveling. She said the show was sold out and the band did a great job. I told her about my evening with Lark, how I had accidently flashed one of the pizza guys from Lorenzo's. She laughed. And how I got too drunk and passed out in my bathroom. I neglected to mention the massive drug intake and outer body experience as a result of almost overdosing. She knew that I had done cocaine before, but I didn't want her to think it was a problem for me. It wasn't, at least not anymore.

Theresa had never met Lark, had only seen pictures, and had the impression that she was a sad person. I'm not sure why she thought that, but she was right. Lark had a certain gloom about her, which was why I had been her friend despite her snide comments about others. There was always a hint of misery behind her smile and I could tell she did drugs to cover her own sadness. I never questioned her about it, though; I didn't think my consideration would matter.

The next week went by slowly. We had six residential closings at work and I had to go to the courthouse to have the Condominium Declarations notarized. That was hell. The courthouse reminded me of an asylum, officers and patients everywhere. The patients were grubby, blue collar workers that had unfortunately been victimized by the law as a result of the American class system.

It was always the people who barely made above minimum wage that were getting caught with traffic violations, failing to appear at court, or getting slapped with warrants for not updating their vehicle registration. And because they were not cooperating with the law, they were hit with fines, perpetuating the financial problem they may have had to begin with. It was a never ending cycle of the American lower class; everyone was stuck in that web, stuck in the cycle of hopelessness, never able to reach above the dividing line between poor and middle class. It was sickening, sad.

On Thursday, Theresa had a study group at our apartment. I walked in from work to find three unfamiliar faces sitting on the floor, discussing social democracy. They were her peers at Columbia, in her Social Research class. I waved to Theresa in the kitchen, who was filling a bowl with freshly popped popcorn for the group. I put my briefcase in my room and changed into sweatpants, then slipped quietly onto the couch, listening to the conversation. A tall guy with dark curly hair and green eyes was speaking. He wore a brown cardigan and a burgundy scarf dangled around his neck. His long legs were crossed, pulling the already tight jeans even tighter against his thighs. His eyes sparkled behind square glasses with thick plastic frames. He was very stylish. He spoke emphatically with his hands, gesturing each word. I found out later that his name was Karl.

He was discussing the importance of human emancipation and emphasized how the push to secure civil liberties was important in the struggle for social democracy. His opinion reminded me of the people in the courthouse who just couldn't get away from their troubles, with the law or otherwise; whose struggles didn't seem far off from my own in that I was also stuck in a web of unhappiness, struggling to find my own sense of place in society. And though I didn't necessarily agree with Karl's flagrance, his passion on the subject of human liberation was refreshing. I talked briefly with him at the end of the study group and we decided that he would have dinner with me and Theresa on Sunday.

On Saturday, Theresa invited me to Fat Cats, a game bar that had live music, to listen to Darryl's band play. I agreed and went with her. Sometime during the night I slipped off to the bathroom between one of the bands' songs, trying to rush so I wouldn't miss the rest of the set. I wasn't doing coke anymore, so it almost seemed like the trip to the bathroom was useless. I checked my hair and makeup and hurried back out to Theresa who was sitting on the couch, watching Darryl and his band perform but was stopped by a familiar sound.

"Ingrid!" A squeaky voice called.

I turned around and saw an old friend of mine from college in North Carolina. She and I had a class together during my first semester, but I had completely forgotten her name. I smiled, hoping she wouldn't try to engage in conversation for very long.

"Hey!" I exclaimed.

I gave her a hug and we chatted for a bit; apparently she was in the city for the weekend visiting a cousin. The conversation wasn't the least bit intriguing, but I tried to pay attention. A few more girls came over to us to chat, her cousin's friends, but not wanting to converse with them all night, I said goodbye and headed back to Theresa on the couch. But as I turned, I collided into a very handsome young man about my height with big brown eyes and a dashing smile.

"Oops! Sorry." I said, brushing past him.

I didn't think twice about it as I was always bumping into people.

"It's alright." He said, letting me pass.

I could feel his eyes following me as I walked away. I smiled to myself, walking up behind Theresa who was stretched out on the long leather couch facing the band.

I sat with her, watching Darryl perform a few songs. A group of people sat around them, listening and bobbing their heads to the music. The band was good, easy to groove to. Theresa looked up to Darryl on the guitar, smitten. I smiled, wishing I had that kind of connection with someone, hoping I would find a Darryl for myself. We sat through three more songs, then the band stopped playing and the deejay began to spin more upbeat music. People danced. Darryl and another band mate came over to me and Theresa upon greeting a few fans. We hugged and the four of us spoke about their new album and upcoming tour.

When the conversation ended, Darryl asked if Theresa and I wanted a drink from the bar, as the performers were given free drinks.

INGRID DARLING

Theresa asked for a Red Hook. I asked for the same. Darryl nodded, gave Theresa a kiss on the forehead, then headed off towards the bar. Theresa and I stood talking about their travel plans for the rest of the year until he returned. He came back several minutes later and handed our drinks to us. We thanked him and each took a sip of our beer which had a bold, nutty flavor.

Sudden Theresa gestured to someone behind me. Confused, I turned around and was surprised to see those big brown eyes from earlier, staring right into mine.

"Theresa, look who I bumped into!" Darryl exclaimed, who apparently knew Handsome Brown Eyes. "Ingrid, this is Thomas. He and I were in school at Columbia together," he said, introducing the two of us.

"Hi." I said.

He extended his hand.

"What's up, I'm Thomas." He said through a wry smile.

We shook hands.

"Nice to meet you" I smiled, blushing and taking another sip of my drink.

Oh yes! I thought. *I am definitely red and definitely hooked.*

Seven

December, 2006

"I think I'm falling for him." I said to Lark. She was on the other end of the phone line.

"I knew that was gonna happen. You've been talking about him nonstop for months." She said, I heard her blow into the line and figured she was painting her nails.

Of course she knew it was bound to happen, I knew it was going to happen eventually, especially considering his persistence in pursuing me. Since our first encounter at Fat Cats, Thomas had befriended me on Facebook and sent me a message asking me to dinner. We went to a fancy Spanish restaurant uptown and discussed philosophy, where we'd travelled, where we wanted to travel, life, and what we each wanted in the future. From that point on, he would come over to mine and Theresa's apartment with Darryl and the four of us would play board games and watch movies together. Every time I would accompany Theresa to watch Darryl play at a gig, she would give me a sly expression when I'd tell her Thomas was coming. She must have known how much I liked him too, yet neglected to make it obvious to me. I wasn't planning on having a boyfriend, my work load was too much to burden someone else with, and I had only really seen him as a friend. But there was something that kept me intrigued, attracted, and it was now clear why I was keeping him around.

"I've been seeing him for a few months now. I didn't really think much about our hanging out at first, but now that I've spent so much time with him, I can see our relationship really blossoming. I really like him."

"Well I'm happy for you, Darling." Lark said.

There was an ounce of hostility in her voice.

"Thanks, we'll see what happens. I guess I'm just gonna wait for him to make the first move."

"Good idea. It's better to wait these things out." Her tone hardened then more blowing.

"True. So how are things with that guy you're dating?" I asked, hoping to divert her enmity away from my future relationship.

"Ugh. He's a dick, just like the rest of the male species. He got arrested for drug possession and tried to blame that shit on me when the cops busted into his house. I was at work when they caught him and that asshole said that the drugs were mine. The cops found all this paraphernalia for making heroin and crack in his basement. I didn't even know the bastard had a basement! The cops questioned me and luckily figured out that the house was in his name and released all charges against me. I've had it with men!" She huffed.

"Wow Lark! When did all of this happen?"

"Two weeks ago. I'm telling you, all guys are jerks. Make sure you can trust this Thomas guy, because when shit hits the fan, they are the first to run away." She said.

I could tell she was only saying that because of her lack of judgment in men, but in case there was slight truth to her words, I decided to store that message in the back of my mind.

"I'm sorry. So what are you doing now? Where are you staying?"

"With my parents. It sucks. But I was thinking of moving to New York. They got a manager position at a Hooters up there that I was thinking about applying for. Hey, do you think I could come and stay with you for a week or so while I look for a place to live?"

"Uh," I paused, not sure if I was more stunned that she was moving to New York or that she was applying to Hooters, especially since she was slightly overweight and wore an A-cup.

"It would just be for a week. I'm sure your roommate wouldn't mind." She cooed.

There was desperation in her voice.

I found her imposition slightly annoying. I didn't want her in New York, calling me every weekend, tempting me with drugs, especially not now that I felt I finally found someone who took my mind off of that empty feeling that I used to fill with cocaine and excessive amounts of alcohol. I wanted to tell her no, that it would be inconvenient and unfair of me to ask Theresa if she could stay with us for a week. And besides, what would happen if she didn't find an apartment, she couldn't just live on our couch for the next few months, I was past that phase of my life and she should have been too. But her desperation exceeded my selfishness and I agreed.

"Fine, you can stay with me. But you really have to find a place soon, because it's really not convenient for Theresa. Her boyfriend comes over all the time and she has study groups in the evenings." I said.

The last part was a lie. Theresa hadn't had a study group since the night I met Karl, and he never ended up coming over for dinner that Sunday either.

She squealed.

INGRID DARLING

"You're the best, Darling! I should be up there in a few weeks. I'll let you know when I'm coming once I finalize my flight plans. I gotta go. I'll talk to you soon." She said.

I told her goodbye and hung up. Nausea swept through my body, tugging at my gut. I really didn't want her to come, or to move to New York, it was too dangerous in too many ways.

I should have told her no, I thought. I should have, but I didn't.

"My old roommate is coming to stay with me." I said to Thomas, taking a bite of my mashed potatoes.

We were having dinner at Planet Hollywood in Times Square.

"Oh?"

He looked up from his plate, chewing the lump of steak in his cheek. His brown eyes widened behind thin wire framed glasses. He looked adorable sitting there with his collared shirt and khakis, like he just won a spelling bee or something. Thomas was very bright, currently working on his masters in Business Finance at Columbia, his alma mater which he also graduated with a 3.9 from. He usually only wore his glasses during the day when he was in class, but we decided to have an early dinner tonight and he didn't have time to put his contacts in before we left. I liked it when he wore his glasses because it showed how comfortable he was around me.

"Yeah." I said, chewing. "She is moving up here and needs a place to stay while she finds an apartment."

"When is she coming?" He looked back down at his plate.

"Three weeks." I sighed.

"Are you not excited about it?" He asked, cutting into the

steak on his plate.

He sliced it with ease.

"Not really. She's my friend, has been for years, but she's not the best person for me to hang out with." I said, bracing myself for the conversation to get deeply personal, something I had been avoiding for a while, but decided it was time Thomas knew more about me than what he saw on the surface.

"How so?" He asked, raising an eyebrow.

He took a bite of his steak.

"Well, let's just say, she's the serpent in that story we all know."

He laughed.

"You mean in the Bible?"

"Yeah. I tend to do bad things around her." I said, taking another bite of my mashed potatoes.

"I don't think that's the right story to use. The serpent, in many cultures, represents wisdom, and it only suggested that Eve become wiser by eating from the tree of knowledge. I don't think that was such a bad idea in her case. It's too bad half the world thinks her attaining wisdom is a sin, but then again, we live in a patriarchal society. I mean, what's the big deal, why wouldn't anyone want to be wise?"

"Because ignorance is bliss." I said, not prepared for my drug confession to become a religious lesson.

"Not in my world," he said, flatly. "Tell me what it is she tempts you to do."

I told him. I told him about the first time I tried cocaine, and how it became priority over my school work, how I spent my paycheck on it instead of saving up for an apartment, how it consumed my days and nights, how I tried to stop once I'd moved to New York but Lark's visit tempted me to do it again, and how I'd almost overdosed which was why I didn't do it anymore. By the time I finished my confession, he had finished his entire steak and two glasses of wine. I was embarrassed by revealing such personal information about myself, especially since my closest friends didn't even know the extent of my addiction. He smiled and told me he was proud of me for telling him, that he admired my strength in the face of compulsion. Though Thomas had never smoked marijuana in his life and definitely could not relate to the sensation of cocaine high, I had the feeling he understood me, more than anyone else would ever be able to. I loved him for that, and I told him that, later on in the night once we'd gotten back to my apartment.

We had reached a new level in our relationship. Thomas was now spending the night every night and we spent every free moment we had with each other. I loved him deeply for his affection and care towards me, for wanting to know about me and for teaching me about him. He told me of a previous relationship with a girl named Yvonne that ended abruptly when she moved to another state. And I learned he was originally from a small town in New Jersey, went to Columbia at the request of his parents, both lawyers, and had family members in prestigious positions in business and law.

"You caught a good one", my mother told me over the phone one night when I was telling her about Thomas.

Granted both of my parents were also lawyers, my grandparents were professors with PhD's and all of my cousins were in some field of law or business, it still was an exciting prospect for my mother to have a son-in-law with a similar familial background. We got along well with everything, shared ideas, clothes, and even toothbrushes. We were comfortable with each other and a deep trust formed between us. Then Lark came.

    She was only in town for two days when my mother called to give me grave news. My godfather had passed away. The funeral was in Union, New Jersey, two days from then. Thomas agreed that I should go despite my feelings of insecurity of having to leave Lark by herself with him, Theresa and Darryl for the day and possibly the night. I reluctantly arranged to meet my family at the airport after which we took a rental car to New Jersey, staying the night in a hotel not far from the church where the funeral service would be held the next day. I didn't like being away from Thomas, and I especially didn't like leaving him with Lark. Though he was staying at his place while I was away, I knew that night Darryl and Theresa were going to Darryl's gig and Lark was going along with them. Thomas told me he had already promised a friend of his from Columbia, that he would go to the show also. I didn't mind because I trusted Thomas, but I was still uneasy about the situation.

    I settled into my hotel room and I decided to go to bed early considering how early I had to wake up for the funeral service the next day. I called Thomas and talked to him for a few minutes before telling him I loved him and hanging up. The TV in my room was still on when I drifted off to sleep.

    It only seemed like I'd been asleep for a few minutes when I woke up to the sound of my phone buzzing. I'd put it on vibrate. I reached over to the nightstand, half asleep, glancing at the clock:

INGRID DARLING

3:15am. It was Thomas. I sat up in the bed and rubbed my face.

"Hello?" I said, groggy.

"Ingrid," I heard Thomas say.

Something in his voice didn't sound right. My stomach tensed then knotted itself.

I knew it, I thought.

He didn't even have to respond.

"Lark t-t-tried to have sex with you?" I stammered.

He was silent. I was miles away so I couldn't do anything about it.

Damnit, why am I in fucking New Jersey right now!

I hated her at that moment. I hated her because I knew she was going to try to have sex with Thomas, even though I said he was off limits. That's how I had to put things to her. "He's off limits, Lark" is what I'd told her before I left; it was all she could understand. I started tearing up. I didn't understand why someone who I considered to be a friend would try so hard to take something from me. My insides tightened. I swallowed hard, trying to mask the pain of the betrayal.

"Are you still there?" Thomas asked, apprehension overcoming his tone.

I could tell he was upset about having to tell me about Lark, about the fact that I was right about my friend, about her being a bad influence on the people she was around.

"Yes, I'm fine but I need to sleep. I'll talk to you tomorrow." I said, wiping the tears from my cheeks.

I did need to sleep. It was after 3am and I had to get up for the funeral in less than four hours.

"Alright, but I promise nothing happened. You're not mad,

are you?" He asked. His voice was sincere.

I wasn't mad at him. I was angry that it happened, but I wasn't mad at him.

"No, I'm not angry with you. But I really need to sleep. Goodnight."

I shut my cell phone and laid my head down. The bed beneath me was uncomfortable.

Why the hell did he have to tell me this tonight, of all nights?!

I was pissed because I had to get up so early. My phone rang again. It was Thomas.

"I wanted to say goodnight," he said. "Have a good day tomorrow. I love you."

He was so sweet and I loved him for that.

"I love you too. Goodnight." I said, hanging up.

I looked up at the ceiling, shadows danced on it, reflecting from the TV. After some time, I finally fell asleep.

The next day at the funeral I was tired. I didn't sleep well the night before; all I could think about was Lark throwing herself at Thomas, desperate to have something good in her life, desperate to have what she thought she deserved. I didn't cry at the funeral, but my heart squeezed in my chest upon seeing my dad upset at the sight of his best friend, dead.

I sat in the front row with my family and my godfather's family. Before the ceremony started we walked to the front to view the casket, it was open. I looked down at my godfather. He wasn't related to me, but I had grown up with him in my life and I loved him like family.

"Blood isn't the only thing that bonds people together", my dad used to tell me. "Friends are the only family you get to choose, so choose wisely", he'd said.

    I only looked into the casket to see his face and then I took my seat on the pew. There was no need for me to stare at him for long; I already knew what it looked like to have no soul.

    Lark went back to North Carolina before I returned from New Jersey. She didn't find a place in New York and most likely left because she couldn't face me knowing what she'd done. She knew I'd never talk to her again if I found out. And even though she threatened Thomas that she would lie and tell me that they had slept together if he told me about her desperate attempt to have sex with him, he didn't care and told me anyhow. How after Darryl's show she took the cab with him home and pretended to be too drunk to go upstairs alone, how he helped her into my apartment, how she threw herself on him and begged him to have sex with her, how she told him that she would give him oral sex if he wanted her to, that I wouldn't mind if they had sex because we were friends and friends shared everything.

    But he didn't have to tell me. I knew what kind of person Lark was, she was unconfident and used others' weaknesses to combat her own insecurities. I still never understood why she would try so hard to take him from me. Thomas said it was because she was a little off, not quite right in the head.

    "To be loved is to be hated," he'd said.

    He was right. As much as Lark praised me, she envied me more. I didn't understand, I was so nice to her, but I guess that's just how it was. She didn't call anymore after that week.

INGRID DARLING

Eight

Christmas came and passed. I flew to North Carolina on Christmas Eve, arriving in time for our yearly dinner with my entire extended family. I missed Thomas. He was in New Jersey with his family. I wouldn't see him for four days, and by the time I'd opened my gifts on Christmas day, I wanted to return to New York to be with him. We talked on the phone every day and night, longing to be in each others' presence but I had to wait. Patience is a virtue, I remembered saying to Emerald in our phone conversation a few months ago. She was right and I wanted to be virtuous. I thought about Emerald, that it would be nice for us to see each other while I was in town. I called her and we decided to meet for breakfast the next day.

  I was supposed to meet her at 10:15am outside of the restaurant, but I was running late. Before I left my house I'd decided to roll a joint in the car and smoke it in the driveway, hoping to catch a quick buzz since I wasn't smoking marijuana in New York anymore. Thomas thought it was unladylike and didn't like it when I smoked. And despite the fact that I lived with Theresa, who was always at our apartment smoking with Darryl, I stopped joining them to appease my new boyfriend. I valued his opinion more than I cared to be high. Besides, I was noticing an improvement in my performance at work, which my boss appreciated as well. He gave me a raise last month.

  The ride was only eight minutes from my house but the drive seemed endless. Waves of rain splattered against the windshield, skewing my vision. I was suddenly very high. I'd just pulled into a parking space when it hit me, my head felt heavy and my stomach tensed.

"I don't feel so good." I said, pulling the rain jacket close to my body as I walked up to the entrance of the restaurant.

Emerald stood under the awning, wearing a bright yellow rain coat. She looked like sunshine.

"Maybe you should eat something," she laughed, pulling me into a tight hug. "How are you babe? It's been a while since I've seen your face."

I smiled and followed her into the restaurant.

"Yeah, maybe I'm just hungry. I missed you." I said, still not feeling quite right.

We walked inside and stood in line. For some reason the place was packed, as if everyone decided to come to this restaurant, this morning, at this time. It irritated me, I wanted to eat something immediately so the uncomfortable feeling would pass, but it would be a while before we would have our food. I could feel a dizzy spell coming on, and fast. I started to panic.

"You know, I think I'm just gonna sit down." I gushed.

I didn't know what was going on and my vision was getting blurry. Emerald looked at me with a worried expression.

"Are you alright?" She asked.

"Uh, yeah, I need to sit though." I said, focusing on searching for an open table in the restaurant.

"Alright, I'll order for you," she said. "The same thing you always get?"

I nodded.

She turned back towards the menu on the wall. I squeezed between her and an older woman and walked over to an open table by the window. It was on the other side of the restaurant and the fifty feet seemed infinite. I took eight steps and suddenly all the color in the room faded to gray. My arms and legs began to tingle and I couldn't walk straight. I took five more steps, trying to keep my balance, and then there was silence.

Oh my god, not again.

I wanted to cry but it seemed like every ounce of life was draining from my body. The gray room quickly turned to white and I could no longer see anything. I could feel myself swaying back and forth as I took the next three steps, bumping into tables and knocking over chairs that were in my way. I reached out, hoping to grab onto something yet touched nothing but air, fell forward then slammed to the ground.

I woke up several minutes later. There were six faces above me when I opened my eyes, all with nervous expressions. It was the first time I'd fainted. I had assumed it was because my breakfast was a joint rather than a meal, but it turns out I had a fainting problem. The next time it happened I was with Thomas in FAO Schwartz, and I woke up a few minutes later in a wheelchair with a candy bar in my hand, and again after that I was in my apartment typing on my laptop and woke up a minute later face down on the floor. It always scared Thomas when I'd faint and he'd get angry with me when I would laugh about it once I woke up. He truly cared about me, Emerald made that clear.

When I finally came to, she made me confess that I had smoked a joint before leaving my house that morning. She sipped her coffee and gave me a pitiful look. I hated it when she judged me, because she was always right.

INGRID DARLING

"Ingrid, I thought you stopped smoking pot. Didn't you tell me that last week?" She said.

I could sense the disappointment in her voice.

"I didn't lie to you." I said, taking a sip of my tea, courtesy of the restaurant.

Perhaps fainting wasn't such a bad idea considering how I received a free bagel with cream cheese, orange juice, and a hot beverage of my choice. I guess it was their way of preventing a liability lawsuit. It wasn't making me feel better though, the tea was bland and my head still hurt. I wasn't high anymore, but the dizziness was still there.

"Well you lied to Thomas." She said bluntly.

She put her coffee on the table and cut into her cinnamon bagel. Steam rose from the middle when she pulled it apart.

"You're right, but marijuana doesn't hurt anyone and studies have shown that it actually has cancer curing properties. I would know because I did a project on it in sixth grade." I said, taking a bite of my bagel.

It was warm in my mouth.

"Well you don't have cancer and it doesn't matter what studies have shown. You said you were going to stop smoking, so you should stop. Don't just say things for the sake of saying them. You need to take responsibility for your own words and actions." She said, biting her bagel.

"Yes, mom!"

I swallowed and laughed.

"I'm not trying to be your mom. I just want you to live up to your own expectations. Do what you say you want to do, anything other than that is just laziness." She said, licking the cinnamon from her lips.

Her short hair framed her delicate face and freckles covered every ounce of blank space on her cheeks. Her white cardigan was buttoned to the top, perfectly pressed, revealing not so much as a wrinkle. She was very careful with everything, even paid attention to where the crumbs were falling from her bagel. It always made me smile at how precise she was. She never wanted to make a mistake, to do anything foolish that could have been avoided with common sense. Lack of good judgment is the only failure in life, she would say. She never wanted anyone to fail. I appreciated her for that.

"You're right. I'm so glad you're my friend, Em. Sometimes I need the advice when I don't want to hear it from myself. I'll stop, not because I necessarily want to, but because I said I would and I promised Thomas." I said, taking another bite of my bagel.

She smiled.

"Glad to hear that," she said. "So, tell me what you were upset about last week. You said you would rather tell me in person than over the phone. What's up?"

She took another bite of her bagel and leaned forward, waiting for me to tell her something interesting. I sighed and took a sip of my tea, it was still bland.

"Well, you remember my friend Lark, right?"

"Yeah, from college. What happened?"

I reached over the table for a packet of sugar, deciding that my tea would taste better with a sweeter flavor and poured it into the cup, stirring with my spoon. I told Emerald about Lark's decision to move to New York, how she came up for the week, how

INGRID DARLING

I had to leave for my godfather's funeral, and how she tried to sleep with Thomas while I was gone. Emerald kept the same expression throughout the entire story, never flinching despite the pain she could see I was feeling from having been betrayed by my friend. When I was finished, she sat back in her chair, placing the bagel on her plate and wiping her hands with a napkin. I looked at her, waiting for a response, curious as to what she was going to tell me.

"She is obviously jealous of you." She said, flatly.

I stopped stirring my tea and put the spoon on my plate.

"I know this. But why would she try to sleep with my boyfriend? I mean, I even told her that he was off limits!" I cried.

My eyes started watering at the thought of Thomas and Lark together without me. I turned and faced the window. Splashes of rain painted the glass.

"Because she is not comfortable with herself, and the only way for her to mask that discomfort is by trying to take it from you. The only reason why we're jealous of others is because we're not where we want to be." She said.

Her voice was reassuring.

"But why my boyfriend?" I asked, wiping a tear from my cheek.

I wanted to continue eating my bagel but I was no longer hungry. The dizziness was beginning to fade away.

"Because she wants the drama. She is aroused by the drama, which is why she tried to take what didn't belong to her. Life is temptation, and there are those of us that keep getting drawn to the fire, regardless of how much pain it will inflict on ourselves or someone else."

A memory of Lark and I doing lines in the bathroom stall

crept into my head.

"I guess you're right," I said, facing her again. "Why do people do this? Why don't they stop being so dramatic, stop living out their own tragedies? "

"It's easy. Human drama is inevitable. No matter how far you try to run from it, it will always be there."

She shrugged her shoulders, taking another sip of her coffee.

"Well so how is it possible for us to escape the tragedy of life?"

"Life isn't tragic. Life is beautiful. You have to realize this. You can't get so caught up with the bad things in life, because they are ultimately there to teach you a lesson. I had to learn this the hard way. When my dad passed away, I thought I was being punished, but in fact it was a lesson I had to learn about life."

"What lesson?" I asked, feeling myself returning to normal.

I was no longer dizzy and my nausea was gone completely.

"That life is something to be cherished rather than thrown away, because you never know how long you have on this planet. So stop wasting your time and live your life to its' ultimate potential."

"How does one do that?" I asked, looking down to my tea.

I picked up the cup and held it to my lips.

"Perfection can only be achieved by facing your imperfections. You can't tell if something is sweet without realizing that it used to be bitter, right? So you have to step away from temptation and find the beauty in life, without having to take it from something or someone else."

I smiled at her and nodded, taking a sip of my tea, no longer bland. It was sweet, just how I liked it. We sat and talked for another hour, and by the time we left the restaurant, the rain had stopped and the sun was shining. I was happy I'd had breakfast with Emerald because she always seemed to brighten my day.

    I returned to New York the day after I had breakfast with Emerald, Thomas picked me up from the airport. He surprised me with a gift, handing me a blue box with a white bow when we got back to my apartment. It was a diamond tennis bracelet.
    "I couldn't stop thinking about how nice it would look on you, so I decided to get it for you for Christmas." He said, taking it out of the box and fastening it to my wrist.
    I was shocked that he had spent so much money on me, but happy that he had chosen such a beautiful present. I fished through my suitcase and pulled out my gift to him which I had carefully wrapped in snowman print wrapping paper. He opened it, revealing the cufflinks I had found at a men's boutique in North Carolina. He thanked me and hugged me tight, telling me that he missed me while I was away.
    The next few days were spent making up for lost time, we had sex until we were exhausted, told each other about our families and laughed about what our relatives had gotten us for Christmas. His aunt had given him a gift card to a hunting store, convinced that he loved to hunt based on a picture of him fishing with his friend when he was ten. I told him how my uncle gave me a pink plastic makeup trunk, similar to what children use with they're in grade school to put their pens and markers in. Apparently my mom told him that my favorite color was pink and that I wore makeup and he just ran with it. It always amused me how my relatives knew who I

was but didn't know anything about me. It seemed that blood was the *only* thing that kept us bonded.

INGRID DARLING

Nine

By the time New Years Eve came, Thomas and I had solidified our plans for the evening. We decided to go to a party that was being thrown at some club uptown by his cousin, Martin. Martin graduated from Yale in 2004, worked for an investment banking firm in New York for two years, and was currently in law school at Harvard. He was one of those people that believed having a 'D' behind your name was some significant achievement, dismissing anyone who didn't or wasn't on their way towards attaining one. His arrogance was the only thing he had achieved in my mind.

After showering and getting dressed, wearing a fitted black dress, black pea coat, and black knee high boots, Thomas picked me up and the two of us drove through the horrendous traffic uptown in his black Mercedes coupe. He wore a gray cashmere sweater, a white collar poking through the neck, and black slacks.

"You look nice." I said, looking at him in the drivers' seat.

"Thanks, Darling. You look incredible." He said, flashing me a smile.

His eyes sparkled from the city lights dashing past. I smiled and grabbed his hand.

We stopped at a street vendor so I could pick up a neon green headband with flashing lights and a big '2007' molded on its' top. When we arrived at the party destination, Thomas valet parked his car so no one would "ruin the paint" while we were in the club, and were greeted at the entrance by a swarm of bodyguards and blaring music. Each of us were searched because evidently some celebrity was inside then granted entrance after which we immediately looked for Martin.

He was at the bar, talking to a girl wearing a bra and panties. She apparently was one of the table dancers for the VIP section. I felt sorry for her; she was so exposed, so exploited, for the pleasure of high paying guests. Cameras flashed. I grabbed Thomas' arm, pulling myself close to him, the party was too crowded and the music was too loud for me to lose him. The model in bedtime apparel walked off as Martin and Thomas embraced. I waved and smiled to Martin while the two of them talked.

I glanced around the party and shifted uncomfortably as I waited for their conversation to end. Loud, intoxicated people danced to the music, bumping into me without apologizing, without even noticing I was there. I listened to bits and pieces of their conversation, hearing Martin say he was planning a trip to Egypt with three guys he worked with from JP Morgan. The guys stood behind him at the bar, all with glasses in their hands, and Martin introduced them to Thomas. I couldn't make out the first guys name, but I heard the other two, Brian and Charles. Martin didn't consider introducing them to me, although I was standing right next to Thomas.

Typical.

The one in the middle, whose name I didn't hear, glanced at me. His dark eyes sparkled under dark eyebrows. He was very handsome. I pulled my gaze from his and leaned into Thomas, hoping to break him away from the conversation and towards the bar so I could get a drink. But the five of them stood talking for a few more minutes. I felt ostracized, like I wasn't allowed into the men's club, like the conversation was only permitted to investment bankers and financial analysts. Some drunken girl wearing a shiny mini dress bumped into me, spilling her drink all over my boots. Once again, no apology.

    The six of us finally migrated towards the middle of the club where a VIP section was reserved for Martin and his guests. There were five bottles of champagne and two large bottles of vodka sitting in silver ice buckets inside of a roped in lounge. We entered the lounge, stepping down and seating ourselves on plush white couches. Across from ours was another VIP section but I couldn't see who was in it, people were crowding around it like paparazzi, trying to capture the guest on their iPhone so they could most likely blast it all over some blog. It was pathetic.

    I sat between Thomas and Martin, across from Brian, Charles and the handsome no-name. We made ourselves some drinks from the vodka bottles, mixing them with the purple liquid that was also sitting on the table. The guys continued talking, this time about their stocks and investments. I nestled into Thomas and glanced around the room, catching a few jealous expressions from girls that were standing around our section, trying to figure out who I was to be there with all those men in VIP. For a moment I was pleased to receive such envious looks from strangers, but then I realized that it made no difference who I was, to gloat about success was childish.

    I turned away, focusing on the ambiance of the club and the music that was being played. The handsome guy was talking but I couldn't hear what he was saying, I just watched his lips move. He sat forward with his elbows on his knees, his hands holding a glass. His black cashmere sweater was pulled tight around his torso, slightly revealing his muscular build. His black slacks were fitted around his legs and I could tell he used to be an athlete. My eyes moved towards his face, locking into his. I could feel him staring into me as he talked, like he was reading my soul. For a moment everything in the club was quiet, as if he and I were the only people there, staring at each other. My heart quickened its pace. I pulled my eyes from his and focused on the drink in my hand.

"James Frederick Blake!" I heard a girl shriek over the loud music.

Apparently that was his name. He stopped talking and turned around to see who was yelling at him. She had short brown hair and wore too much makeup. She nearly fell into the rope as she leaned forward to hug him, clearly drunk, trying to force an invitation into our VIP section.

Just another gold digger, I thought, rolling my eyes.

I looked at Thomas. He followed my gaze towards the girl, who was now trying to invite three of her scantily clad friends into the lounge with her. He knew exactly what I was thinking. We both laughed.

I didn't pay too much attention to what was going on around me for the rest of the evening. After three drinks, my equilibrium was off and the club looked more lopsided than perpendicular. I danced to the music in our VIP lounge, occasionally catching James' eyes. He kept sneaking glances at me while he sipped his drink. The drunken brunette was now licking his face, trying to secure herself the evening in his bed, but it seemed he had other plans. He eventually left the lounge and disappeared to the other side of the club, I didn't see him anymore after that.

At midnight, Thomas and I kissed. It wasn't as romantic as I'd hoped and I was slightly disappointed. By 2am I was ready to go back to my apartment. My feet were tired from dancing so much

INGRID DARLING

and my head hurt from drinking all that vodka. Thomas wanted to stay and talk to people he'd run into from his classes. I'm not sure what he wanted to talk about in the noisy club, but instead of arguing I just sat on the couch in the lounge, now empty, and waited. I waited for forty-five minutes. Four very inebriated men approached the lounge at different times asking me to dance, all offers of which I declined, before Thomas reappeared with my coat, telling me he was finally ready to leave.

Though the party was planned to last until 6am, I was exhausted and not thrilled to be there anymore. We said goodbye to Martin and Brian, who were both by the bar talking to a different group of scantily clad girls, left the club and took the elevator down to the valet garage. We stood outside, shivering in the cold, waiting for the valet driver to arrive with the car. A few flurries trickled from the sky, my breath formed clouds in front of my face. I huddled close to Thomas, hoping to warm myself with his body heat. I looked down at my boots which had been stained with cranberry and vodka, ruining the suede.

Oh well, so much for preserving the finish.

A few minutes later, the black Mercedes sped around the corner then screeched to a halt in front of us. The valet driver threw the driver's door open, nicking the rail between the curb and the garage wall. The sound echoed through the garage and Thomas let out a gasp as he ran to see if the paint had been scratched. He nearly screamed, grabbing his face with his hands and falling into his car. The door was dented in. I looked at the valet driver who didn't seem to care about damaging the car, he handed Thomas his keys and sauntered around to the valet stand. It wasn't the best night, but I would say that the New Year definitely started off with a bang.

Ten

June, 2007

London. I stretched out on the couch, staring out the window as drops of rain trickled down the pane. The sky was overcast, as it had been for the past three days. John Coltrane played on the sound system, filling the condo with sophistication. Thomas sat in the recliner opposite the TV, watching a football game on mute: England versus Portugal. Theresa appeared from the kitchen with three glasses of red wine, handing one to me, one to Thomas, then sitting on the couch opposite me. I took a sip and found it was a full bodied Cabernet. The three of us sat for a few minutes, quietly sipping our wine and enjoying the ambiance of the afternoon before Darryl came in, holding a glass of wine and a magazine, breaking the silence.

"So what should we do for the rest of the day?" He asked, throwing the magazine onto the coffee table. He sat down next to Theresa and threw his arm over her shoulders.

Thomas shrugged.

"Doesn't matter to me," he said, keeping his eyes locked onto the screen.

More rain splashed onto the window. I turned towards the group and sat up.

"Well it's kind of gross outside."

Theresa laughed.

"It's always gross in London," she said, taking a sip of her

INGRID DARLING

wine.

    In early May, the four of us decided that a summer trip to London would be a great way to get the travel bug out of our systems. The condo belonged to Theresa's grandfather who lived in Manchester. He bought it a few years ago, deciding that his children and grandchildren would want to visit London when they came to see him and it would be more cost efficient to purchase a place rather than waste money on hotel rooms. It seemed logical, but the condo was located in one of the fanciest areas of London, which didn't actually make it a money saving purchase. It didn't matter to him though, he lived in a medieval estate on four hundred acres, with horses, a lake, and a landing pad for helicopters, so saving money wasn't something he was concerned with.

    He made his money as a wine vineyard owner and distributer. Sixty of his four hundred acres was where the grapes were grown, processed, and distributed. He started his company when he was 21 and still continued to produce and distribute wine to this day. When Theresa called to tell him that we were coming to England, he agreed it would be lovely for us to stay in his condo as long as we paid him a visit.

    We took the train to Manchester the next day after we'd arrived, spent the afternoon lounging by the lake and driving four wheelers on his land. His chef prepared a five course meal for us and mixed our favorite smoothies from the fruit grown in the orchard on the other side of the lake. Her grandfather was very refined and had a sharp English accent. The conversation at lunch was entertaining as he told many stories about how wild he was when he was our age. Theresa's grandmother passed away a few years ago and I could see that he still carried the pain of her death with him. His brow was heavy and his eyes looked sad, despite how happy he was to see Theresa. Apparently she was his favorite grandchild as she was the only of who spent the weekends on his estate as a child. Having lived in London for her father's job for a few years, Theresa was much closer to her grandfather than her other cousins were. We stayed until sundown then decided we would return to London. He hugged each of us and had his driver take us to the train station.

We spent the next day being tourists. Darryl and Thomas and I had never been to London before so we went to the typical tourist sites: Big Ben, The Tate Modern, The London Eye, Buckingham Palace and Harrods. We took pictures in the red phone booths and posed with wax celebrities at Madame Tussaud's. I always thought it was eerie that someone would take the time to make a wax statue of a famous person. It seemed to take the reality out of their existence, as if they weren't really human beings like the rest of us. After Darryl and Thomas posed with Michael Jackson, we left the museum and walked around the city. We went to a pub after dinner, getting drunk and taking the bus back to the condo. We all woke up late this morning, ordering lunch from the concierge, drinking mimosa's and now wine.

Portugal scored. Thomas didn't flinch. I'm not sure if he knew who he wanted to win. It seemed as if he was only watching the game because there was nothing else to do.

"So? We need to decide on a game plan." Darryl said, more annoyed this time.

He obviously didn't want to sit in the condo all day, unlike the rest of us who didn't seem to care. I took another sip of my wine.

"We can relax today, since it is raining. And why don't we plan a day trip somewhere for tomorrow." Theresa said, running her hands through her long hair.

"Oh that'd be fun!" I exclaimed. "How about Paris? I've always wanted to go there."

"That's a good idea." Darryl said.

"That could be cool." Thomas said, eyes still glued to the TV.

He hadn't touched his wine.

"Great! Paris it is. We need to book our tickets at the train station. Do you guys want to go down there in a few hours?" Theresa said, standing up from the couch.

She walked into the kitchen and reappeared with the bottle of wine and refilled her glass.

"Sure." I said, extending my glass.

She poured more wine into it and placed the bottle on the coffee table.

"Great, this should be fun." She said, sitting back on the couch next to Darryl.

He smiled and kissed her on the cheek.

An hour later, the four of us piled into a cab and rode down to the train station. We sat down with a travel agent and booked four tickets for the 5am train to Paris. Our package included train seats and a guided bus tour of the city. None of us had been to Paris before, so we were all very excited. We spent the rest of the day wandering around Trafalgar Square people watching, which was amusing.

In the evening we went to an exclusive Asian restaurant that was hidden down an alley and whose only indication of existence was a bouncer standing in front of a windowless, sign-less door. It was a popular restaurant with celebrities and socialites and usually took knowing someone to actually book a reservation. Theresa's grandfather must've known someone because he called earlier in the day and booked us a table for the night. We arrived for our reservation twenty minutes late which meant we would only have the table for an hour and forty minutes; that's how it worked in London, your reservation was only good for two hours, then they kicked you out. We barely finished our dessert before the waitresses were handing us our checks and ushering us out the door. We decided not to do anything extravagant later in the evening considering how early we had to wake up to catch our train so we each had a glass of wine before heading to bed.

    The next morning my intention was to wake up early, shower and blow dry my hair, but it seemed the odds and the European outlets were against me. My blow dryer blew three times before I gave up on drying my hair.

    It will just have to be curly today. And so it was.

    Not sure what the weather would be like in Paris, we decided to dress for summer in London. Theresa and I wore dresses and lightweight jackets, Darryl and Thomas wore jeans and t-shirts. By the time we arrived at the train station it was time for us to board. The ride took a few hours. I sat by the window, watching the landscape change as it rushed by. Darryl and Thomas slept while Theresa read a book. After some time, I must have fallen asleep because the next thing I knew, we were arriving in Paris.

INGRID DARLING

*E*leven

Berets, poodles, accordions playing sweet Parisian music, beautiful women in little black dresses, fancy intellectuals smoking cigarettes in a café. That had always been my image of Paris, pure elegance. This, however, was not the image we were greeted with upon exiting the train station. Rather, we were welcomed with the Parisian national guard parading along the sidewalk holding rifles the size of small children, refugees from Kosovo or Albania or some eastern European country asking people to hold their baby so they could pick pocket them, and Haitian street vendors yelling in French at tourists, trying to make a sale on knockoff designer handbags. A woman with rotted teeth wearing a head scarf bombarded me on the sidewalk, speaking some Slavic language, and forced a sign written in broken English into my face.

Try to getting me in America, it read.

Her breath smelled like sour milk. Thomas grabbed my arm and pulled me away from her before she could reach into my handbag. Another woman in a similar outfit rushed to Theresa, grabbing her hand and pulling her away from us. Darryl nearly pushed the woman to the ground before seizing Theresa's hand and guiding her away from the commotion of the immigrants. There was chaos outside the train station, people were everywhere, rushing past and yelling in French, it wasn't romantic like I'd pictured, like I'd expected. The sky was overcast and the air was chilly, and every building around us looked like it could be a part of the red light district, dirty and polluted.

Welcome to Paris.

I sighed, walking with Thomas, Darryl and Theresa to the edge of the sidewalk. We had no idea where we were going, but it seemed like a good idea to hail a cab and decide from there.

Our driver spoke English, so my horrible attempt to communicate that we wanted to go the Notre Dame didn't matter. I'd taken French in high school, but it had been four years since I'd actually spoken the language, so the only thing I could really say was "bonjour", "s'il vous plait" and "merci". That was all that was necessary anyway, especially when all we had to do was point to a map. At least I was able to be polite after pointing out where we wanted to go. The driver took us to Île de la Cité where he said we'd be able to walk to Notre Dame, Pont Neuf, which is one of the oldest bridges in Paris, and the Place Dauphine, a public square that has been around since the 17th century. All of these places were located along the Seine, which flowed through central Paris. By the time we paid our driver and got out of the cab, the sun started shining.

We spent an hour walking around Île de la Cité, taking pictures of the church and the bridge and rummaging through the trinkets on the street vendor tables. I bought a compact mirror with a cat on it for my mom. Thomas bought a painting of the Eiffel Tower for his brother. I stopped into a small bookstore, hoping to find something worth purchasing that would make me look like an intellectual back in New York. I found a Harry Potter book in French and decided it was worth buying since I was a fan of the series anyway.

We stopped at a café and ordered omelet's, crepes and

cappuccino's, figuring we had to order French food while we were in France, and breakfast was appropriate considering it was only 10am. Again, I communicated our orders by pointing to the menu and saying "s'il vous plaît". The waiter smiled, something I wasn't expecting, and took our menus. Our food came soon after, it was delicious.

    We spent the rest of the day on the bus tour which had come with our package. It felt funny sitting on the roof of a red bus with a huge sign on it that screamed "Tourist". I hated drawing attention to myself, especially being an American. I didn't want the natives to think I was some Da Vinci Code breaker on a mission in Paris. However, the bus ride was fun. It circled the city, drove up the Champs-Élysées, where the Bastille Day parade is held yearly, and around the Arc de Triomphe, which was created in honor of those who fought for France during the Napoleonic Wars. There was so much history around us, something I never saw in America. The bus rode us through the streets and around buildings and monuments. The city was beautiful under the bright sun. I leaned into Thomas, watching the people on the street below. Fancy women strutted by walking their poodles and men sat on chairs outside of café's smoking cigarettes, no doubt having some intellectual conversation.

    Now this is Paris, I thought, smiling and admiring the scene around me.

    We got off at Champs de Mars to see the Eiffel Tower, which was much bigger than I'd expected. We ate lunch at a pizzeria then decided that we wanted to see the Louvre. We took the bus back to the first arrondissement and walked up to the museum. Darryl and Theresa decided they would rest outside the museum while Thomas and I ventured inside.

We entered through a giant glass pyramid, took an escalator down to the ticket booth, purchased entry tickets, and made our way through the museum. Thirty minutes of walking later we realized that we were still in the first half of the first wing. At 650,000 square feet, there was no possible way we would be able to see the entire museum, so we chose three particular pieces on the museum map that we would see while inside: the Venus de Milo, the Nike of Samothrace, and the Mona Lisa. The first two happened to be in the next hallways which made them easy to find, the Mona Lisa, however, as we discovered, was not as simple to locate.

Upon following signs advertising the painting for ten minutes, we realized the painting had to be the largest attraction and therefore must be somewhere in the middle of the museum, so we quickened our paces. We saw more signs, but no sign of the painting. Our brisk walking became a power walk and then we eventually broke into a jog. It had already been an hour since we entered the museum and we didn't want to keep Darryl and Theresa waiting while we browsed, so we hurried along. Our jog gradually became a sprint and we laughed as we ran past people through the museum, following the signs for the Mona Lisa.

I nearly collided into a group of Asians huddled together pointing to a map. I laughed as Thomas and I kept dodging people and sculptures. I felt young and excited and alive, as if all I ever needed to do in life was run through the Louvre. Paintings rushed past in a blur of color. We ran through hallway after hallway, amused and happy. I counted fifteen signs before we finally came to the hallway leading into Leonardo da Vinci's work. We slowed our pace, laughing and panting. Thomas pulled me into a tight hug and kissed me on the forehead. His body was warm.

"I love you." He said, smiling and breathing hard.

"I love you too." I said, grabbing his hand and stuffing the museum map into my purse.

The two of us waited in line to view the painting, during which I heard three different languages buzzing around my head, suddenly making me feel very foreign. I had already forgotten that we were in a different country, with a different culture and language.

It is easy to pretend that everyone is just like you when you feel happy and carefree. Running through the museum made me forget how different we as humans are, because it all looked the same from the outside, it all was the same colorful blur. We all are pieces of art, expressing something deeper beyond the surface, something beautiful which artists try to express in their sculptures, in their paintings, hoping to capture what we as humans exude in our everyday existence.

We inched forward in line. The man in front of us pulled a camera out of his shoulder bag and began snapping pictures, speaking to his wife in Arabic. I looked at the sign near the entrance. It had a picture of a camera with a slash across it. This man must not have understood the drawing.

The line broke and Thomas and I walked around the room, which was small with extraordinarily high ceilings. Several paintings lined the walls with small captions beneath them, seeming to lead up to the main attraction which was centered in the room on a free standing wall. A group of people stood huddled around the Mona Lisa behind the red velvet rope. A security guard paced in front of the painting holding a club, clearly ready to hit anyone who tried to cross the rope. I peeked through a tall man and a short woman, catching a glimpse of the painting. It was much smaller than I'd expected. The crowd eventually cleared and Thomas and I stood examining the painting.

I could see why it was such a famous piece of art. Leonardo da Vinci impressively captured the reality of the woman. Everything from the way her eyes followed me when I moved from side to side, to the delicacy of her fingers was accurate. The finish on the canvas gave the painting a real look, like she could actually be sitting inside the frame, watching everyone admire her beauty. The only odd thing I noticed about the painting was that she had no eyebrows, which was bizarre only because it made her look like a man, rather than a woman.

Perhaps that was the point, to reveal the beauty of humanity, rather than any particular man or woman.

We gazed at the painting for a few more minutes and then decided it was time to leave the museum. Ten minutes later, we were outside, walking towards Darryl and Theresa who were seated against a statue in the courtyard. They had fallen asleep. I approached Theresa and nudged her shoulder, jarring her from sleep. They stood and stretched then the four of us walked toward the Arc de Triomphe, deciding that we would have a drink while we were in the city. Darryl suggested the Buddha Bar, which was the sister bar to the one in New York that his band mate had spoken highly of. He said it was pretty cool and had a funky ambiance, so we all agreed to go and made our way towards the metro station. Theresa searched for the location on her Blackberry, discovering that it was located in the 8th arrondissement, and we were currently in the first.

The metro was crowded and stuffy. The four of us huddled

together in a corner, feeling ostracized by our inability to communicate with the Parisians in the car with us. I laughed at the image plastered on the door of the train. It read:

Attention! Ne mets pas tes mains sur la porte: tu risques de te faire pincer tres fort!

Beneath the letters was an image of a rabbit with its hand caught in the door. I figured it was warning of some sort, unsure why the French had used a cartoon to express the message. Apparently it's easier to follow the direction of a rabbit.

The train pulled to a stop and the doors flew open. We made our way down the corridor and up the stairs to the street, trying not to get pushed over by the rushing Parisian mob. We took a few turns, following the map on Theresa's phone and finally found the entrance to the Buddha Bar. I followed the group through the large oak doors, adjusting my eyes to the dim lighting inside. They waited for me before they said anything to the hostess. Even though I could only say three things in French, it was three more than them, so they let me do all the talking.

"Combien de personnes?" The hostess asked through red lips and a perfect white smile.

Her long brown hair framed her delicate face. She wore a black corset and black fitted pants and stood with her hand on her hip next to the hostess stand.

"Quatre." I replied, nervously.

I felt strange speaking a foreign language so badly. Luckily she didn't ask anything after that. Another hostess came over, grabbed four menus from the stand and ushered for us to follow her.

"Amusez-vous bien."

The first hostess said as we walked past her. I smiled and nodded, not exactly sure what she'd said.

We followed the other girl towards our table. She had short black hair, wore a black mini dress and black flats and smelled like jasmine. She led us through a dark hallway. I had the impression that the Buddha Bar was only a bar, but it was, in fact, a restaurant. Mosaics were painted along the walls and lamps cast red tints over the tables and chairs. The hallway wove around a central seating area which was a level below. As we followed the hostess around, a giant golden statue of a sitting Buddha appeared on the floor in the middle of the room. It was the height of the entire restaurant with its head nearly touching the ceiling. Despite the low lighting, the statue radiated a sort of power, like it was watching over everyone who dined in its presence. Moroccan style music drummed throughout the restaurant, giving it an air of chic sophistication. The hostess walked us to a low table with bench style seating and oversized pillows. We sat and she handed us our menus.

"Votre serveuse viendra dans une minute." She said, smiling.

"Merci." I said, opening my menu.

She turned and disappeared around the corner. The lighting was dim and it was nearly impossible to read our menus.

"We're only getting cocktails, right?" Theresa said, making a funny face at her menu.

"Yeah. I can't read this thing anyway. Where is the cocktail list, Ingrid?" Darryl said, throwing his menu on the table between the four of us.

INGRID DARLING

I laughed.

"I think where it says 'Boisson', on the back side." I said, pointing to my menu so Theresa and Thomas could find where the drinks were.

We each tried our hardest to pick a cocktail in the dim light and foreign language before our waitress came. She walked up to our table, wearing a loose blouse and dark fitted pants and flats. She didn't smile.

"Prêt?" She asked, looking down at the pad she was holding.

Her stance was stiff and she avoided eye contact, like she was disgusted with having to take our orders.

"Um." I hesitated, glancing again at my menu. I looked toward Darryl, Theresa and Thomas. "Do you guys know what you want to order?"

"Yeah, I want this one." Theresa said, pointing to a cocktail on the list.

"I'll have the same." Darryl said, reclining back on the bench.

"Get me this one." Thomas said, pointing to his menu.

I looked up to the waitress. She shifted on her feet and sighed loudly. Her annoyed attitude made me flustered.

"Uh, nous voudrons deux, uh, these." I said, pointing to the drink that Theresa and Darryl wanted. "Et, je voudrais one of these." I said, pointing out the drink I wanted to order. "Et, il voudra this one." I said, pointing to the drink that Thomas wanted.

My broken French was the best attempt I could give, but she wasn't impressed.

"Comment?" She said, forcefully.

INGRID DARLING

I repeated my order, slowly this time, hoping she would understand my French better than I could. She scribbled something on her pad, and collected our menus, never once looking up at us.

"Ces stupides américaines! Ils viennent en France et n'apprennent pas notre langue. C'est comme on parle à un singe!" She said to another waitress that walked past.

The other girl laughed and looked at the four of us and then the two of them sauntered away.

"Oh my gosh!" I gasped, leaning back against the bench. "That bitch was talking shit about us!"

"What?" Theresa cried.

A confused expression formed on her face.

"Yeah, she was like 'these stupid Americans can't even speak French, blah blah blah'." I said, unsure of what exactly she'd said but certain it wasn't nice.

"What a bitch! What does she expect, for us to know what the hell she's talking about? I mean, how rude! She isn't getting a tip from me." Theresa said, flipping her hair.

Thomas and Darryl looked at each other and laughed.

"You girls are so funny." Thomas said, shaking his head.

"Why are we so funny?" I asked, looking at him.

"Because you're in their country, speaking in English! I'd be pissed too if someone was trying to order in my restaurant in a different language."

"Well, at least I tried to speak French! Some people don't even do that. They move to another country and never try to learn the language. So she shouldn't have been so nasty to us."

"We're in France. What did you expect?" He replied, leaning forward to examine the candle on the table.

INGRID DARLING

"I expect her to be more cordial, especially because we're paying guests!" I said, slightly annoyed that he was scolding me for reacting to the haughty waitress.

I crossed my arms over my chest and focused my gaze across the table to Theresa and Darryl. I could barely see their faces in the dim lighting. I wasn't exactly sure why the lights were so low, unless they were trying to make sure guests never actually saw their food while they were eating. Darryl was leaning into the table, playing with the wax that was overflowing from the candle onto the wooden tabletop.

"If you ask me, language is a sort of barrier. It keeps people from understanding one another. Our waitress was speaking French about the same thing we were talking about in English, but we just couldn't understand each other because of the barrier between us." He said, peeling off a piece of wax and dancing it between his fingers.

The waitress suddenly appeared with our drinks. She placed them on wooden coasters and disappeared without asking if we needed anything else. I wasn't surprised. I reached for my cocktail and took a sip, trying to avoid the large yellow flower hanging over the edge of the glass.

"That's one barrier she certainly doesn't want to break down. Her sour attitude is stronger than my drink" I sighed.

"You shouldn't let what people say bother you." Thomas said. "Someone talking about you is like them having a different view on things. Most people are ignorant and would rather believe that others can't understand them so they can do and say whatever they want and get away with it."

"I think that different languages give people different views on things." Theresa said, thumbing the pink flower hanging over her glass.

"They definitely give people a different view point because each language expresses a different idea, kind of like a symbol, so with each there is a particular way of understanding something." Darryl said, taking a sip of his drink.

"All language is symbolism anyway. A word is essentially a verbal sign for whatever it is expressing." He continued. "Chinese characters, for example, are perfect symbols for the words they express. I mean, each character describes what they actually saw. So the symbol for sun is basically just a square, and the symbol for tree looks like a 'T'."

"I didn't know that." I said, swirling the yellow flower with my finger.

"Yeah, I mean it basically symbolized what they saw. Then as the language became more complex, or descriptive, they began to add on to the characters, and they also became more complex." He said, finishing his cocktail.

"It's so strange to think that a language derives from pictures. It's like the pictures represent reality." Theresa said.

Darryl placed his empty glass on the table.

"Exactly! That's the point. If you were creating a language, wouldn't you make it so anyone could know what each symbol was and represented?"

"I guess I would," Theresa said.

"But the problem with language is that not only does it take away from the essence of the object, but the symbol only projects an imitation of the real thing. It's like art. Art is only a representation of reality so it inevitably falls short of the original."

INGRID DARLING

I thought about the Mona Lisa, how she looked so real, but was still just a painting.

"And all symbolism harbors the curse of mediocrity," he continued. "Even linguists say that language as a symbol is bound to obscure what it seeks to reveal, it doesn't reveal the life and individual fullness of existence, only a dead abbreviation of it."

Our waitress is clearly a dead abbreviation of the French language, I thought, fingering the yellow flower in my cocktail.

Darryl was still talking.

"It's like the traditional Chinese characters that derived from the simple characters that became more complex as the language evolved. Then as generations became more descriptive with language, the characters followed suit and eventually lost their true meaning. Then they came up with simplified characters, which had less brush strokes in order to abbreviate the symbol, and so the root of the character, the root of the meaning, was lost.

"Even the fact that people attributed a word for tree gave the tree less essence. It's like what the Tao Te Ch'ing says, that naming fragments the mysteries of life into ten thousand things and their manifestations," he concluded.

"So what's the point then? If language just complicates things and removes the mystery of life, why can't we just get rid of it altogether?" Theresa said.

Thomas took the last sip of his drink and laughed, placing the empty glass on his coaster on the table.

"You want to go back to grunting and sending smoke signals?"

"Well, maybe then we'll be able to understand each other. You can't grunt that you hate someone." She said, slurping the last of her drink and placing the empty glass on the table.

"Oh, you can grunt that you hate someone, and you can definitely grunt when you love someone. As a matter of fact, you can grunt all you want around me." Darryl said, growling and nuzzling his nose in Theresa's neck.

She slapped his arm gently and laughed.

"Well grunting or not, our waitress asserted her language as the authority in the situation because we're in the country where her language is dominant. I mean, it takes patience to learn a language, it takes patience to understand people. Our waitress not having patience caused her to speak badly of us when she doesn't even know us." I said, still mildly annoyed with our waitress' haughty attitude.

"True. But Darling, you can't get frustrated because of someone else's impatience." Thomas said, sliding me towards him on the bench.

I took a sip of my drink which was nearing its end.

"You're right. I'm over it now." I sighed.

At that moment, our waitress appeared around the dark corner. She approached our table and took Darryl and Theresa's empty glasses. I took one final sip of my drink and handed her my glass. She placed a black leather envelope on the table. It contained our check and a ballpoint pen. I looked at her and smiled.

"Merci," I said as sweetly as possible.

I hoped my sincerity would have an impact on her snotty attitude. It didn't, the smugness on her face remained. She picked up Thomas' glass from the table, grunted and sauntered off.

INGRID DARLING

Twelve

We arrived back in New York two days after our day in Paris. Angry with our waitress at the Buddha Bar, Theresa and I decided to leave her a less than generous tip, throwing pennies and Canadian coins on the table for her as a token of our appreciation. Only later did we discover that no one actually left a tip in Paris, so our attempt to piss her off was actually a monetary gain for her. Thus, I came to the conclusion: revenge isn't worth it, literally.

    We'd returned to London, spent the last day on a ferry ride and wandered around the outskirts of the city, before we boarded our flight to New York. The flight was long. I'd slept most of the way and occasionally stood to stretch my legs. Thomas and I talked about traveling to other places in Europe and decided the next place we would visit would be Italy. The plane landed at 3am at JFK Airport. The four of us retrieved our bags from baggage claim and wearily made our way by taxi back to mine and Theresa's apartment.

    The next day at work I gave my boss the gift I had gotten him from a souvenir store in London, a glass ash tray with the flag of England on its' base. He was thankful that I'd thought of him while I was across the ocean. I told him it was just my symbol of appreciation for letting me take a week off from work. He responded by saying that an idea is fixed and held when it is embodied in a symbol, much like language. I chuckled at his shrewdness, thinking back to the conversation I'd had with my friends in Paris, and thinking that a simple thank you would have sufficed.

    The week went by fast. I tried to ignore Mary's comments

about my travelling so much, her judgments were more covetous than sincere. But it didn't bother me; she'd never been outside of New York City so I couldn't blame her for being jealous.

On Friday I met Theresa at a cigar bar called Sullivan's for a drink after work. Inside, it was smoky and reeked of pretentiousness but I squeezed my way through the crowd and found Theresa sitting at the end of the bar talking to someone on her phone. She waved at me as I approached. I gave her a hug and sat waiting for her to finish her conversation. A few moments later, she hung up the phone and turned her attention to me.

"Apparently someone broke in and stole two paintings from my mom's gallery today." She said.

"Oh gosh, that's terrible!" I cried, thinking of how devastated Theresa's mom must be feeling.

"I know. People should have some decency to leave art galleries alone, those paintings were someone's work and who knows how long it took them to create them." Theresa huffed, staring down at her hands.

"I'm sorry to hear about your mom's gallery." I said, putting my purse on the bar top.

"It's alright. My mom didn't sound too worried about it, so I'm not gonna worry about it. I just think it's ridiculous that all these other places that should be stolen from, like banks for instance, never get touched, but small galleries are always the first to get broken into."

"You're right, but they only steal from galleries because it's easy. It's not so easy to break an institution, especially one that has a monopoly over the entire world. I mean if you think about it, banks control the world, that's what Karl Marx was trying to show people. Too bad they didn't really get it."

Theresa laughed. "Speaking of Karl, we never had that dinner with him. He would definitely love to talk about this. He is obsessed with Marx's theories and ideas."

"When is the last time you saw him?" I asked, picking up the menu that was on the bar.

"Just after December finals. He said he was thinking about joining the Peace Corps."

The faint jazz music grew louder as the bar filled with more people.

"Don't you have to be a graduate to join the Corps?" I asked, reading through the martini specials on the back of the menu.

"Yeah, he graduated in December. I haven't seen him on campus or heard from him so he must've joined." She said, flipping her hair out of her face.

She wore a faded t-shirt with a guitar on its front, a black mini skirt, and black gladiator sandals. My knee length sundress and heels made me feel stuffy next to her and I wanted to change into more comfortable clothes. A bartender came over and asked if I wanted anything, I ordered a raspberry martini. Before I could hand the menu to him I heard Theresa cry out and jump from her barstool.

I turned around, puzzled by her animated gesture, and saw her wrap someone in a tight hug but was unable to make out who it was through the crowd. They talked for a second before Theresa ushered the two of them over to where we were seated at the bar. A girl with a pixie haircut, lace cardigan and Bermuda shorts walked up behind Theresa.

"Ingrid, this is Jada. She and I had a class last semester

together. Jada, meet Ingrid, my roommate." Theresa said, motioning between the two of us.

I smiled and shook her hand.

"It's nice to meet you." I said.

Jada smiled back, revealing a perfect set of teeth.

"You too!" She exclaimed.

She took a seat at the bar on the other side of Theresa. The two of them began talking quickly, catching up on what they were doing for the summer. I overheard Jada say that she was waitressing at some bar uptown and was considering going back to Columbia for her master's degree in the fall. I didn't hear much more of the conversation, Thomas called.

I answered my phone but could barely hear him in the noisy bar so I grabbed my bag and pushed through the crowd to the front door, opening it to a blast of heat. I stood on the street talking to him for a few minutes, holding my hand over my other ear, trying desperately to shield the noise from the sidewalk construction and blaring traffic. He told me he was going to New Jersey for the weekend and wanted me to come with him. I agreed and told him I would meet him at his apartment after I left Sullivan's. My heart skipped in my chest as I hung up the phone.

I'm finally going to meet his family, I thought, shaking my head with nervous enthusiasm.

INGRID DARLING

Thirteen

March, 2008

Florence, Italy. We stood in line outside of the Galleria dell 'Accademia. The warm air was in stark contrast to that of New York. Thomas and I had arrived in Rome two days earlier. After meeting his family in New Jersey several months ago Thomas' parents became smitten with us as a couple and insisted we visit as often as possible. We'd visited several times through the fall and I chose to spend Thanksgiving with his family rather than mine. As a token of their appreciation, Thomas' dad offered to pay for our flight and hotel accommodations while we traveled through Italy. He was so proud of his son finding a "woman worth marrying" that he wanted to give us a trip that we could use for discussing our future together.

We spent the first day of our arrival in Rome touring the ancient city. We went to the Coliseum and other tourists spots, before taking a train to Florence. We would spend the rest of our week in Florence, making a day trip to Venice, before flying home. Now we stood in front of the museum that housed one of the most famous statues in history.

I licked the dripping ice cream from my cone. The wait was supposed to be an hour before we would be allowed entry so I'd asked Thomas to get me some ice cream from the vendor on the adjacent street. It took him twenty minutes to return, and the ice cream was now practically melting in my hand. I didn't mind however, I loved Thomas for being so attentive. He shifted on his feet, his impatience glaring next to the Zen-like older couple behind us.

"Ugh, how much longer to see this thing?" He asked, irritation beginning to overwhelm his normally calm persona.

"I'm sure it won't be much longer." I lied, hoping to relax him.

It would actually be another twenty minutes, but keeping that information to myself would be more helpful than hurtful in this situation. I took a seat on the stone wall beside the museum. Thomas sat with me. We waited, watching people in the street hurry along. The sight was similar to that of New York: business men speed talking to clients on their phones while mini cars dodged the pedestrian traffic crowding the busy square. It was loud and busy and the only difference was the antique architecture and construction workers shouting in Italian, otherwise, it was just another city.

Fifteen minutes passed and the line began to shift. Thomas and I stood, pulling our entrance tickets from our pockets. We inched along until we came to the front doors of the museum. A tall man with a long nose and sunken in face mumbled something in Italian, scanning our tickets. We followed the line through the double doors. A cool draft swept over my body as we walked up the stone steps inside the museum. We looked at the statues along the walls, reading the captions and taking pictures with each. We gradually made our way through the museum, down the halls and through the rooms filled with paintings and sculptures. We had already spent an hour wandering through the museum before deciding to see the last piece, a sculpture I had wanted to see my

INGRID DARLING

entire life.

"Were you saving the best for last?" Thomas asked as I pointed out the location of the statue on the museum map.

I smiled and folded the map.

"Of course," I said, grabbing his hand and pulling him down the hallway towards the center of the museum.

We turned a corner and I stopped, staring down the long corridor. Along the walls were other statues by Michelangelo, but not the one I had come to see, not the reason why I was in Florence. Sunlight streamed through the dome ceiling above a nude man standing on a marble base, David. Thomas and I walked slowly up to the famous statue and I could feel a chill crawl up my spine. As we got closer, he got bigger. I was aroused by the thought of walking towards such a famous statue, such an amazing piece of art. I was amazed by its history and presence in the room, standing seventeen feet taller than everyone else around him.

The light shone on David's face as he stood forward, facing left, like heaven was shining down on him, overwhelming him. His poised stance exuded power and exalt and radiated through the room. I didn't see anything else, I didn't hear anyone else, Thomas's voice faded into a quiet mumble. All I was aware of was David, standing there in front of me, like a god among mere mortals. The heat from the sun bounced from his chiseled marble body and onto my face, warming my cheeks. He was carved in 1501 by a twenty-six year old Michelangelo and was a true masterpiece. The idea that someone, only three years older than the age I was, had created such an exquisite piece of art by hand awed me.

The only thing I could feel at the moment was emotion, my body shuddered as a tear streamed down my face. I gazed up at the man in front of me. He was perfect, flawless, carved from stone to portray victory over a beast, victory over vice. I wiped the tear from my face before Thomas could see me crying. He was observing the statue from the other side. He didn't understand my love for art, the intimate connection I felt with such amazing skill, how it reminded me of when I used to paint and how much I'd loved it. Thomas appeared from behind David's legs.

"Okay, I've had enough of this naked guy. Can we leave now?" He said, rubbing his temples.

I could tell he was exhausted, we'd been on our feet since 9 am and it was now almost 6pm. I smiled at him and kissed his shoulder.

"Yes. I've seen what I came for. We can go now." I said, wrapping my arm in his.

We turned around and walked down the corridor towards the front of the museum. I glanced back at David, watching him growing smaller but still radiating light through the large room. I smiled to myself as we turned the corner and exited the museum, my cheeks were still warm.

We spent the rest of the week eating ravioli and spaghetti, buying souvenirs and taking pictures. We visited Il Duomo, Piazza della Signoria and Piazza Vecchio. We took a ferry to Venice before our last day, spending the majority of the day in Piazza San Marco, eating ice cream and watching the pigeons. It was interesting to observe the birds, as they behaved the exact same way as the pigeons in New York did. I wondered if the Venetian pigeons were able to communicate with the New York pigeons, or if they were like humans and had a different language because they lived on the other side of the Atlantic. I asked Thomas but he just laughed and said of course they could communicate with each other, they were just birds. But I didn't agree with him, because after all, we were just humans and communication was our biggest source of conflict.

We spent the rest of the afternoon on a gondola ride through the streets, which were in fact waterways. Venice was interesting simply because it was a floating city. The unfortunate part was that it was also a sinking city and would one day be under the Adriatic Sea. Our gondola driver looked like he'd come directly out of an Italian movie, striped shirt, red scarf and all. He even sang while he drove us. Thomas took pictures while we rode through the city, I wished he would put the camera down and put his arm around me, but I didn't dwell on it, I just sat back and enjoyed the moment, listening to the deep Italian vocals from our driver. The day seemed to be idyllic, I told myself it was. We ate at a pizzeria before heading back to Florence, oddly the pizza wasn't as good as Lorenzo's back in New York. Apparently Sicilians truly have the best pizza in the world, no matter where they are.

We arrived back at our hotel room in Florence and ordered room service and a bottle of wine. We spent the rest of the evening sitting on the balcony watching the Italians on the street below, and drank until we fell asleep. Although we didn't talk about our future like Thomas' dad wanted, we did have a memorable time in the Mediterranean boot.

The next day we flew back to New York. We had dinner with Theresa and Darryl the following night, which was Sunday, telling them about our adventures through Italy and about all the great food and wine the country had. I gained a few pounds from eating so much pasta that week, but I didn't mind, and Thomas didn't seem to care either. The rest of the month went by fairly

INGRID DARLING

quickly and before I knew it, it was almost Spring.

Fourteen

Time continued to pass and my relationship with Thomas and my friends was pleasant. But I had once again grown tired of the redundancy in my life and began to feel the empty feeling I'd had once before. By April I was restless, and I was having dreams that were becoming increasingly vivid, some disturbing, others suggestive. It was early May when I sat at my desk at the office, thinking about my latest dream. I sat staring out the window at the flowers blossoming on the trees. It was 10:18am and I could hear Mary in the background talking to me, but I wasn't listening. I was thinking about my dream from the night before. I didn't really know why I was so captivated by it, I'd had interesting dreams before, but this one stood out.

I sat at my desk, shaking my foot, like nervous people do. I was supposed to be revising some Condominium Declarations, but I couldn't concentrate. I wanted to tell someone about my dream, I had to tell someone about my dream, I needed another interpretation of its meaning. I looked at my computer screen and then at my phone. I thought about Emerald but decided against calling her. I hadn't spoken to her in almost six months and she would fuss about my absent phone calls before listening to what my dreams were about.

Maybe Thomas? I thought, but figured it wouldn't be worth it.

He always said that there was no biological definition for dreams, that it was just your mind recalling events during REM sleep. He didn't believe that dreams could be interpreted as a source of insight into unconscious desires, like what Freud had observed. I didn't rely on Thomas for anything other than scientific or biological explanations; he was too rigid in what he had learned in school.

I'll call my mom. She'll know what this means, if it means anything at all.

I thought it best since psychology was her major in college. I picked up the phone and dialed her number. My boss had left the office for a minute, so I wasn't worried about him catching me not doing work. Mary was still talking, and I still wasn't listening. The phone rang twice then she picked up.

"Mom!" I exclaimed.

"Ingrid!" She cried back to me.

I swiveled in my chair so Mary couldn't eavesdrop.

"So, I had a weird dream last night." I said, hushing my voice.

"Okay, what happened?" She asked.

She loved stories, especially ones she could interpret.

"It's too much to say over the phone."

I didn't want to tell her the dream over the phone, especially since Mary was hovering over my shoulder at her desk on the other side of the room.

What a nosy bitch!

"Can you email it?"

"Sure. I'd have to write it out in Word and then attach the file. Will that work?"

"That'd be fine. Besides, I can't talk long, I have a few clients to see. Just email me the file and I'll read it."

"Great, I'll do that." I said goodbye and hung up the phone.

INGRID DARLING

I was elated. Now I had another reason not to work on those Declarations, and I could still look like I was doing something.

"What happened in your dream?" Mary asked, as soon as I hung up.

Damnit, she is so fucking nosy!

I rolled my eyes and turned in my chair to face my computer.

"Well it was interesting, I met God." I said.

I didn't want to have a discussion with her about my dream, especially since she was particularly closed minded about spirituality. She always said there is no God but her God, which I always found to be quite disturbing. I could never understand people who believed that there was only one way of interpreting the divine, especially those who believed that anyone who didn't agree with them was going to hell. That's how Mary was, she was ignorant in my eyes, and as much as I tried to open her up to understanding other religions, she still maintained an egotistical view of "her Christian God". She began to tell me about what she'd heard in Church this past Sunday, but I didn't really care. I gave her a half smile and turned back towards my computer screen. I opened a blank Word document and began to type:

Part One, The Island.

I woke up to the sound of waves crashing against a wall. I was on a boat with twelve other people. None of us knew how we came to be on the boat, we were just there. I looked around and didn't recognize anything and I had no idea where I was. The boat then came upon a huge mountain in the middle of the ocean and we realized that the mountain was part of an island. As our boat came to a smaller rock, we all got out and started climbing to the top of the mountain. As we climbed, a man started to tell a story about an island in the middle of the ocean with no beaches, just a mountain on one side and a waterfall and lagoon on the other.

"The island was occupied by people for some time, but no one knew it existed. And though people lived there, the only place on the island was a huge building which served as a school, a hospital, a recreational facility, and housing for all of the people on the island." The man said. "Then one day, all of the people on the island disappeared. They all got up at the same time, left everything behind, and started walking to the edge of the island where the cliff became a waterfall and had the lagoon at the bottom. One by one, they all dove off the cliff and plunged into the water below. When the island was discovered, there were cars on the roads as if people were in them, but they weren't. No bodies were found on, around, or near the island. It was completely deserted with no trace of human life."

By the time he finished the story, we were at the top of the mountain. A few people asked him questions, but he didn't know anything else. That was all he had heard of this mysterious island.

Part Two, The Asylum.

At the top of the mountain, I looked around and saw beautiful rolling hills with meadows of flowers and lush green grass. It looked like heaven and the sun shone down so brightly that I had to squint to see. There were no animals, birds, or bugs anywhere in sight. It looked as if there should have been life around us, but there wasn't. We all decided to split up to explore the island. I found

INGRID DARLING

myself in the middle of what looked like a town, with streets and cars, but no other people around. By this time the sun was going down, so I got into a white two-door car and started driving towards the sunset. By dark I reached the driveway of what looked to be leading up to an estate. I drove down the driveway and realized that I had come upon the "huge building" that the man had described earlier in his story. I parked the car in the grass under some trees and started walking towards the entrance of the building. As I walked over a bridge towards the glass double doors, I noticed that the building looked like an enormous green house. It was hard to imagine that people lived in this building, but as I got closer, I saw that it stretched for miles to my left and right. The odd thing was that the entrance appeared to be the only way to get in and out of the building, so if people did live here, they were all trapped.

Part Three, The Blue Lagoon
I sat in the car at a red light. I waited for the light to change and the cars in front of me to move, but they stayed in place. I honked my horn a few times before realizing that everyone had gotten out of their cars and were standing in the street. It turns out that I had flashbacked into time when people were living on the island, including myself. I got out of the car and looked around at the others who stood staring into the sun. It was bright, too bright. Then a sublime light came down and blinded everything. I could only see a haze of green from the traffic light as everything else turned a pale white color. The light came down and shone so brightly and swallowed everything and everyone with its presence. As soon as the light faded, everyone in the street started walking towards the sun and before I knew it, I was at the end of the island

looking down a massive waterfall which fell into a beautiful lagoon and into a vast sea of bright blue water that stretched out toward the sun. It was beautiful, it looked like heaven. I watched as the people one by one walked toward the edge of the cliff, stretched out their arms, and fell towards the water, their bodies disappearing over the edge. And every time someone would fall, the sky would light up. I asked several people why everyone was diving off, but no one could give me an explanation. I asked if the people who fell over had died and if I was going die if I fell off too. Even though I never got an answer, I walked up to the edge of the cliff and stretched out my arms, unafraid. A bright light once again came down from the sky, and it got brighter and brighter until I couldn't see the blue sea anymore. Then I closed my eyes.

    Part Four, God.
    I opened my eyes and saw a long hallway in front of me. The walls and ceiling were decorated with ornate finish. At the end of the hallway was a set of elaborate double doors with glass windows that looked to lead to another hallway. Fear crept into my body but as I started walking, something told me that there was nothing to fear, that I was by myself. As I approached the doors, they opened, revealing another long hallway with an identical set of double doors at its end. I stopped after the next set of doors and thought about returning, but a voice spoke to me, saying that I should keep going and it would be worth it. It said that God was at the end of the hallway and I had to keep going if I wanted him to answer all of my questions. I was confused because I didn't know where the voice had come from, but I kept walking down the hall and didn't question it. When I finally got through another series of

hallways and doors and came up to a set of large elaborate double doors with large glass windows, an extraordinarily tall man in a tuxedo walked towards the doors to greet me. The room behind the doors was decorated with gilded mirrors and fancy furniture. I tried to see the man in the tuxedo's face, but I could not make out who he was. He opened the doors and motioned for me to come in. As I entered, he said, "God has been waiting for you."

He led me into another room which was smaller, but big enough for a large white bed, huge armoire, and a tall table. I walked in and sat on the bed, the man in the tuxedo disappeared. Suddenly a shadow appeared in the corner, the silhouette of a man. He told me, through my thoughts, not to panic, and that I could ask any question and he would answer it.

"Are you God?" I asked.

"Yes." He answered.

I took a deep breath and asked him about the island and why I was on it, what happened to the people on the island, and why were they diving off the cliff.

Then he explained that all of the people were on the island for a reason. He said that he was the light that came down from the sky and during that time he would determine if the people were ready on to go to the next life or not. Depending on what they accomplished in their present life, the people who he felt were worthy would walk to the edge of the island and fall into the lagoon, leaving this life to go onto a better life. He said that those who were listening would hear him when he called for them, no matter who they were or their position in life. He said that in order for those to become worthy, they must understand themselves, and they would hear him call, and he would lead them to the next stage in life, he would lead them to freedom.

    I nodded and laid back on the white canopy bed, closing my eyes, listening to his voice in my mind.

    Then I woke up.

    I finished writing and saved the document to my personal folder on my computer. I opened an email to my mom and attached the file, then clicked send. A wave of relief washed over my body, like I had just spoken to a shrink and now understood what my life was about. But I was still confused by the dream.

    What was the significance of my meeting God and why did everything else happen in the dream?

    However, before I could dwell on it, my boss walked in, demanding me finish the Condominium Declarations by 4pm, it was already 2. I closed my email and started working on the Declarations, and by the end of the day I had forgotten about the dream.

INGRID DARLING

Fifteen

It seemed as though my mom had forgotten about my dream as well. I didn't get a response from her about it, so my wish to understand its meaning went unfulfilled. I met Thomas that afternoon at his apartment. Darryl and Theresa were having a dinner date at our place and I didn't want to disturb their romantic evening together so I packed a bag and brought it with me to work so I wouldn't have to stop home at all that day.

Thomas lived in Gramercy, which was much closer to my office than my apartment was, but he lived with his messy brother which made staying with him less tolerable than sitting next to the sweaty bald guy on the subway every day. I always mentioned to Thomas that his brother's two week old dirty dishes in the sink were disgusting, but he never said anything about it, just let them pile up until he was forced to clean them for sink space. Since I was staying at his place that night, Thomas took the liberty of cleaning his apartment before I came so he wouldn't have to hear me complain about the filthy habits that ran in his family. I was surprised to enter into a tidy den, organized office and made up bed. I put my things on the floor of his bedroom while he ordered take out, Indian.

Our food arrived not long after had Thomas ordered it. He paid the delivery boy and brought the food, wrapped delicately in tin containers, and opened the package on the counter. A disoriented looked appeared on his face as the potent fumes of the Indian cuisine escaped the packaging. A few moments later, his entire kitchen and den filled with the scent of the India. Though I'd never been, I figured it mostly smelled of curry and cow dung. He prepared our plates and I hungrily began eating.

"I've always wanted to go to the Middle East." I said thinking of travel.

I spooned the sauce from my tandoori chicken into my naan then took a bite.

"Where?" He asked, cutting into the curried lamb on his plate.

"Dubai could be fun, and of course Egypt is at the top of my list." I said, licking the sauce from my fingers and taking another bite of my bread.

"Egypt would be cool. I'm not sure I'd want to go to Dubai though." Thomas said, taking a bite of his lamb.

His tone suggested that he was uninterested in visiting either place.

"It's one of the best places to go on earth. They just finished building all these enormous hotels and attractions to get people to visit it. I'd definitely go if I could."
"Well, not me. Europe was enough, and I don't want to go anywhere in the Middle East."
I was right.

"That's not very open minded of you, Thomas. You should want to visit more places to see how other people in the world live and understand things. I think Americans are jaded in that our country is so new that we can't appreciate history the same way Italians and French and Asians and Africans can." I said between chews.

"You might be right, but I am an American and if I chose to be jaded, then that's what I'll be." He said, cutting another piece of his lamb.

INGRID DARLING

I rolled my eyes.

"That's pretty ignorant of you, and what did you say to me once? That ignorance is a situation in which a person can be enclosed as narrowly as in a prison?"

"Actually, Simone de Beauvoir said that. I never agreed with her."

"Well you certainly quoted her with robustness. Don't quote people to prove your point unless you're going to agree with them. But that's beside the point, I think you could be more open-minded, you just don't want me to be right." I said, taking another bite of my naan.

He chuckled.

"You know me so well, Darling."

Before I could say anything else, his phone vibrated on the table. He leaned over to look at who was calling and immediately silenced it. He sat up straight and cut into his lamb again, his cheeks flushed. A suspicious feeling whisked through my body.

"Who was that?" I asked, drizzling the tandoori sauce over my rice and spooning it into my mouth.

"No one, just an old friend." He replied, taking a bite of his lamb.

"Who? Do I know them?"

Something didn't feel right about his answer.

"No. It's just this girl I used to talk to." He said, focusing on his plate.

"What's her name and why the hell is she calling you?" I exclaimed, placing my spoon on the table.

I told myself to remain calm, there was no reason to get upset over a phone call.

"It's not a big deal Darling. Her name is Yvonne. I talked to her for a few months before I met you."

"Oh yeah, I remember you telling me about her. Why is she calling you now though?"

He put his fork on the table and took a sip of his water.

"I don't know. She calls me every month just to say hi or whatever." He said, gulping.

Heat rose to my face.

"What the hell? Why does she call you every month? She knows we're together right?"

I crossed my arms over my chest and glared at him. He smiled nervously.

"Yeah she knows. We talk about you sometimes. I told her we just went to Italy together. She's a nice girl, I feel bad not being her friend."

"Well that's disrespectful, Thomas. No girl just calls some guy she was dating because she wants to be friends with him. I didn't realize you were still talking to that girl. I want you to stop talking to her, now." I said, irritated that I had to tell my boyfriend of two years not to talk to some girl he'd dated before me.

"I never dated her! We only talked for a few months. I mean, she lives in DC so there was no way it would've worked out anyway. I'll stop talking to her though, I'm sorry." He said, giving me an earnest smile.

I still felt uneasy.

Why would she continue to call him every month if she knew that he and I were together? And why would he entertain conversations with her unless...

I stopped my thoughts. I didn't want to think about my boyfriend cheating on me with some girl who lived in DC, besides

INGRID DARLING

there was no possible way he's even had a chance to see her because he and I have been attached at the hip since November of 2006. I took a deep breath and got up from the table, I wasn't hungry anymore. Thomas could sense my anxiety about the situation so he kept quiet. I went into his room and changed into running pants and a tank top and lay on the bed. I wanted to go for a quick run around the block, to get my nerves back in order, but I was tired from work and in five minutes, I had fallen asleep.

I woke up to an ambulance blaring past the window. It was dark outside.
I wonder how long I've been sleeping.
The bedroom door was cracked and light streamed through from the den. I rolled off the bed and walked over to the door, peeking through the opening. Thomas was stretched across the couch, watching TV. I thought about joining him but decided against it. I walked over to the table in the corner of his room and opened my purse, rummaging through the contents for my phone. I had three missed calls, all from my mom. I guessed she wanted to talk about my dream and prepared to call her back but hesitated for a moment then decided to call Emerald instead. I knew she would probably complain to me about not calling, but I wanted to talk to her. I missed her voice and her insight, so I dialed her number.

"Hello?" A tired voice answered.

I looked at the clock on the night stand, it was 11:40pm.

"Emerald. It's Ingrid." I said, biting my lip, preparing for the angry comments.

"Hey Darling. How have you been, babe?" She said, sweetly.

The line rustled.

"I've been alright. Did I wake you?"

"No, I was just lying down." She said, more rustling.

"I'm sorry I haven't called, it's been a busy few months for me." I said.

"It's alright. I've been really busy too. How is Thomas, are ya'll still together?"

"Yes we are." I said, sitting on the edge of the bed.

She must have sensed my hesitation.

"What's wrong?" She asked.

I looked to the door and thought about closing it, but the TV was too loud for Thomas to overhear my conversation. I sighed and told her about the girl who had called his phone that night and how he had dismissed her as a friend, that I was still uneasy about the situation and how I was unsure of his relationship with her.

"Listen babe, love is an emotional tournament where both skill and character are tested and perfected." She said. "You love him, right?"

"Of course" I said, lying back on the bed.

I propped a pillow under my head.

"Then you have to trust the love you have with him. If you feel uneasy about the situation, ask him. Otherwise don't stress about it, I'm sure he's not cheating on you." She said.

Her calm approach helped ease my anxiety.

"He did say he would stop talking to her and I know he hasn't seen her since we've been together. I guess it's not that serious. I'll stop worrying about it. Thanks Em, I can always rely on your advice."

"It's not a problem at all. I just hope you call me a little more often now. I miss your voice, babe." She said.

I smiled, knowing that she would mention my absent phone calls.

"I will, I promise. So tell me what's new with you."

We talked for twenty minutes about her having graduated from UNC this past fall with a degree in psychology, her new job, her boyfriend and friends of ours in North Carolina who were getting married and having children. Talking to her reminded me of the calm nature of my home state, I wanted to visit my family, see my old friends. I missed my home and the comfort it gave me.

We said goodbye to each other and I hung up the phone, staring up at the ceiling. I laid on the bed for a few minutes, contemplating whether to stay in the room and go back to sleep or join Thomas in the den. It seemed he heard my thoughts because the door opened and he entered before I could decide.

"Are you okay?" He asked.

His eyes looked sad, as if he could feel my emotion.

"I'm fine." I said, unsurely, but he could tell I was still upset about the phone call.

"She is just a friend, and I promise I won't talk to her anymore." He said, walking over to the bed and sitting on the edge.

He stared at his hands.

"I believe you." I said, pulling him down onto the bed with me.

He kissed me and caressed my hair, staring into my eyes. We had sex, but it wasn't the same. Something had changed between us, and I could feel it.

INGRID DARLING

Sixteen

It still felt like March, when we were sightseeing in Italy, but it was August already. My birthday came and went. Thomas bought me a leather journal and some perfume. The journal was for writing down what I couldn't say out loud, and the perfume was so I could smell good even on my saddest days. I was sad. I missed my family in North Carolina and my job was making my anxiety worse. I had been having panic attacks every few weeks, waking up in the middle of the night feeling like I couldn't breathe, and fainting more often than usual. Thomas said I should see a doctor, which I did, only to find out that it was just stress.

"It's amazing how stress can do physical things to people", I told Thomas after my appointment.

He responded by saying that our problems and anxieties are like particles of sand in between our toes, and depending how we walk they either grind at us or massage our feet. I asked him where he came up with that and he said he'd heard it from a homeless man a few years ago. I asked him what else the man had told him and he said that the man also told him freedom is not a natural inheritance of man, that in order to possess it we have to create it. I asked Thomas what the man meant by that, but he didn't know.

"He's just an old guy who's been living on the streets for too long," Thomas replied.

But something in the man's words rang true to me, I just couldn't put my finger on it, not yet at least.

The weeks drummed on. I tried writing in my new journal,

but nothing substantial came out, so I began recording my dreams. They were getting more and more vivid, with similar themes: imprisoned, trapped in a dark room, betrayed by my friends, abandoned by my family. I told Theresa about a dream I had one night about Thomas, I couldn't remember what happened in the dream, but I woke up feeling sad and nauseous. She told me not to worry about it, that dreams are only what you interpret them as, but I wasn't convinced. I asked her if she would have a girls' night in with me and she agreed and invited Jada.

When Jada arrived at our apartment we ordered a pizza and talked about how we first met each other. I told them that time was a funny thing, that years could feel like days, and minutes could feel like hours.

Jada responded by saying that time is all relative.

"If you're constantly thinking ahead, then you're living in the future and if you're constantly thinking about what you've done, then you're living in the past. But if you view everything as it happens, then you're living in the present. Therefore, in reality, time has no meaning. It is all relative to how you see yourself in a certain situation."

I said that all I could think about was my future and how unsure I was of the direction I was currently taking, that every minute felt like I was losing in some aimless endeavor to live my life.

Then Theresa said, "the amount of time that one minute lasts was simply a creative idea developed by someone long ago. The only time that does exist is this present moment, and even the past and future are mere fabrications of the mind."

INGRID DARLING

I asked her what that meant to my situation and she replied that I shouldn't worry about the future because it wasn't happening at the moment, that I should focus on what was happening now and only then will the future present itself. I smiled at her perceptiveness. We finished the entire pizza and talked for a few hours. Jada left fairly early and Theresa and I and talked a little longer. I slept well that night and when I woke up, I couldn't remember anything from my dream.

INGRID DARLING

Seventeen

November, 2008

The plane pulled steadily into the tarmac and stopped. I waited for the 'fasten seat belt' sign to turn off, ignoring the flight attendant over the speaker and baby crying in the seat behind me. I was tired. I had to go into the office this morning to file and seal some paperwork before rushing to catch my flight to North Carolina, a flight that was delayed for three hours on the runway due to mechanical issues. Despite my weary sentiment I was very anxious to be home to see my family. It was the day before Thanksgiving and my boss was generous enough to give me the entire week off after he'd overheard my complaining to Mary that I hadn't seen my family in almost a year. The seat belt light turned off and I jumped up, grabbing my small carry-on that I was able to stow under my seat. The aisle immediately crowded with people so I was stuck waiting for the slow overweight passengers to gather their belongings and de-board.

    I met my mom outside the terminal, she rushed over to hug me before I had the chance to notice that she'd cut her hair. I hadn't seen her in a long time and her age was beginning to show, the lines on her brow were more defined and a few gray hairs were visible in her full auburn curls. Despite her physical appearance, she was still very beautiful. I smiled and hugged her back then followed her through the airport to the parking lot. My dad was waiting in the car for us, in the driver's seat. He asked me how my flight was. I told him it was alright, that I was delayed on the runway for an eternity. He laughed. He too, looked like the victim of old age, as his hair was thinning and more gray than usual.

    I laid my head back against the head rest and pulled my phone from my purse, no missed calls. I thought it was unusual for Thomas not to have called, especially since I should have been in North Carolina a few hours ago.

    He should have called at least to see if I got home safely.

    But rather than calling him I decided to wait until we got back to the house, so I could change into more comfortable clothes and grab something to eat.

    I ate dinner with my parents in the dining room, something we rarely did when I lived at home. After dinner I watched a movie with my dad in the den. Thomas still hadn't called. Halfway through the movie I decided to call him, to make sure everything was alright, it was unlike Thomas not to check up on me. I walked to my room and grabbed my phone from the bed then sat down and dialed his number. I figured he would be busy with his family, preparing food for Thanksgiving dinner, eating or whatever. No answer. I left him a message telling him to call back and leave a voice message, something he never did. That didn't matter though, he called me right back.

    I told him about having to go into the office before my flight, how I was delayed forever on the runway, that I was happy to be home but that I missed him. My words, however, meant little because after a thirty second hesitation he said those dreaded words:

    "Ingrid, I don't think I can do this anymore."

    My instincts had already told me that something wasn't right, that something was about to happen, but I hadn't listened. An enormous lump rose from the bottom of my stomach to the back of my throat. I let out a stammered gasp, my lip quivering.

"What do you mean?" I asked, biting my lip.

"I mean, I want to break up." He said.

His voice was as cold as ice, expressionless. I gasped again.

"I knew you were going to do this to me!" I bellowed, opening the dam.

Tears streamed down my face as I cried into the phone.

What was happening, was this really happening, were we really breaking up? My thoughts spun in my head.

It made no sense, just four days ago we were having lunch with Theresa and Darryl and talking about when we planned on having kids and where we should plan our next joint vacation.

No, this isn't happening! This couldn't be happening, especially not over the phone!

All I could think about amidst my confusion and the pain gripping my soul was whom he might have spoken to, to convince him to do this.

"No one," was his first response, then he stuttered a little, not knowing how to react to my sudden emotional explosion. "Well I talked to Martin, and my parents." He finally said. "This isn't easy, Ingrid. This has been the hardest two days of my life, but I feel like I need space." He said.

There was no sentiment in his voice, as if he didn't care about the relationship we'd had with each other.

"You don't have to do this, why are you doing this? I know we talked about taking a break from seeing each other so much, but now this?" I cried.

We had discussed spending less time with each other

before he left for New Jersey two nights ago. It wasn't that we were tired of seeing each other, it was so we could each have a little more space than we'd had over the past two and a half years. We needed it, but his decision to break up was out of the blue and it felt like the ocean had collapsed over my body. My arms and hands were shaking at the thought of not being with him anymore, of him breaking up with me. The idea sickened me and I wanted to vomit. I said a few more words through emotional outbursts and hung up, remembering the last thing he said.

"I'm sorry. I hope life treats you well."

But it wasn't what he said that hurt, it was the ice in his voice. I couldn't believe what had just happened, how he could suddenly be so cold towards me. I sat at the edge of the bed staring at the cell phone in my hand. Tears poured from my eyes and my body shook with heart wrenching sorrow.

I didn't have to tell my mom what had happened. She could see it in my eyes. After crying for the entire night I came down to breakfast the next morning and ate in silence.

"What was his reason for wanting to break up?" She asked, hesitantly.

"I have no idea. He said he needed space, which is what we had already talked about. I need space too, but breaking up was not part of the plan. I feel so lost." I said, forking the eggs on my plate.

"Well eat up, we don't want you fainting over some boy." My dad said wryly.

I chuckled, he always knew how to make me laugh.

"Well why would you two talk about having space?" My mom asked, taking a sip of her coffee.

INGRID DARLING

"Because I was feeling trapped, and I suggested it so we wouldn't argue about little things, like the dirty dishes he keeps in the sink for weeks." I said, taking a bite of my eggs.

My stomach turned and I wanted to throw up, but I held it down.

"Do you think your dreams have been telling you that lately?" She asked, eyeing me suspiciously.

"What do you mean?" I asked, putting down my fork and taking a sip of my orange juice.

"In that dream that you emailed to me, you mentioned something about a building that people lived in but they were trapped in it. Do you think your subconscious was giving you a sign about your waking life?" She looked down to her plate and took a bite of her sausage.

I thought about that dream. I had completely forgotten about it once I'd sent her the email. I was feeling trapped in my waking life, which was most likely why I kept having dreams about being imprisoned and trapped in dark rooms. I remembered the dream I had about Thomas a few months earlier. I had woken up sad and sick, the same way I felt now, only this time there was a reason behind it.

Are my dreams telling me something?

"What about the part when I met God, what was that supposed to mean?" I asked, picking up my fork and picking at my pancake.

"God is the indwelling soul of the universe." She said, taking another sip of her coffee.

"What does that have to do with my dream?" I asked.

"That is something for you to discover on your own." She

said.

"How?" I asked, looking at my dad across the table.

He had already finished his eggs, pancakes and sausage. He picked up the bacon from his plate and took a bite, eyeing my mom.

"There is more than one way to interpret the divine." She said. "I can't tell you what your dream meant to you."

I wasn't surprised at her interest in the divine aspect of my dream. My mom had always been interested in spirituality, following signs and listening to her subconscious. My dream encounter with God meant more than what I was able to comprehend at the moment, but she knew what it meant, she just wanted me to figure it out on my own. Dreams are messages sent from the depths of your soul, is what she'd say. But I had lost my soul, Thomas had taken it along with my heart.

I took another bite of my eggs then got up from the table. I wasn't hungry and forcing food down was only making me more nauseous than I already was. I walked into the den and lay across the couch, flipping through the channels with the remote.

"Are you not going to finish your breakfast?" My dad called from the kitchen.

"I'm not hungry." I replied, stopping on the Lifetime channel. *Ghost* was on. I laughed to myself at the irony. Then I cried.

INGRID DARLING

Eighteen

I cried for the next two days, stopping only to have Thanksgiving dinner with my grandparents, cousins, aunts and uncles. My uncle who'd bought me the pink makeup kit for Christmas asked if I had been using the makeup lately because I had bags under my eyes and I looked like hell. I told him no and that he was an asshole. My mom apologized to him for my comment, but didn't say anything to me about it. She knew how upset I was and didn't want me to cry in front of the entire family.

I returned to New York on Sunday, Theresa picked me up from the airport and I told her that Thomas had broken up with me. She asked when it happened and I told her that he had called me the day before Thanksgiving and we broke up over the phone. She was appalled by the fact that he hadn't waited to face me to do it and said that he should be ashamed of himself for being so inconsiderate. We arrived at the apartment and I went straight into my room. It was cold and empty. Thomas' shoes were strewn all over the floor by the closet next to the stereo his dad had given me for my birthday earlier this year. I threw my bag on the bed and sat down, staring at the pictures that lined my dresser, all of me and Thomas. He and I standing in front of the Eiffel Tower, sitting on the gondola in Venice, and laughing in front of the Coliseum in Rome. We looked so happy. I thought about how much I loved him and before I could work myself to tears, Theresa knocked on the door. She said she wanted to talk to me when I had a moment. I told her I'd come out there in a few minutes.

"I'm really sorry about Thomas, Ingrid.". She said when I

left my room and walked into the den.

"It's okay. I'm sure we'll be able to work it out or something." I said, not entirely convinced with my own words.

I stood facing the TV, it was on mute.

"Well, I wanted to tell you this because you're my roommate and you need to know." She began.

I looked over to her with curiosity. She combed her hair behind her ear and smiled.

"I've been thinking about this for a while now and I started looking for places with my mom last week, and well, I'm moving to Brooklyn with Darryl." She said.

I stared at her blankly and sat down on the couch.

"I wanted you to know now before I move so you can find another roommate or somewhere else to live. I'll be moving out next month. I hope that is alright."

I was in shock. I didn't want her to move out, and especially not all the way to Brooklyn.

I need her now more than ever, I thought, not wanting to believe she would be gone soon.

"Ingrid?" She said, crossing the room to where I sat on the couch. "Are you okay with that?"

I nodded. "Sure, I'm really happy for you two." I said, forcing a smile to my face.

"Thanks, and I want you to come visit me all the time." She said, bending down to hug me.

I hugged her back. Then I cried.

INGRID DARLING

Nineteen

January, 2009

I moved out the week after Theresa did. I'd found a one bedroom apartment in Washington Square and put the down payment on it immediately. I spent my weekends with Theresa in Brooklyn, helping her unpack her things into the old brownstone she and Darryl had purchased together. It was lovely and rustic and reminded me of what the 1970's would have been like. She let me talk about Thomas, something I did everyday to anyone who would listen. I needed another interpretation of our break up, because it didn't make sense to me. He and I were no longer speaking to one another. I'd sent him a few emails asking if we could get together and talk, but he never responded, he refused to communicate with me. His absence was glaring and all I did was cry.

I deleted him as a friend on Facebook to keep myself from stalking his page, and as much as I wanted to know what he was doing, I didn't want to obsess over us not being together. I hadn't spent much time on Facebook since we'd been together, there was no reason for it, only to keep in touch with my friends in North Carolina, but now that he was gone, I was spending more and more time online, trying to fill that void with something I could only find in cyberspace.

My mom suggested I go to the library, that perhaps I'd meet a nice, intelligent man there. But I didn't want to meet anyone else, I wanted Thomas, I missed Thomas. I wondered if he missed me, thinking that he had to. I was such a big presence in his life that it would have been emotionally impossible for him to forget about me so suddenly. But I was wrong. It seemed he filled his void with someone else, something I could have only found in cyberspace.

I had gotten home from work that day, changed into a velour track suit and heated some leftovers in the microwave before opening my laptop to my email. I usually checked my personal email at home since I was occupied at work most of the day with legal paperwork and real estate closings, and today was no exception. I opened my inbox and gasped, seeing an email from Thomas. It was a response to the last email I'd sent him, the day before the New Year.

Ingrid,
I hope that you understand why I haven't responded to your emails. I know that this is really hard for you and I would rather if we didn't see each other. I wanted to tell you that I have been out of town with Yvonne for the past week and that it is probably not appropriate for me to talk to you anymore. I'm sorry if I have caused you any pain.
Take Care,
Thomas

It read. I sat back against the couch and gasped in disbelief. *Oh my god, he's been out of town with that girl!*

A deafening silence echoed through the room, my heart drummed in my ears and my eyes throbbed in pain. A wave of nausea rose through my body and my head felt heavy. I stood from the couch and stumbled into the bathroom, feeling a fainting spell approach. I splashed my face with water and stared into the mirror above the sink. A familiar face stared back at me, the same face that stared at me from the night I almost overdosed, the same face from my godfathers coffin, a face that had no soul. I wanted to scream, to run back into time where Thomas was laying on the bed in the next room, waiting for me to join him. But as I'd learned, time was a funny thing, in that it was only limited to what it was perceived to be. The only thing I could think about was going to Thomas' apartment, to see him face to face, so he could tell me where he'd been, how long he'd been seeing Yvonne, and if he had been cheating on me.

I don't remember changing clothes, or hailing a cab, but suddenly I was in Gramercy outside of his apartment building, standing on the snowy sidewalk. I hurried up the steps to the front entrance and buzzed his apartment. No answer. I pulled my phone from the pocket of my coat and dialed his number. Oddly, it felt strange dialing it, like he was just another friend in my phone, not someone I had loved for the past two and a half years. He picked up after the third ring.

"Hello?"

"Let me in." I said then hung up the phone.

There is no way he would just let me stand out here in the cold, I thought, shivering.

Snow trickled from above, as if appearing out of nowhere in the black sky. A minute later, the door opened. Thomas stood in the doorway with a bitter expression on his face.

"What do you want, Ingrid?" He demanded, impatiently.

"I want to talk to you. Let's go inside, it's freezing out

here." I said, pushing past him and into the hallway.

He huffed and closed the door, following me up the stairs to his apartment.

"Why are you here?" He asked, trying to hurry past me, but I reached his door first, letting myself in.

It was dark except for the light in the kitchen. Two large suitcases sat on the floor in the den, one was opened, a mound of clothes pouring out of it. My heart pounded in my chest. I walked across to the den and sat on the couch, unraveling the scarf from my neck. He closed the front door and stood in the area between the kitchen and the den, hands on his hips. He glared at me from behind his glasses. He looked tired, as if he had just gotten back from a long day of travel.

"What do you want, Ingrid?" He said again.

I reached across the couch and turned the lamp on.

"Where have you been?" I asked, dryly.

His expression turned from bitter to angry, as if he were mad that I wanted to know what he'd been doing these past few weeks. It probably wasn't my business considering we weren't together, but I wanted to know anyhow.

"I don't want to tell you. And didn't I say it's best for us not to see each other?" He demanded, angrily.

His sudden change in tone bothered me, but I remained calm and repeated my question.

"I'm not leaving until you tell me where you've been." I said, crossing my arms over my chest and leaning back against the couch.

He sighed and sat on a barstool in the kitchen, facing me.

"Dubai." He said, holding his head down.

INGRID DARLING

My face went numb and my lip quivered.

"Where?" I stammered, suddenly noticing the color fade from the room.

"Dubai." He repeated.

I tried to stand but lost my balance, falling back into the couch. My ears rung and my heart pounded in my throat. *Did he just say Dubai?* I asked myself, thinking that I had to have heard him wrong, that there was no way he had been across the world, in the Middle East, no less, with that girl.

"You went to Dubai with Yvonne?" I asked, more to myself, to make sure I'd heard him correctly.

"Yes!" He barked, standing from his chair. "I didn't want to tell you, Ingrid. Why did you have to come over here?" He yelled.

The color returned to the room and I stood, suddenly very composed. They say that the eye of the storm is the calmest place to be, and it seemed as though my third eye was wide open and very present amidst the gale that was brewing inside of me. I crossed the room to where Thomas stood, pushing him back into his chair. I stood above him, looking down, my thoughts went blank.

"You are going to tell me everything." I said.

The eerie calm in my voice resounded through the room. Thomas's eyes widened and he straightened his back. He sighed and told me how after he'd broken up with me, he called Yvonne, that Yvonne was going to Dubai for a trip with her grad school class, that he decided to go because he wasn't doing anything else, how he had been gone with her for ten days and just got back this morning, and that he didn't want to tell me because he knew it'd upset me.

I stepped back and let him finish. He told me that his

cousin Martin was the only one who knew he was in Dubai with Yvonne, that Martin had encouraged him to go, and that he was certain he didn't want to be with me anymore. I asked him how he knew if he was certain about me and if he loved Yvonne and wanted to marry her. He said that he just knew that it wouldn't work between us, that he did love Yvonne and that he might want to marry her. His last statement was like a dull knife slicing through my heart. My head ached and I had a sudden vision of cutting Thomas to pieces with a sword. But I had no sword, just a body frozen to stone, thinking how someone I loved, could do something like this to me.

"I told you I wanted to go to Dubai, Thomas. I told you I wanted to go with you, and you went with her!" I exclaimed, remembering the conversation I'd had with him in his kitchen several months ago.

I had a feeling then that Yvonne was more than a friend to him, but my delusion had kept me from prying. I could feel the storm pick up. Heat rose in my body.

"I don't remember that." He said, looking away.

"I can't believe you would do this to me." I said, trying to hold back the explosion that was coming on.

"I didn't do anything to you, Ingrid. We are over." He said, standing.

I wanted to cry, to punch him in the face, to throw him out the window, to watch his body bury under the snow. It didn't matter though, his heart and words were already cold, he was already buried, and I wasn't digging him out.

I walked back over to the couch and grabbed my scarf, struggling to hold back the tears that were welling in my eyes.

INGRID DARLING

"You are going to regret this," I said, wrapping the scarf around my neck. "What goes around, comes around. And karma can be a real bitch."

I pushed past him to the door.

He grunted.

"Whatever."

I whipped my head around and faced him, staring into his eyes.

"You know what Thomas? I loved you with all my heart and you just used me and wasted my time, and now you're frolicking around with her like nothing ever happened between us. This really shows your true character, and I'm done with you."

I opened the door and walked out, slamming it behind me. The tears burned my eyes but I didn't want to let them out, I didn't want to cry about him anymore. I remembered what Emerald had told me months ago, about love. That love is an emotional tournament in which both skill and character are tested and perfected. And it seemed as though Thomas had cheated in that game. I ran down the stairs and opened the door to the street. The snow was falling hard and fast now. An old man walked by on the sidewalk, bundled under multiple coats.

"It's gonna be a blizzard tonight.' He said, hurrying past.

I looked up to the sky at the snow falling from above. A flake fell on my forehead and slid into my eye, opening the floodgates. I bent forward allowing the tears to rush out, crying out in heartache, from betrayal and pain. The old man was right, there was definitely going to be a blizzard tonight, and it already started.

INGRID DARLING

Twenty

I took the next week off from work. I was too upset to do anything, much less roll out of bed and grab something to eat. I couldn't eat, I was too nauseous to force anything down. I tried to focus on reading but nothing was holding my attention, all I could think about was Thomas and how much he'd hurt me. I called my mom, telling her that this was the worst thing he could have done to me, how I told him I wanted to go to Dubai and he purposely went with Yvonne instead. She calmly told me that breakups are hard and to let go of something you love so much is a very difficult thing to do, especially when it is a person. But that people walk in and out of your life at the moment they are supposed to and every moment happens as it should. I didn't want to think about Thomas's moment with Yvonne on the other side of the Atlantic. The idea sickened me, but I was thankful it was just an idea and not something I had to be faced with. At least not until Thursday.

My phone vibrated on my dresser that day, waking me up. It was Theresa.
"Ingrid?" She asked, nervously.
"Yes?" I replied, rolling over to look at the clock.
It was 1 in the afternoon.
"Have you been on Facebook today?"
Her tone jolted me awake, it didn't sound pleasant. My stomach tensed then turned.
"No, why?" I said, wanting to cry.
I didn't know what it was about, but I knew what it was

about, and it had something to do with Thomas.

"I think I'm gonna come over there in a little while." She said.

"Okay." I said, hanging up the phone.

I threw on a sweatshirt and ran out of my bedroom to the kitchen, flipped open my laptop and logged onto Facebook. I clicked to Thomas' page. He didn't have his privacy settings activated so I could see everything I had been avoiding since we broke up. I clicked on his wall and nearly fainted. Not only was his relationship status visible, revealing that he was now in a relationship with Yvonne, but fifty new pictures were plastered all over his page, all of him and Yvonne in Dubai and Egypt visible for all of our friends to see, including me. My heart jumped from my chest to my throat as I clicked on each picture, one by one, staring in horror.

He didn't tell me he went to Egypt too! I thought, still clicking on the pictures.

I shouldn't have looked but I did. Nausea filled my veins and gripped my stomach as I stared in shock at the pictures on the screen, pictures of him and her hugging in front of the pyramids, riding camels in the desert, smoking hookah pipes in a bazaar, and kissing by a candlelit dinner on the sand. I continued looking in disbelief while the color faded from the room. This time I couldn't hold it back, the fainting spell hit me and I collapsed to the floor.

I woke up to heavy knocking on my front door. I lifted my head from the ground and it pounded between my ears.

"Ingrid?" I heard Theresa call through the door. "Are you in there? Is everything okay?"

"I'm coming." I called weakly, lifting my limp body from

the floor.

I stood and wobbled over to the door, unlocking it. Theresa bounded in and hugged me.

"Did you see the pictures?" She asked, holding me tight.

I nodded, unable to speak.

"Oh hunnie, you're as cold as ice!" She cried, walking me over to the couch.

I rubbed my temples, sitting down. I had no idea how long I'd been passed out, but it wasn't long enough to forget what I'd just seen. My body shook, still horrified by the public display of affection between my ex-boyfriend and his new girlfriend. I could feel the betrayal stabbing my insides. Then I cried.

Theresa stayed for the rest of the day. Darryl came over for dinner and the three of us sat and talked. I was much calmer than I had been earlier in the day, but my soul had escaped, leaving an empty feeling in my heart. We ordered Chinese take out and sat on the floor between the couch and the TV, talking about relationships and heartaches. I asked Darryl if he'd known about Yvonne, if Thomas had ever mentioned her to him, but he said no. But even if he did know about her, I didn't expect him to tell me. Sometimes ignorance really is bliss.

Theresa couldn't understand how Thomas could be so inconsiderate and hurtful just five weeks after he and I had broken up. She said inconsideration wasn't in his nature and that she was disappointed in him. Darryl told me to be strong, something I had been trying since Thomas and I had broken up, but it was difficult, especially since everything I did reminded me of him. Theresa said that it always hurts more to have and lose than to not have in the first place. I told her she was right, that Thomas' absence felt like someone close to me had died. Darryl left after dinner and Theresa stayed the night with me. I loved her for being such a great friend.

The next day I called my mom and told her what had happened. She said problems are only spiritual teachers in disguise, providing a message that can only be heard by opening your eyes. I told her that I couldn't see anything except Thomas because his face was clouding my head and I couldn't focus on anything else.

"Pay attention to what is underneath the mental chatter that's happening in your head because it's pointing you in the right direction," she said. "Each issue in your life repeats itself when it is unlearned and ignored, but once you pay attention to what you're being shown, your problems will dissolve immediately."

I asked her how I could stop the mental chatter and she said I had to still my mind. She suggested I join a yoga studio or take some classes to finish my degree. I decided it wouldn't be a bad idea to go back to school and told her I would look into universities in the city to enroll in for the fall.

The next week I visited the Admissions office at NYU and glanced through some brochures, figuring it would be a good place to finish my undergraduate degree and take some interesting classes, especially now that I had no distractions. After speaking with an Admissions advisor, I was ushered into a meeting which was being held for applicants interested in becoming full time students in the fall. I was put into a group of four people, two guys and a girl named Anna.

Anna was from the Upper East Side and spent her summers in Europe with her cousins who were European royalty and global socialites. Anna was a New York socialite herself, clad head to toe in designer clothes and always invited to exclusive events thrown by fashion designers and industry moguls. She was arrogant but she and I got along well during the group information session. We exchanged numbers and met for coffee the next day. I learned that her parents were divorced and her dad lived in Los Angeles, that she had just started dating a financial analyst on Wall Street and was bored from spending the entire winter in New York City. She invited me to a party which was being thrown by a well known deejay that night, but I passed. I wasn't ready to mingle with people yet, I was so too fragile from my break up. I told her I'd go to the next party with her, she smiled and told me she understood how hard breakups can be. She asked about the details of my breakup with Thomas. I told her how he had broken up with me over the phone, gone to Dubai and Egypt with the girl who had been calling him the entire time we were together. That he put the pictures on Facebook for everyone to see, how humiliated I was to show my face around our mutual friends, and how devastating his actions had been for me. She told me I was a strong person for not allowing the pain to show outwardly, that if she were in my shoes, she would have burned his apartment down with him in it. She said that betrayal is worse than anything, especially when it is with someone you opened your life up to. I asked her if she had even been betrayed by a boyfriend. She said no, but her eyes lowered, as if there was someone who had hurt her in the past. Only later did she tell me that her current boyfriend wasn't the faithful type, and though she insisted it didn't bother her, I could tell she was hurt by his actions. But I didn't want to dwell on it, so I changed the subject. I was happy that I could talk to her, happy that I'd met a new friend.

By the time May came, I'd enrolled full time for the fall

semester, choosing French as my major. I figured it would be a chance for me to learn how to communicate with people differently than I had been before. I told my boss that I was returning to school in August and that I would no longer be working for him. He told me he was proud that I decided to finish my degree and it was worth it to have that piece of paper but to never lose sight of what I was trying to understand. I asked him what he meant and he responded by saying that according to Plato, the task of education was to help people to recollect what they implicitly knew but had somehow forgotten. It was more about drawing knowledge out from the hidden depths of the psyche rather than simply putting knowledge in. I shrugged in response, thinking I just wanted something else to focus on, to take my mind off of the past, even though I knew it could never be erased.

INGRID DARLING

Twenty-One

July appeared sooner than I'd expected. It was still hard for me to eat. I had already lost fifteen pounds, and the nausea was overwhelming. Even though it had been eight months, I was still thinking about Thomas. I'd heard somewhere that it takes half the amount of time that you're dating someone to get over them. I still had a few more months to heal and it was a very slow process.

Hoping it would take my mind off of my ex, I had gone to a few parties with Anna once she returned from Europe, meeting all of her rich socialite friends. They were all the same, substitute runway models with cocaine addictions and hefty trust funds. But for some reason their habits didn't bother me. I told Anna that I used to rely on cocaine as my source of happiness and when Thomas filled that void I never thought about the rush it used to give me. I hadn't thought about cocaine in almost three years, and now I sat in a private room with a mound of it on the table, sparkling in the dim lights. My mouth watered watching the skeletal models indulge in my favorite pastime, but observing the scene made me think of them more as scavengers feeding from the powdered bones of the dead than beautiful figures airbrushed in magazine ads.

Anna offered me a line. A lump raised in the back of my throat as I recalled the last time I did cocaine.

Fortune only smiles once, I remembered telling myself.

I told her "no" and sipped my champagne, watching everyone else indulge in something that only reminded me of death. Cocaine won't fill that emptiness, it can never replace a soul, is what

INGRID DARLING

I had concluded.

While I occupied myself with Tetris on my phone, tuning out the noisy banter between the rich socialites, I thought about Lark and wondered if she was alright. The last time seeing her was like spending time with a heroin addict in denial.

"I'm not doing that stuff!" she'd repeatedly told me, whilst scratching her arm and twitching her shoulder.

I'd shrugged off my concern after she tried to sleep with Thomas, but it was clear then she had a serious drug problem. I hadn't heard from her since she came to visit and I certainly wasn't interested in calling to see how she was doing. I remembered what my mom had told me about people; how they walk in and out of your life at the moment they are supposed to. Lark had walked out when Thomas walked in, and Anna walked in when Thomas had walked out. The circumstances were paradoxical, but it didn't matter because I wasn't doing coke anymore, I made that clear to myself two years ago. And though I seemed to find a new friend with my old habits, the difference between Anna and Lark was that Anna actually respected my decision to refrain from doing the drug, something I appreciated considering the amount of cocaine that was sitting on the table as temptation in the first place.

In August, I decided to go with Anna to Atlanta, hoping the rest and relaxation would distract me from my growing emptiness. She had just gotten into a fight with her mom about her overdraft issues and thought it was wise to stay at her dad's condo for the weekend to take her mind off of it. The R&R, however, only prompted her to go shopping. We perused the department stores at the mall until Anna finally found a turquoise and navy silk blouse that cost a mere $1,700.00.

    I was in awe of her spending, considering the delicate financial situation she was in to begin with. She swore it was for her back to school shopping, but I knew it was truly because she had a problem, materialism. After her material binge, we phoned her dad's driver to pick us up. We waited at the valet entrance, Anna furiously texting her unfaithful boyfriend in New York, me staring at the parking lot filled with Maseratis, Porsches, and Bentley's, slightly disgusted with the amount of pretentiousness in my presence.

    I thought about my ex-boyfriends cousin for a moment. Spending all of my time with Anna was helpful in that I rarely thought about Thomas, but everything we did reminded me of Martin: the arrogance of her friends, the amount of money they spent on unnecessary things, and the way they looked down upon people who didn't have what they had.

    As if on cue, a black Rolls Royce pulled to a stop in front of us, the silver dancing figure on its hood glistened in the sun. The windows were tinted so I couldn't see who was inside. But just standing next to it made me feel more like a snob with a trust fund than a paltry college student.

    As the back door opened, Anna let out a loud shriek. Startled, I turned my attention to her and saw her practically jump on the tall attractive guy with gelled blonde hair and well manicured hands who'd stepped out of the vehicle. He wore a black silk shirt and dark slacks, black sunglasses perched on the collar of his shirt. His spicy cologne penetrated my pores, it smelled of money. I immediately realized who the Rolls Royce belonged to.

    He hugged Anna and shifted his weight, revealing a shorter,

INGRID DARLING

stockier friend behind him. I smiled at the friend while Anna squealed and chirped to blond. The friend had dark hair combed neatly to the side, his pink and white polo shirt was tucked very delicately into his khakis. His white loafers were perfectly polished and almost reflected the arrogance off from his body. He too reminded me of Thomas' cousin Martin.

The two young men looked as though they had just stepped off of some yacht in the Mediterranean and landed at the valet entrance of the shopping mall. An awkward moment passed. I wasn't interested in introducing myself to the friend and considering the vanity searing from his smug expression, and he had little interest in introducing himself to me either. Another minute passed, Anna still chirping, before the blond asked for an introduction. She paused mid-sentence and looked at me as if she didn't know who I was before laughing shrilly and grabbing my arm.

"Oh my gosh, I'm so sorry! I was just blabbering on and on," she cried, slapping her knee with another shrill laugh.

My body jolted forward with her exaggerated expression.

"Ingrid, meet Dane."

"Dane, this is Ingrid, one of my new friends at NYU." She said, waving me to him as if she were showing off her prized pedigree poodle at the Westminster Kennel Club.

"Nice to meet you, Ingrid," he said in a faint English accent.

I hadn't even noticed the accent because Anna had done all of the talking. He extended his hand. I smiled and shook it back. He stepped to the side and motioned to his friend who'd stepped towards the three of us.

"This is Allen, he and I grew up together in England. We

came to America to see my uncle who just so happened to leave this morning for Miami, so Al and I decided to come to Atlanta for the weekend. What do you have planned for this evening?" Dane said, facing Anna.

She looked at me and squeezed my arm, which meant that our original plans for ordering a pizza and watching a movie just went out the window. We would now be spending the rest of our night with the English boys. Despite the fact that I was taking a break from men at the moment, her excitement exceeded my distaste so I gave her the okay with a nod and a half-hearted smile.

"We don't have any plans," she gushed, stepping closer to Dane and dropping my arm.

"Right, well Al and I are going to shop around, then return to the hotel for a whisky. We're staying at the Ritz, room 1340. Come around 10 and we can decide what to do from there."

"Perfect!" Anna said, pushing her body against his.

He kissed her on each cheek then stepped away.

"Great. See you later," he said, winking at us.

The two of them turned and strutted into the mall, leaving a faint trail of cologne behind them. Anna turned to me and jumped up and down, clearly excited about spending the rest of her evening with the Englishman.

"Oh my god!" She squealed. "I haven't seen him since I went to St. Tropez with my cousin last year. I met him at this party and we totally had sex in the bathroom and I spent the rest of my vacation with him on his mom's yacht in Lake Como. He's so fucking hot! Oh my god, I'm definitely having sex tonight!"

"Um, hate to be the bearer of bad news, but you have a boyfriend, in New York, remember?" I said, picking up my bag that

INGRID DARLING

I'd put on the ground beside my feet.

She picked hers up too.

"Screw that cheating bastard!" She snorted, rolling her eyes. "Besides, Dane's parents are billionaires, and that's much more important than some puny Wall Street financial analyst." She said, fishing for her Blackberry out of one of the shopping bags.

I rolled my eyes.

"Whatever," I said.

She found her phone and began texting again. A black Mercedes pulled into the car port, our driver was finally here.

Later that evening, Dane's diamond cufflinks sparkled from the marble counter over the butler's pantry in his enormous suite. He picked one up and fastened it to the sleeve of his crisp white shirt.

"I *love* your cufflinks, Dane." Anna gushed, pouring herself a glass of vodka into a crystal tumbler on the counter.

She splashed two ice cubes into the glass and took a huge sip.

"Thanks love, they were a gift from mum for my birthday last month."

He said, fastening the second cufflink to his other sleeve. Anna pressed her body up to his and began nuzzling his neck with her nose.

It had taken Anna the entire two hours once we'd gotten back to her dad's condo to figure out what she wanted to wear for the night. I'd tried to take a 20 minute nap, hoping to re-energize myself for the evening, but Anna's constant complaining that she didn't have time to dry clean her dress kept me awake. She finally decided on an outfit and we quickly did our makeup and had the driver pick us up. We arrived at the Ritz at the same time as Dane and Allen, meeting them in the lobby. We all took the elevator up to the suite with Anna clinging to Dane like he was the last dollar she would ever see. Allen's pretentiousness seemed to come down a notch as he did the majority of the talking once we got into the suite.

"I think everyone should wear diamonds." He said in response to Anna's brown nosing to Dane.

I glanced at him from the other side of the suite, which was very plush and smelled of the spicy cologne Dane was wearing. Dark wooded cabinets lined the walls and an enormous flat screen TV was mounted on the wall. A huge suitcase sat opened on the bed with what seemed like a truckload of clothes pouring out of it. Six pairs of shoes lined up along the foot of the bed. Dane fastened his tie while Anna followed him around the room like a Shih-Tzu followed its owner.

I poured myself a drink then crossed the room and sat next to Allen on the couch who'd busied himself with the TV remote. He clicked to the channel for X-box then picked up a second remote and started playing a video game.

I sipped my drink, thinking about Allen's inconsiderate comment.

"Most people can't afford diamonds." I finally said.

Allen laughed.

"That's unfortunate for them."

"I like diamonds, but I think people should stop wearing

them." I said.

Allen looked at me as if I had just shot the Pope.

"What! They are such a commodity, not to mention a growing industry, that my family makes money from, I might add." He said, focusing his attention back to the TV.

"Yes, well the industry began at the expense of others who were exploited and had their lands taken from them so people could have fancy jewelry."

Anna walked in the direction of the couch, noticed that the conversation had dramatically changed then quickly decided that she was more interested in Dane, who was now busy changing his shoes on the edge of the bed.

"My great-grandfather helped pioneer the diamond industry and he was a great man. Smart too, they guy went to Oxford." Allen said, smugly.

"So did Cecil Rhodes, and that guy was an arrogant prick." I said, more forcefully than anticipated. "I mean, he deliberately took land from those Africans, whom he called "despicable specimens of human beings who should be brought under Anglo-Saxon influence". I mean, the guy had the nerve to write a book that promoted racist expansionism and European imperialism. It's because of people like him that racism and social oppression exist in the first place."

I had only just learned about Cecil Rhodes in my summer reading book for philosophy class. Though I'd only skimmed a few chapters, the section on Rhodes stood out to me and got me thinking more and more about the growing materialism in the world today.

"Well, my great-grandfather knew Rhodes and worked with him, and I have them to thank for my wealth. I mean, I have a decent life and I'm not complaining about it. I'm not saying that what Rhodes did was right, but to be a good businessman sometimes there have to be sacrifices." Allen said, frantically pressing the buttons on the remote.

"You're saying that the entire African continent should have been sacrificed so your great-grandfather and his comrades could make a profit?" I queried, feeling my cheeks flush.

"I don't believe he took the entire African continent! Give the man a break." Allen snorted.

"No, not the entire continent, but he had the audacity to convince the king of Matabeleland to give complete and inclusive charge of all the metal and minerals in his land in exchange for financial subsidy and weapons. Then he named the land after himself, in the name of colonization! And what for, so his great-grandchildren could sit on a yacht in the south of France while African nations deal with apartheid and civil wars over the land and minerals which European nations stole from them!"

Heat rushed into my face I could feel anger rising in my chest.

"You sure are angry about this, eh?" He laughed, haughtily.

He paused the video game and dropped the remote onto the coffee table in front of the couch then crossed the room to the butler's pantry. I saw Anna climb onto Dane on the bed out of the corner of my eye.

"It's always women who get all bent out of shape about things like this." Allen continued, pouring himself a glass of whisky into a crystal tumbler.

"Are you suggesting that only women are capable of understanding human degradation and civil inequality?" I asked, sarcasm breaching my tone, unsure why I was carrying on a conversation with someone who was clearly jaded.

"No, we men see it too. We also see the bigger picture. Sure, a few Africans were hurt at the expense of an industry, but that's what has to happen if you want to succeed. I mean, let's look at your country for instance. The natives of your land were practically extinguished and America is now the most powerful nation in the world. Sacrifices are always made for greatness to expand."

Allen crossed the room and resumed his spot on the couch, replacing his tumbler with the remote. He resumed play on the game.

"I can't believe you think its right for people to be sacrificed for an industry or for some imperialist motive. It was wrong for those settlers to take over North American lands just as it was wrong for Europeans to divide up Africa and devour its people and natural resources like some birthday cake."

He picked up the tumbler from the coffee table and took a sip, eyeing me.

"I never said it was right. I said it was what had to be done. And men are made just for the job. Women are too emotional. That's why you don't see women at the heads of powerful companies like Microsoft. The only reason for women to exist is to please men." He huffed, turning back to the TV to resume his video game.

INGRID DARLING

Appalled, I looked over to Anna, hoping that she would fire a rebuttal back at him, highlighting his ignorant comment amidst intelligent women. Despite her belief that women should marry rich men so they didn't have to work, she was avid women s' rights supporter. But she was straddled over Dane's legs, her tongue down his throat. She hadn't even heard Allen's statement. Too stunned to respond, I let him continue.

"I mean, they make a national holiday whenever women do something because women never do anything!"

His thumbs witlessly pressed buttons on the remote while he bent and swayed into the TV, as if acting out the characters on the screen.

"So, you're saying women should be egotistical materialistic wealth magnets, like those men who run major corporations and suck the blood out of nations in the name of capitalism?" I demanded, hoping to throw him from his stupid video game.

I didn't know why I was so angry with Allen but I wanted him to lose the game.

"Huh? No, they won't ever make it to the top. It's not in their nature," he said. "Women have always been inferior, even the Bible says it."

My jaw dropped open.

"The Bible was also written by men." I said flatly.

His ignorance reminded me of Lark, whose only motivation was pure indulgence, regardless of what kind of affect it had on others. I usually wasn't bothered by ignorant statements, but for some reason Allen was getting under my skin, perhaps it was the English accent or the perfectly polished loafers. I took a deep breath and exhaled, hoping the rage that was boiling under the surface would cool itself down.

"Why does it matter how successful or wealthy a person is?" I asked. "Can't someone still live happily without those things that drive them to wealth and power? I mean, Einstein rode a bike everywhere, and he was one of the most brilliant minds in Western history."

"Whatever, Einstein was poor. His little theories were the only things that made him famous." Allen snuffed, pulling out a small baggie from his pocket.

Pausing the game, he poured the contents of it onto the coffee table. A mound of cocaine spread across the glass.

I shook my head as he cut several lines and indulged in my favorite past-time. I watched him with disgust.

Suddenly I realized why I had allowed myself to become so involved in a conversation that had no resolve. Though I was upset with his viewpoint, my argument with Allen wasn't why I was so angry. I was angry with Thomas and Martin and Yvonne, and taking it out on Allen was my way of dealing with the anger. A moment passed and I decided it wasn't worth the effort to argue with Allen anymore. I rubbed my temples and turned towards Anna, who was now dry humping Dane on the corner of the bed.

I sighed and slumped back into the couch. I didn't know why I had decided to come to Atlanta with Anna. I knew that a weekend away from New York would rejuvenate me for school, but

INGRID DARLING

I felt silly discussing civil equality with someone who snorted cocaine and frivolously spent money all day. I didn't need to surround myself with ignorant people. After my petty friendship with Lark and disheartening relationship with Thomas, I'd decided to cut out all nonsense from my life, and I needed to stick to my decisions. At that moment, I was ready to leave that room of fools, ready to go back to New York where my friends actually had some sagacity, actually cared about others, regardless of how much their trust fund was worth.

INGRID DARLING

Twenty-Two

When we returned to New York I tried my best not to think about Thomas. The interesting weekend in Atlanta left me more anxious than relaxed and I couldn't stop thinking about how Thomas helped mask that anxiety. But it was over and he had moved on. On Wednesday, Anna and I ate lunch in Times Square, hoping to find some cute tourists on the streets. We had no luck. Her dingy chatting kept me distracted for the time being, but there was never any substance to our conversations.

After lunch, we drove around midtown in her black Range Rover. I spotted Theresa and Darryl on the sidewalk and told her to pull over after which I introduced the three of them. Theresa told us about a party she and Darryl were throwing to welcome themselves to Brooklyn, despite the fact that they had been living there for seven months already. It was going to be the approaching weekend and she insisted we come. She told me I needn't worry because Thomas wouldn't be there. I thanked her and told her we would come, and that she and I needed to have dinner together sometime before my classes started. She said that would be nice.

On Saturday, Anna picked me up and we drove down to Brooklyn.

"Who will be at this party?" She asked, once we were comfortably on the road.

"I have no idea." I shrugged.

"Aren't you friends with these people?" She asked sharply, leaning towards the steering wheel.

She wore a bright blue silk dress with a rope tied around

the midsection as a belt, white gladiator sandals wrapped around her calves. The enormous sunglasses on her face made her look more like a bug than a socialite. I chuckled to myself thinking her get up was probably five times more expensive than my cotton sundress and leather sandals. My shoes were from Italy but I had fished them out of a thrift store in Venice, whereas Anna's shoes were made in Italy but came from the Prada store on Fifth Avenue. The funny thing was that both pairs looked like they came from the Gap. But I kept that notion to myself, she would have definitely thrown a fit if she knew I thought her shoes looked cheaper than they actually were.

"I know some of Theresa's friends, but not all of Darryl's," I said, turning my attention back to the road.

"I'm sure it'll be fun, besides, I need a break from uptown. Those socialites are too much sometimes," she sighed, gripping the wheel tighter.

Traffic picked up and all of a sudden we were bumper to bumper with every car on the road. The light turned red, Anna slammed on the brakes.

"Ugh, I hate New York drivers!" She exclaimed.

I laughed.

"Yeah, I'm sure we'll have fun. You'll like their brownstone, it's very different, it feels like you stepped out of New York and went to India somewhere." I said.

"I don't think I'd like India." Anna said flatly, rolling her window down.

The light turned green but the car in front of us didn't move. She honked her horn and gestured out the window with her hand.

INGRID DARLING

"Why not?" I asked, gripping the handle above my seat.

Her impatience was making me uneasy.

"Too many bums."

She turned to face me then laughed.

We arrived to the party 45 minutes later. Anna nearly killed a homeless man walking across the street, but slammed on the brakes in time. She shouted out the window at him, telling him that a job and house would help him see better. I told her that her comment was mean and she apologized for being so rude.

"I'm an anxious driver," was her response for her outburst. I thought obnoxious was a better word for how she acted on the road, she didn't seem to understand that other people were trying to get somewhere as well. By the time we arrived in Brooklyn, my nerves were on edge and I had broken a sweat, mainly out of fear for my own life. She parked on the adjacent street and we walked around the corner and up the steps to the brownstone. I could hear people and music through the door. My nerves settled and I was now excited to see some of my old friends and meet some new ones.

I knocked and a moment later Theresa opened the door. She wore a loose shirtdress and flats, her hair swept to the side in a messy bun. A huge smile formed on her face when she saw us. Anna and I entered, each giving Theresa a hug. We were suddenly hit with the aroma of barbeque chicken and loud strumming from the bass guitar.

"Glad you two could make it." She called, over the music, closing the door behind us. "Darryl's band is playing in the den and there are wings and drinks in the kitchen."

People crowded the hallway, talking and laughing. Theresa

pushed through towards the den, pulling me and Anna along with her. We cut into the kitchen, towards the counter lined with bottles of wine and liquor.

"What do you want to drink?" She asked loudly, pointing to the variety we could choose from.

"I'll have a dirty martini." Anna said.

"Vodka and cranberry would be great." I said, looking around the room for anyone I may have known.

Theresa poured me and Anna a drink then walked into the den, disappearing into the crowd. I spotted Jada leaning against the refrigerator, talking to a tall guy with dreadlocks. She caught my eye and cried out in excitement.

"Ingrid, you're here!" She said, pulling me into a tight hug.

Her short hair was swept to the side and held in place by a large pink bow. She wore a pink blouse, white shorts and white sandals.

"How are you doing, sweetie?"

"I'm good." I replied, hugging her back. "How are you?"

"Ugh, busy with work as always. I'm so glad you could come," she said. "I missed you."

"I missed you too. Let's get together for lunch this week." I said.

She nodded.

"Definitely!"

Anna pinched my side, making me wince. I had already forgotten she was there.

"Oh, Jada this is Anna." I said, introducing my two friends to each other.

"Nice to meet you." Anna said, shaking Jada's hand.

INGRID DARLING

"You too. Cute shoes!" Jada exclaimed, staring down at Anna's feet. "Are they from Gap?"

Anna's cheeks flushed red and a horrified expression appeared on her face. She took a sip of her martini and swallowed.

"No, they're Prada." She said through grit teeth and a half hearted smile.

"Well they certainly are fancy." A voice from behind me bellowed.

I raised an eyebrow, thinking I recognized that voice. I turned around to see Karl with a huge grin on his face.

"Hey Karl!" Jada, who'd known Karl from their classes at Columbia, exclaimed. "I thought you were in the Peace Corps."

"I just got back." He said, straightening his shoulders.

His green eyes beamed under the curly mop on his head. He wore a fitted t-shirt and short khaki shorts, leather sandals.

"I was wondering when we were gonna have that dinner." I said sarcastically.

He laughed.

"Sorry about that, Ingrid. We'll have to reschedule."

He gave me a hug and looked at Anna. She shifted on her feet, avoiding eye contact with him.

"Karl, this is Anna." I said, grabbing her arm.

"Pleasure." He said extending his hand.

She smiled and shook it.

"Nice to meet you."

We waited for Karl to make himself a drink then the four of us migrated into the den, mingling with other people we knew and watching Darryl and his band perform. They played for another hour before switching to the stereo. Hip hop filled the brownstone as people danced and drank for several more hours. Anna and Karl stood near the bookcase the majority of the night, talking. After dancing with one of Darryl's band mates, I shuffled over to the two of them, slipping in the on the conversation.

"Our society has become the media," Karl was saying. "Everything is entertainment to Americans. How is it that what we see and read in the news can become a blockbuster movie within the same year? I mean, take Rwanda for instance, there is a civil war going on over there and Americans are busy making movies about it rather than helping end the situation."

"Well I would say that does call attention to the situation. Some people don't know what's going on in Africa and the only way for them to know is by watching movies or TV shows about it." Anna replied, sipping her martini.

"Yeah, but there is an obvious parallel to reality and reality TV, and people are getting confused between the two." Karl said.

"I definitely agree. I'd even say that entertainment has become reality for most people." I said.

Karl looked at me and smiled.

"Of course, especially our generation," he said.

He placed his drink on the bookshelf and continued.

"Our generation is so numb because of the media and all that garbage they throw at us to keep us from revolutionizing our society. I mean, when is the last time people had a riot in this country? Minimum wage went up a dollar! A fucking dollar! Why are people not protesting for a bigger raise? It's ridiculous, people need to stop watching this fucking reality TV and stand up for something. Why is the gap between the rich and the poor so big?

INGRID DARLING

Because no one is trying to make it smaller!" He exclaimed, crossing his arms over his chest.

The guy I was dancing with came up behind me and grabbed my waist. I pulled away from him, more interested in the conversation between Karl and Anna than dancing with a sweaty drunk guitar player.

"Wow, Karl, you seem pretty adamant about this. Why don't you start a riot right now? We can go to Duane Reade and stock up on be-be guns and start breaking people's mailboxes." Anna said, sarcastically.

He grunted.

"They probably won't even notice, they'd be too busy tracking their stocks. Exactly why there is a wealth gap in this nation."

"There isn't a huge gap between the rich and the poor because that's where the middle class is."

I knew what I'd said was false, but I hoped my comment would ease the resentment Anna was beginning to build towards Karl.

"The gap between the rich and middle class is getting bigger and bigger, and there is definitely a gap between the rich and the poor. I mean, some real estate mogul is sitting in his Upper East Side condo, deciding on which pair of expensive shoes he wants to wear on his vacation in Dubai which he flies to on his private jet, while some family of four lives on welfare 30 blocks away. It's ridiculous, the wealthy just don't seem to care about the poor or middle class in this society."

Karl's mention of Dubai made my stomach turn. A wave of nausea swept over my body. I swallowed, trying to avoid thinking about Thomas. I didn't want to have a reason to be upset that night.

"I resent that. My mom is heavily involved with charity organizations and networks for underprivileged children in Manhattan." Anna said, placing her glass on the shelf next to Karl's tumbler.

It was her third or fourth martini and she swayed back and forth in Karl's face, trying to make her point.

"In Manhattan! But guess what sweetie, the poverty in Manhattan doesn't compare to the poverty in Africa, in Indonesia, in India, or in South America. And your mom only does her charities what, six months of the year, and only because she'll get a tax cut. The other six months I'm sure she spends on some yacht in the Mediterranean." Karl huffed.

Anna gasped.

"You're an asshole." She snorted.

"At least I'm an asshole who cares more about helping others than whether my shoes are from Prada or Gap!" He said, loudly.

The couple on the couch next to the bookcase looked up towards us, obviously hearing the conversation which was turning into a battle between Anna and Karl.

"What makes you so great? You harp on about doing good for others, what good have you done recently?" Anna demanded, moving her face closer to Karl's.

I awaited the explosion that was building up. I didn't know Karl that well, but he was predictable. His face turned red then he grabbed Anna by the arm.

"For your information, rich girl, I just spent the past two years of my life in Sudan helping others. What have you done

INGRID DARLING

lately?" He said sternly in her face.

She pulled her arm out of his grip, took her martini off the shelf and pushed past him, grabbing my hand.

"C'mon Ingrid, we're leaving!" She huffed.

"Sorry." I mouthed to Karl as Anna dragged me away.

He nodded and turned back towards the bookcase. He reminded me of the homeless man on the street Anna had almost run over. She had a way of doing that with people, of colliding into them until she was forced to turn in a different direction.

INGRID DARLING

Twenty-Three

Karl and I had exchanged numbers before his quarrel with Anna and agreed to have breakfast the next day. We met at Jives, a 24-hour Diner that had just opened up near our apartments. It turned out Karl lived three blocks away from me, which made it easier for us to spend time together. I arrived a few minutes late and found him seated in a booth near the window. He saw me from across the restaurant, smiled and waved me over to him. He wore a white linen shirt and sunglasses sat atop his curly hair.

"Sorry about last night." I said as I slid into the booth.

I put my purse next to his messenger bag between us on the seat.

"It's alright, I had a feeling that conversation with Anna wouldn't end well. She just irritated me you know, with the 'my shoes are from Prada' and all."

"She's an Upper East Side socialite, what'd you expect?" I said, picking up the menu on the table.

"I guess I figured she'd be a little more down to earth." He said, picking up his menu.

A waitress came over and asked what we wanted to drink. She had short red hair and bright green eyes. I ordered orange juice, Karl ordered an iced tea. She nodded and shuffled away.

"I think earth is too common for socialites." I said, glancing through the menu.

He laughed.

"At least you two got home safely." He said, placing his menu on the table.

INGRID DARLING

"Yeah it took some effort to convince Anna that I should drive us back uptown. She finally handed her keys over after I told her that she couldn't even walk straight, much less operate heavy machinery." I said, putting my menu down.

The waitress appeared with our drinks and asked if we were ready to order.

"I'll have the western omelet, without ham please." Karl said.

"I'll have the pancakes with a side of fruit." I said.

She nodded and took our menus then walked off.

"So what got you two started talking about all that anyway?" I asked, taking a sip of my orange juice.

"She asked me where I was for the Peace Corps and I told her I had been in Africa, then she started talking about all these movies she'd seen about Africa and how she thought it was cool that diamonds came from there. I mean, it's sad that someone our age is so obsessed with material things." He said, slumping back against the seat.

"Yeah, I know. It bothers me too sometimes but I just block it out."

I thought about my conversation with Allen in Atlanta and how I almost let his pretentiousness affect my sentiment.

"It's hard to block it out when you're around it all the time." He said.

I looked over to him, curious as to what he was going to say next.

"I mean, I grew up in a really nice neighborhood, my parents were part of the country club, we went on vacations three times out of the year, my brother and I went to private school and my parents paid my tuition in full to Columbia and everything. We had a good life." He began.

"So why are you so against it if that was how you were raised?" I asked.

He took a sip of his tea.

"Because my dad got so wrapped up in how much money he was making and how much his stocks were worth and would go ballistic if they went down. He would take it out on me and my brother and my mom to the point where she had to get divorced from him. He was so obsessed with what he had in the bank that he forgot about what he had in his home, his family."

Karl held his head down. It was obvious how painful it was for him to talk about his family.

"I'm sorry to hear that Karl." I said, rubbing his shoulder. "Though it's not just your family, most people in this society are that way. They are so busy thinking about what they can buy that they lose sight of what is really important, like the value of life."

"I completely agree. It's unfortunate that people create a truth for themselves that their material goods will provide them with the ultimate comfort, the ultimate freedom. In actuality, they become a slave to their passions and ignorantly perpetuate its dominion over their lives." He said.

I thought about what Thomas had told me once about freedom, how freedom is not a natural inheritance of man, that in order to possess it we have to create it. We are not free unless we allow ourselves to be. The homeless man whom he'd quoted was right, and even took the liberty to divorce himself from material possessions. I wondered if Thomas understood the wisdom the old man had passed along. Karl continued.

INGRID DARLING

"And that's why I have issues with my dad. He never calls to see how I'm doing, and my mom is still having a hard time dealing with the divorce and all the pain and drama he put her through. It was humiliating for her to leave her husband because he was so obsessed with artificial things. He turned into such an ugly person that it's hard being in the same room with him, even now."

"Wow." I said, taking another sip of my orange juice.

"Yeah, and apparently he threw a shit fit when he found out that I didn't want to go into banking, like him, and that I wanted to study society and help others around the world. He would call my mom and yell at her, telling her that she raised a son who wasn't worth anything. He is such a pigheaded asshole. I mean, who cares about the fucking banking industry!"

"Seriously, there are much bigger problems in the world. Isn't there a civil war going on in Darfur?" I said, remembering what I'd heard on the news a few months ago.

"Yes, there is. And what my dad fails to acknowledge is that the banking industry is what fuels all these wars. Without banks there would never be enough money to pay for all the war equipment, because it costs billions of dollars to go to war. And unless billionaires are secretly funding every war in the world, then the only other source for that much money are the banks." He said.

"It's pitiful to think about that. I hate that there are wars now, after all the time humans have been on the planet to make peace with one another, it's ridiculous that it still continues." I said, shaking my head.

Karl took another sip of his tea.

"It is terrible, that's why we have to change it. We have to change how people think otherwise this cycle of ignorance will never end."

"I agree, but what can one person do to combat all the ills in the world?" I asked, looking into his eyes.

"Do you know who Margaret Mead is?"

I shook my head no.

"Well, she said "Never doubt that a small group of thoughtful, committed citizens can change the world. Indeed, it is the only thing that ever has." We could change the world."

"How?"

"We have to start with ourselves." He said.

Just then our waitress appeared with our food. She placed Karl's omelet on the table in front of him and put my pancakes and fruit in front of me. She asked if we needed anything else, we told her no and she walked off. I took a bite of my pancake, thinking about what Karl had just said.

Was he right, could we really change the world?

I thought about what difference I was making and how I was helping others, then realized that I wasn't doing anything but laying around watching TV when I wasn't at work legalizing the sales of extravagant homes in New York City. It was ridiculous, and I didn't want to be a part of it anymore. I took another bite of my pancake, deciding that I was going to turn my cable off so I wouldn't be distracted by reality TV shows anymore. I didn't need to watch some materialistic person live their life on television, that wasn't my reality. My reality was my family and my friends and eating breakfast with Karl right here, right now.

"I'm going to cut my cable off." I said, mouthful of pancake.

Karl smiled, cutting into his omelet.

INGRID DARLING

"That's a good idea. I never watch television anyway, I'm too busy living my own life to follow someone else's." He said.

"That's exactly why I'm getting rid of it." I said, sticking my fork in a strawberry from my fruit bowl. "Besides I'll be able to focus more on my schoolwork and do some reading, there are a few books I want to read before the year is out."

"That's a good idea. Start with yourself, you can only be a better person after that. I wish more people would focus on themselves because when you know who you are, you can understand others a whole lot better. More good things would happen in the world, and there wouldn't be so much anger." He said, eating the omelet from his fork.

He chewed for a few seconds then spit it out onto his plate, groaning in disgust.

"What's wrong?" I gasped, startled that he'd just spit his food out.

"Ugh!" He moaned.

It seemed that pigs were everywhere these days.

"There's ham in my omelet." He said.

INGRID DARLING

Twenty-Four

September, 2009

A door-bell rang, it was my phone. I flipped it open. It was my mom, most likely calling to make sure I was registered for classes and had all of my books for the semester. I pressed the send button and she immediately spoke.

"I just wanted to make sure you were all set for classes," she gushed.

I chuckled to myself, she was so predictable.

"Yes, I have everything I need." I said, walking from my kitchen to the couch.

I propped a pillow against the armrest and sat down, laying my head against it.

"Are you sure you have everything you need? I put some money in your bank account. I hope you didn't shop too much when you were in Atlanta," she said, the last sentence conveying skepticism.

It seemed I too was predictable.

I thought about Atlanta. After spending the rest of the evening with the English boys, Anna who drank too much vodka and ended up vomiting all over Dane's clothes, Dane who cried like an infant when he lost one of his diamond cufflinks, and Allen who was slapped in the face by a woman at the bar for grabbing her butt, I'd had enough of frivolity. I'd decided to return the several purchases I'd made at the mall before we left Atlanta and spent the money on a laptop I'd found on sale at the campus store. Other than having lunch with Anna, going to Darryl and Theresa's party, and eating breakfast with Karl, the past two weeks I'd pretty much spent reading a book I bought online and organizing my schedule for when classes started. My first class was on Monday, two days from now, it was Ethics.

"I didn't leave Atlanta with any more than I went with." I said, positioning the phone between my ear and shoulder and reaching for the notebook that was sitting on the coffee table.

I flipped through it, finding the page with my schedule on it. I had a feeling she would ask me about my classes.

"That's good to hear. So what classes are you taking?" She said, as expected.

"Well," I paused, glancing through my schedule.

I probably should have known which classes I was taking, but I didn't. I didn't occupy myself with things that I could otherwise find written down. Eventually it would become routine and I would no longer have to remember, I would just go through the motions.

"I'm taking an Ethics course, Philosophy, Statistics of Psychology and French." I said, closing the notebook and placing it back on the coffee table.

"I thought French was your major. Why are you taking so many other courses that are unrelated to your field?"

"Those classes are required for my major actually. Besides, they're interesting classes and I'm sure I'll be able to benefit from each of them." I said, sitting up on the couch.

I leaned over and picked up my laptop that was on the floor next to the coffee table, opened it and turned it on.

INGRID DARLING

"That's true. You start on Monday, is that right?"

"Yeah, I have Ethics on Monday."

"Okay, I just wanted to check on you. Have a great first week of classes. I'll chat with you later. Love you."

"Thanks, love you too." I said before hanging up.

I opened the internet on my laptop, checked my emails then checked Facebook. I had two messages. I opened the first, it was from Anna.

Oh my god, Allen tagged me in five pictures from that night in Atlanta and I'm throwing up all over Dane in one of them! I was so drunk, I don't even remember doing that! I'm so pissed that he put those pictures up. What a prick! I'm reporting him. PS- Lets have lunch this week. Call me and let me know your schedule. Anna.

The second message was from Theresa.

Hey girl, thanks again for coming to the housewarming party. I'm glad Anna could come too, she's an interesting girl! I have the next two weeks free if you want to come to my house and hang out some time. Have fun with class this week. T

I signed out and closed my laptop. I hadn't been on Facebook very much since discovering Thomas and Yvonne's adventures abroad. I didn't want to be faced with anything else that reminded me of them, and I valued face time with my friends, anything else seemed artificial, unreal. Emerald once told me that she'd had a job interview via webcam for some pharmaceutical company. She was appalled by the sheer separation between her and her interviewer and wondered how it was they were able to judge her ability to contribute to the company when they didn't even know if she was a real person.

"How can people rely on such things as virtual interviews, it's ridiculous, the internet promotes antisocialism," she'd said.

She was right. It was easy to lose yourself in cyberspace, which was why I tried my best to stay away from it.

On Monday I woke up to the sound of my alarm. I showered and dressed quickly, wearing a cardigan, jeans and flats, and grabbed an apple from the kitchen before making my way out of my apartment and down the street. I lived a few blocks from NYU's campus so the walk wasn't bad. Inside the classroom I chose a seat near the front, sitting between a boy and an older woman. The boy wore a white sweater vest and jeans and looked to be a freshman, just out of high school, naïve to college life. He reminded me of how I was when I was a freshman at college in North Carolina, nearly four years ago. The older woman appeared to be in her sixties. She wore a faded pink blouse and navy corduroys, bright orange glasses framed her tired eyes. Her demeanor reminded me of a weeping willow, aged yet full of verve. I felt like the bridge between, filling the gap.

Our professor walked in as the rest of the classroom filled up, pushing through students as he descended the stairs to the front. He wore thick bifocals and walked with his head down, as if avoiding eye contact from anyone of whom he did not wish to speak. He carried a trench coat in one arm, the other securing the shoulder bag to his hip, which was overflowing with papers and books. He made his way to the front and dropped his coat and bag onto the table beneath the chalk board. He spun around and picked up a piece of chalk and immediately began scribbling on the board.

>Albert Bernstein, PhD.
>Ethics 206
>"As intellectual and cultural development progresses, our relation toward the outer world changes proportionately from a passive to an active attitude. Man ceases to be a mere shuttlecock at the mercy of outward impressions and influences; he exercises his own free will to direct the course of events according to his needs and actions." –Ernst Cassirer

He spun back around and put the chalk on the table, wiping his hands together then stood waiting for the conversations in the back of the room to quiet down. I heard a few "Shh's", papers rustling, then silence. Someone coughed. He pulled a book out of his bag, walked to the pulpit and stood behind it, opening the book and placing it on the stand.

"If you're not supposed to be in this class, please leave now."

He kept his eyes on the book, flipping through the pages.

"For those of you in the right place, you should have already printed the syllabus from the course website, if you haven't, do so by our next meeting," he said.

His voice was monotone and he spoke with annoyance, as if he didn't want to be bothered with students who didn't want to learn. He lifted his head to the class. When no one left the room, he continued.

INGRID DARLING

"Very well. The focus of this course is to discuss the nature of man in his environment. I expect all students to participate in intellectual discussions on each topic and include references from outside sources to support your statements. You are expected to prepare and submit a 3,000 word essay as your final exam, the focus of which will be on the ambiguity of the human condition. This essay will be a culmination of what we have discussed in class and what you have learned as a result of those discussions. This is a college level course, any of whom feel it is too difficult to keep up with the assignments, please schedule a meeting with me to discuss how to improve your understanding of the subject matter."

He glanced back down at the book on the pulpit and looked back towards the class, pushing the bifocals up the bridge of his nose. The boy beside me shifted in his seat. Another cough.

The rest of the class time was spent discussing the quote that was written on the board. One student mentioned that man's relation to the outer world has always been active, which was why we were so much more advanced than the first humans. Another student spoke, saying that it was passion that motivated humans, that nothing great in the world has ever been accomplished without passion, but that passion is what ultimately led man to iniquity such as slavery and war because controlling the masses became the object of man's affection.

Another student agreed, saying that slavery was not just physical but it was mental as well. He quoted Michel Foucault, who said, "that bars exist inside our heads, and they have been placed there by the various modern institutions, in particular, the family, the school and the workplace." The student continued to say that most people are still mentally enslaved and are therefore unable to exercise their own free will.

Dr. Bernstein interjected, without lifting his eyes from the book on the stand.

"Plato said that the highest good for anything, human or nonhuman, consists in fulfilling its own nature, in living up to its own form or essence, not following the paths of others. In that case, how does man exercise his own free will?" He said.

"Nature provides free will for all living things, which means that man is born free and remains free, regardless of his circumstance," someone else said.

I thought about the quote Thomas had told me a year ago and decided to speak.

"Well, freedom is not a natural inheritance of man. In order to possess it we have to create it." I said.

Dr. Bernstein raised his eyes from his book and took his glasses off, staring at me.

"That's right," he said. "Ernst Cassirer said that. He also said that if man were simply to follow his natural instincts he would not strive for freedom, he would rather chose dependence. That this dependence also accounts for the fact that in both individual and political life, freedom is so often regarded much more as a burden than a privilege. Can anyone explain why he said that?"

A student raised a hand in my row. I looked over to see a young girl with curly brown hair and glasses.

"I guess it's much easier to depend upon others than to think, judge, or decide for yourself," she said.

"And why might that be?"

"Because most people don't know who they are and would rather have someone else direct them than learn about themselves and become an individual in society." I said, thinking back on my relationship with Thomas.

I hadn't been an individual with him, I was dependent, and because of my attachment to him, I hadn't known who I truly was.

"Humanity is similar to cattle, a herd that follows a herd-like mentality," the older woman to my side said.

I thought about my past herd-like mentality, how willing I was to follow others, then spoke again.

"But humans are aware that something is wrong with their condition, which is why they are constantly searching for freedom in each and every day. It's because they see the ambiguity in their condition and are looking for a way of understanding it. This is why man learns from his own experiences that it is not worth following others, that it is best to trust himself and reflect that inner knowledge onto his own life rather than following what the norms of society suggest to him." I said, more to myself than to the class.

The room was silent for a moment. The older woman on my side turned in her chair and gazed down at me. Her eyes were wide behind the orange frames. I suddenly felt as though a spotlight were shining on me, pointing me out amidst the class. An uneasy feeling swept over my body, I shifted in my seat. Dr. Bernstein put his glasses back on and closed the book on the pulpit. The fluorescent light from above caught his eye and twinkled, and for a moment it looked as if he were smiling.

"That is exactly what this class is about," he said.

The rest of the day went soundly. I bumped into Anna in the hallway in front of my last class and we briefly discussed our schedules. She looked tired and worn-out so I asked her if her classes were going alright. She sighed, telling me that her classes were fine, but she and her boyfriend had broken up. I gave her a hug and told her to be strong. She nodded and told me she would call me when she was feeling better, but I figured I wouldn't hear from her for a while.

    I walked home after my fourth class, ate the leftover pasta I had in the refrigerator and organized my notebooks. I went to sleep thinking how strange it was that I was back in school, finishing my degree. Having worked the past three years, it felt funny returning to a university environment. Everyone either seemed much younger or much older than me, as if I were the only one of my kind.

    I hoped to meet someone new, someone I could identify with. Lark was gone. Thomas had moved on. Theresa was in Brooklyn. Anna was too wrapped up in her own world. Karl was interesting, but we only connected on an intellectual level. I wanted someone who could open my mind and my heart. I wanted someone I could learn from. I wanted someone like me, needed someone like me.

INGRID DARLING

Twenty-Five

"Have you read the Bible, Ingrid?"
I had bumped into Dr. Bernstein at the campus library while looking for a book for Philosophy class. He was sitting on a leather chair in the reading lounge near the Religion section. We'd talked about class for a few minutes; he asked me if I understood the topics, if there was anything I needed help with. I told him no and we somehow got into conversation about religion.

"Not the whole thing," I replied, "just the parts read in church services. That is, when I actually go to church. Why do you ask?" I said, accompanying him through the Philosophy aisle.

"Well, most people who have read the Bible do not quite understand the messages presented in the gospels."

He pulled a bible off the shelf and thumbed through it, stopping and folding the cover back.

"In fact, many of the gospels of the original disciples have been left out of the Bible, done so by vote at the Council of Nicea. But my reasons for asking is that most of the gospels were written in parables, namely by students of the original disciples. I wanted to read one in particular that you might be able to personally relate to at this point in your life. It's from the gospel of Mark and it says, "Unto you it is given to know the mystery of the kingdom of God; but unto them that are without, all these things are done in parables. That seeing, they might see and not perceive; and hearing, they might hear and not understand"."

He lifted his face to me and pulled the book to his chest.

"Which gospel is that?" I asked, not sure why I was

interested in pursuing this topic of discussion with my suddenly very friendly Ethics professor.

"Mark 4, verses 11 and 12," he said, pushing the bifocals up the bridge of his nose.

His black hair was streaked gray and he stood with his shoulders hunched.

"What does it mean? Am I supposed to understand something in that passage?"

"You'll figure it out. I have faith in you, Ingrid. I must go now. When you leave here, look to the left and the message will appear just a bit clearer. Good luck to you. Maybe we will meet again soon, until then I'll see you in class."

He closed the book and placed it back on the shelf, grabbed his trench coat off the back of the leather chair and slung it over his shoulders. He nodded his head and turned towards the end of the aisle, disappearing around the corner. I looked around, puzzled at what had just happened.

Why was my professor telling me that he had faith in me? And what was he talking about; look to the left and the message will be clearer?

I rubbed my temples, closing my eyes.

"I overheard your conversation with Dr. Bernstein," a deep voice behind me said.

I whipped around to see a very attractive young man standing in front of me. He was much taller than I with dark hair and mysterious eyes.

"He comes here a lot but I've never seen him read an excerpt of the Bible to a student. He usually keeps to himself, you must have struck something in him," he said.

"Oh?"

INGRID DARLING

I felt a flutter in my stomach, butterflies.

"He teaches Physics here. Are you his student?"

"No. well, yes, but not for Physics. He's my Ethics professor." I stammered, stuffing my right hand in the front pocket of my jeans and shifting my weight.

For some reason I was nervous around this stranger, maybe it was the way his eyes pierced into mine. I looked down at my feet, feeling my face flush.

"Yeah I had him for Ethics in undergrad. What are you studying?"

"French. That's my major."

"Oui, le français! I took French in high school. Well like I said, Bernstein doesn't converse with his undergrad students. I heard him read Mark to you? What'd you think about it?"

"Honestly, I didn't really understand why he was reading it to me, I'm not even religious." I said, suddenly wishing I had said something more eloquent.

I didn't want tall, dark and handsome to think I was an idiot with no depth.

"I'm sure he had a reason," he laughed. "Have you heard of Georg Hegel, the German philosopher? I'm sure you've discussed him in Ethics. Well, Hegel viewed religion as a way in which the human spirit could become aware of itself as a manifestation of the One, which he also called the mind or consciousness. For him, consciousness was the searchlight for the spirit of mind within humanity trying to know itself. And since it can't find a fixed object for its concentration outside itself, it must turn inward and discover itself as the One. However, until the spirit finally achieves this, it creates images, forms, symbols, and ideas outside of itself as guideposts and reflections of this quest. The Bible is a sort of guidepost for the conscious spirit until it can become aware of itself."

I stared blankly at him.

He is beautiful and brilliant!

He smiled, revealing a perfect set of white teeth. For a moment he looked familiar, as if I'd seen him before somewhere, perhaps in a dream. I smiled back and scratched my elbow out of nervousness. A minute passed, I didn't know what to say. He broke the silence.

"Did I just talk over your head? I tend to do that, especially with pretty girls."

My cheeks flamed.

"No, it's just really philosophical. I'm into that, but I wasn't ready to hear it from you." I said, combing a stray curl behind my ear and looking him bashfully in the eye.

He laughed.

"Yeah I get pretty philosophical."

He looked down the aisle. A group of students passed by, whispering.

"Are you in grad school here?" I asked, hoping to delay him from leaving.

"Yeah I am." He looked back at me, the light caught his eye and I saw a glint of hazel.

"What are you studying?"

"I'm doing my dissertation on metaphysical theories."

"Oh."

"Yeah, it's pretty intense." He raised an eyebrow and shrugged his shoulders. "So what are you doing later? Do you have any plans?"

I thought about my schedule for the rest of the day.

"I actually do." I said.

I had a meeting with my advisor to review my plan of work. *Fuck, why did I have to run into Hercules today?*

"Well, why don't I give you my number and you can call me sometime. If you're not busy tonight, a bunch of my buddies are coming over to watch the game. I live in Soho with a roommate. I think you might like the set-up. Plus, you might be able to benefit from the conversations, a few of them are really into reality and universal phenomenon and all that Hawkings stuff, so we always end up having really interesting discussions, or you might call them tête-à-têtes."

He smiled and winked. My heart melted. I smiled back, imagining him ripping my clothes off.

"Here," he said, pulling out his wallet and handing me a business card. "That's an old business card from when I worked at JP Morgan, but the email and cell number are the same. Give me a call when you have some time. I'd like to get to know you."

He smiled once again and picked up a messenger bag that was sitting on the floor between us. I hadn't even realized it was there.

"Okay." I said, giving him a shy wave as he made his way down the aisle and disappeared around the corner.

I looked at the business card in my hand:

James Frederick Blake, Asset Manager.

His name sounded familiar, as if I had heard it before. I folded the business card and placed it carefully in my back pocket.

Don't want to lose this one, I thought.

INGRID DARLING

I grabbed my tote which was sitting on the floor at the end of the aisle, hung it over my shoulder and walked towards the entrance of the library. A group of students rushed by me, whispering numbers and equations, clearly on their way to a study session. I walked through the revolving door to the outside and a gust of wind blew my hair over my face. I combed it behind my ears.

Look to the left and the answer will reveal itself, I remembered my professor saying.

I did, noticing nothing but the usual lunchtime New York City pedestrian traffic. I shrugged my shoulders and thought that perhaps Dr. Bernstein had said that as a parable to make his point. People hurried past me, heads buried in their Blackberry's and babbling to clients on their iPhones. I thought about James, but before I could imagine him kissing me, I turned around and walked directly into Emerald.

"DARLING!" She screamed, pulling me into a tight hug.

I screamed and squeezed back, in awe that she was standing there in front of me. I was so happy to see her.

We took the elevator up to her room. Emerald was staying at The Mandarin Oriental for the weekend with her boyfriend while he was in town for a business meeting.

"I needed to get out of North Carolina," she'd said was her reason for accompanying him on his trip.

"I'm so glad you're in town," I said. "But why didn't you call me?"

"I'm sorry babe," she said, as the elevator doors opened. We walked out and I followed her down the hall to her room. "I just got here this morning and I figured you were in class or something."

"How funny is it that I ran into you?" I said, still in awe that she was actually in the city.

She unlocked the door to her room and we walked in. I settled down on a chair against the wall as she took her coat off and sat down on the bed.

"Yes, well it was bound to happen." She smiled. "So, tell me something."

I unzipped my coat and put my tote on the floor.

"Well, strangely enough, I met a guy today." I said.

She raised her eyebrow and tilted her head.

"Oh?"

"At the library. It was odd because I was there looking for a book for my Philosophy class, which I didn't find, and I bumped into my Ethics professor who started talking to me about God. So I entertained a discussion with him for a few minutes and when he left, this really cute guy came up to me and sort of picked up the conversation where my professor had left off."

I gave her a detailed description of James, how intelligent he was, how intense his eyes were, and how I felt in his presence.

"Then I ran into you." I concluded.

Emerald smirked then leaned back onto her elbows on the bed.

"What do you think this means?" She asked.

I shrugged.

"I have no idea."

"What about all the drama you went through with Thomas? Do you think this is a sign that you're going through some sort of transition?"

I thought for a moment about the possibility of a connection between the events of the past few years and the present but then passed it off as coincidence.

"Doubt it." I said.

"Well you never know. I think certain things place themselves in our paths for a reason. The universe has a plan for us. God, had a plan for us."

"What do you mean?" I asked, pulling my arms from my coat and positioning it over my shoulders.

"I don't know. It seems as though there has to be a reason for living. I mean, it makes no sense otherwise, to just be on the planet to take up space? There has to be another reason, that's why I believe in God, that's why I believe there is a purpose to life."

"So what's my purpose?"

"I don't know. All I'm saying is that it seems like every obstacle is put in place to point us in a different direction, in a better direction. Perhaps you were meant to meet this guy. Perhaps it was fate playing its role in your life."

"So you're saying that my circumstances are already mapped out?" I asked, thinking about the quote Dr. Bernstein had read to me.

Perhaps I am seeing and not perceiving, I thought.

"There is a definite map to existence," she said. "Everything definitely happens for a reason."

"Then what is my reason for meeting James?" I asked, trying to understand the significance of my encounter with him.

"Who knows. Maybe he's supposed to teach you something or maybe he's the one you're supposed to be with."

INGRID DARLING

"I wish I knew. There was something about him, something I could feel inside of me, like he touched my soul or something." I said, hearing James' deep voice in my head.

She smiled.

"There's an old saying, that love is the soul's recognition of its counterpoint in another."

"I didn't say I loved him. I don't even know him." I said quickly, feeling my face flush.

She eyed my skeptically.

"There is no mistaking love, Darling. You feel it in your heart."

"Emerald!" I gushed. "I don't even know the guy!"

"You don't have to know him to love him. You can love anyone, regardless of their significance in your life," she said.

"Well I am interested in getting to know him. I think I should start with that."

"If you want him, focus on him. Focus on what you want, and you'll eventually get it."

I was quiet for a moment. I thought about James, about his piercing eyes and how warm he made me feel. I didn't want to think about the possibility of loving him though, especially since I hardly knew him.

I could get to know him. I could call him, I thought, reaching into my pocket and touching the business card.

But I hesitated and pulled my hand out. It was too soon.

Besides, I'm sure he doesn't really want me to hang out with him and his friends tonight, I told myself.

I was good at that, of convincing myself that I shouldn't do something. It was the fear talking; it was fear preventing me from taking chances, of living my life.

"I'm hungry." Emerald said, breaking my thoughts. "Let's get something to eat."

"Where do you want to go?" I asked, slipping my arms back into my coat and standing from the chair.

"I don't know. Let's just get on the subway and see where it takes us," she said, jumping up from the bed and grabbing her coat.

I picked up my tote from the floor as she threw her coat on.

"Sounds like a plan." I said, following her out the door.

We took the elevator down to the lobby and walked out into the cold. We walked several blocks to the subway station and hurried down the stairs to catch the next train. The doors of the train flew open as crowds of people flooded in and out. The two of us squeezed through the mass and found empty seats at the back of the car.

"So where do you want to go?" I asked again as we sat between two older men.

"I'm sure we'll figure it out when we get there. Only the journey is written, not the destination. So just ride," she said.

I laughed and leaned my head back.

Emerald is my guiding light.

The doors closed and the train rocked as it sped off.

INGRID DARLING

Twenty-Six

October, 2009

A cold gust of wind blew past me. I adjusted the scarf around my neck. I was on my way over to Karl's apartment; he was tutoring me for my Statistics of Psychology class. I understood the concepts, but as my professor put it:

"If you don't understand one method, you'll never understand the rest".

So I decided that before I got lost, I would have Karl tutor me, especially since Behavioral Research was what he was currently researching for his PhD. I walked quickly down the sidewalk, passing a group of high school kids chatting in front of a Halloween store. I slowed my pace and glanced through the window, spotting a very cute Harry Potter costume that would be perfect to wear for Halloween.

Now I just need a Halloween party, I thought, quickening my pace and rounding the corner.

I walked by Lorenzo's Pizza, waving through the window to Lorenzo, he was behind the counter laughing with another pizza chef. His arms were crossed over the sauce stained apron barely covering his stout frame. He waved back and shouted in his delicious Italian accent:

"When you gonna bring your ma to eat my pizza?"

"Soon," I called through the door.

He smiled and waved me off, turning back to the smaller

dark haired man standing with him. Behind the two men was another thin dark haired man. I immediately remembered him; he had tried to tell me about my revealing breast situation several years ago. Embarrassment flushed to my face as I ducked away and hurried down the sidewalk.

I reached the corner of the street, turned right and cut across to the brownstones on the other side. I rang the bell and a few seconds later Karl buzzed me up. Upstairs I waited outside his door for almost five minutes before he opened it.

"Sorry, I had to pull the pizza out of the oven," he said, kissing me on the cheek.

He loved how Europeans greeted one another so he was always kissing, instead of hugging or shaking hands. He startled a lot of people that way, especially men, but it didn't bother him, he was very comfortable with himself. He was wearing a red knit sweater and fitted jeans, gray socks. His hair was styled but disheveled, the 'in' look. His dark green eyes beamed as he smiled at me. I walked in and unraveled the scarf from my neck.

"So we're having pizza tonight?" I asked, tossing my scarf and tote onto his black leather couch.

"Of course, Darling, its Tuesday night," he said, shuffling into the kitchen.

I plopped down on the couch and faced the TV, picking up the remote and flipping through the channels. The volume was muted. Nothing interested me so I stopped on a commercial for Time Warner Cable, featuring a man and a woman sitting in a classroom with a female teacher who was teaching them about the "more important things in life". On the board behind her was an image of a remote control. I chuckled to myself and thought about what Karl's reaction to this commercial would be. I put the remote on the glass coffee table in front of me and picked up a magazine. I flipped through it, paying more attention to the noise Karl was making in the kitchen.

"Almost ready!" He called.

I could smell the pepperoni and my mouth started watering. I took my eyes off the magazine and glanced around the room, noticing a new book propped forward on his bookshelf adjacent to the couch. I was about to get up from the couch to look at it but Karl appeared from the kitchen holding two plates and two napkins. He handed me a plate then placed the napkins on the coffee table and sat on the couch next to me.

"Thanks. What kind of pizza is this?" I asked, picking up the slice and taking a big bite.

"DiGiorno," he said, taking a bite as well. "I thought about ordering from Lorenzo's, but I already had this in the freezer. Hey, so you want to get breakfast tomorrow? My professor cancelled our meeting so I'm free all morning."

Sauce dripped from his lip, he caught it with his plate.

"Sure. I don't have any classes tomorrow so I'm actually going to Brooklyn to see Theresa, but I can meet you around 10ish. Does that work for you?" I took another bite, savoring the flavor in my mouth.

"Perfect. Jive's?"

He took another enormous bite, his napkin was now a grease stained wad in his hand. He wiped his mouth, chewing the lump of pizza in his cheek.

"Sounds good."

I also took a huge bite, finishing my slice, and almost

choked trying to swallow the cheese. We faced the TV, no longer on commercials. An episode of *Lost* was on.

"I love this show!" Karl exclaimed, grabbing the remote from the coffee table and un-muting the volume.

"Do you watch this show?" He asked, stuffing the remainder of the slice in his mouth.

"Yeah, but I've only seen up to the third season. You know I don't have cable so I have to wait to rent it." I said, putting my empty plate on the coffee table. "Is there any more pizza left?"

"Yeah, on the stove," he said between chews.

I got up from the couch and made my way into the kitchen, wiping crumbs from my turtleneck and jeans.

"Well, in my opinion, the show is genius," he called from the other room. "It brilliantly ties in 17th and 18th century philosophy by incorporating the messages of the philosophers in each character."

"How so?" I asked loudly, pulling another slice of pizza from the pie and placing it on my plate.

I walked back to the couch and sat in the same place.

"Well, you know who John Locke is, right?" He had finished his pizza and was now slumped against the back of the couch, pillow under his arm.

"Yeah, he's the old guy on the island with the bum leg who tried to open the hatch and had his own philosophy about how the island should be governed."

I laughed and took a bite of the fresh slice, thinking of the show and how each character had their opinions about Locke.

"No, I was talking about John Locke, the British philosopher and political theorist during the Enlightenment. It's interesting how the show characterizes Locke, because in reality, 18th century thinkers were influenced by John Locke's advocacy of religious toleration, his concern for liberty, and his rational attempts to understand and improve the human condition. His ideas saturate the American Declaration of Independence, Constitution, and Bill of Rights."

"Oh really?"

"Yeah! Locke believed that human beings are born with the natural rights of life, liberty, and property and that the establishment of the state was to protect these rights, and no legislature had the authority to deprive any individual of their natural rights."

"That sounds like the basis for the Declaration of Independence." I said, taking another bite.

A pepperoni fell from the pizza into my lap. I picked it up and stuffed it in my mouth, wiping the grease stain on my jeans with my napkin.

"Exactly!" He exclaimed, leaning over the arm of the couch and picking up a beer that was sitting on the floor.

He took a sip and continued.

"In his Second Treatise on Government, Locke wrote that "Political power is that power, which every man having in the state of nature, has given up into the hands of society and to the governors. This power, which every man has in the state of nature, and which he parts with to society is to use the means for preserving his own property, as he thinks good and nature allows him. And to punish the breach of the law of nature in others, so according to the best of his reason, is conducive to the preservation of himself and the rest of mankind."

He took another sip of his beer and placed it back on the

floor.

"So you're saying that people give up their natural rights to society with the expectation that their government will uphold the responsibilities of protecting its citizens and their property. Kind of like a social pact, like a sort of trust."

"You got it."

I thought for a moment about the rights I had given up, to Lark and to Thomas. My social pact clearly went unfulfilled.

"Interesting, hence the character Locke's opinions on how the island should be run. But hold on, were you paraphrasing or did you actually remember that word for word?" I said, taking another bite, annoyed that I had just stained my jeans.

He laughed.

"I was paraphrasing, but I actually had to recite the entire treatise for a play I was in a few years ago for drama class."

"Impressive."

"Yeah, well I'm impressed by Locke."

"What about the other characters in Lost?" I asked, between chews.

"There is also Rousseau. You know, the crazy French woman who lives in the jungle and tries to steal everyone's baby."

I laughed.

"Yeah."

"Rousseau's character, it seems, is derived from another 18th century philosopher, Jean Jacques Rousseau. In *Emile*, he suggested that educational reform would cure the ills of society. His educational reform advised that children should experience direct contact with the world to develop their imagination, resourcefulness, and resilience so they would become responsible and productive citizens of society. He said that children should not be treated like adults, and chaining them to desks and filling their heads with outmoded learning was only hindering to their growth. He said, "Nature, not man is his schoolmaster, and he learns all the quicker because he is not aware that he has any lesson to learn"."

"I believe that. For me, taking a break from college to work and experience the world gave me a better understanding of life. I'm obviously back in school now, but I think Rousseau would agree that the world taught me more about myself than statistics ever could."

Karl nodded.

"I wonder if the writers purposely used those philosophers to model their characters." I said, taking the last bite of my pizza, now thirsty.

"I'm sure they did. People are smarter than they get credit for. I'm sure the writers were trying to use the philosophers to make a point, so they adopted their names and philosophies and incorporated them in the story. The whole show is genius in my opinion."

"Yeah, I really like it too." I said, swallowing the final chunk in my mouth. "You got any more beer?"

"Yeah, I'll grab it for you," he said, leaving the couch for the kitchen and returning with a beer.

He undid the cap and handed it to me.

We spent the next fifteen minutes talking about which books we were currently reading. Karl loved to read and was always suggesting books for me in hopes of expanding my political and social horizons that television and the internet could not provide. Luckily I didn't have cable, so books and magazines were truly the only thing that could keep me entertained if I wasn't occupied with school work. We each had another slice of pizza then I pulled out my statistics book and we began study session. Around 10 o'clock we kissed on the cheek and I headed back to my apartment.

    I texted Theresa on the walk:

Going to breakfast with Karl, be at your place around 12.

She texted back:

K, see you tomorrow.

    I hurried through the cold, pulling my tote close to my body and crossing my arms, tucking them into my armpits. I was home a few minutes later and I undressed, putting on sweat pants and a tank top, and stuffing my sauce stained jeans into the dirty clothes basket in my closet. I sat down on the couch and opened my laptop, checked my email for school, and then my Facebook messages. Jada sent me a message asking if I wanted to have dinner with her tomorrow at Sullivan's, the place where we'd first met. I responded, telling her yes and giving her my phone number. I signed offline and closed my laptop then sat back and stared up at the ceiling fan. It rotated slowly. I thought about my conversation with Karl. He was so astute and I loved him for teaching me what I otherwise may not have paid attention to. My mind wandered for several more minutes and before I knew it, I had drifted into sleep.

    Karl must not have sensed my admiration towards him that night, because the next day at Jive's he began our conversation with one of his tirades. We hadn't even ordered our breakfast when he started ranting.

"Can you believe this, some dick on the subway was reading the Times and had the audacity to laugh at a picture of these poor kids from Malawi, and you know what he said? He said that their government needs to figure out a way to be more like America so those kids could have luxury things like us! Are you fucking kidding me? Those kids need water and food, not a Rolex and an expensive trench coat! Luckily for him he got off at the next station before I could go off on him. I mean, what's wrong with Americans? They look at people in underprivileged countries and think less of them because they don't have things. Hell, those people have more *because* they don't have things! They don't have anything to distract them, because all they're concerned about is living! And westerners think, 'we're so powerful because we have so much and we feel so privileged because we have everything and everyone else wants to be just like us!' What the fuck!"

I opened my mouth to say something but it was useless. This was going to be a Karl breakfast. The waitress came to our table but hesitated before asking what our orders were. Karl didn't stop raving. Other people were starting to look our direction. I looked at the waitress and gave her an apologetic expression. She smiled timidly and shifted her weight. She was young and had a petite frame. Her thin blond hair was twisted into a messy bun on top of her head. She kept her head down and avoided eye contact. Karl didn't seem to notice her. I grabbed his hand which was resting on the table. The other was flailing wildly through the air emphasizing each exasperated statement he made. It broke his concentration. For a moment he seemed not to realize where he was, just lost in his own world.

"We need to order." I said.

His menu sat on the table, unopened.

He picked it up and glanced through it for half a second.

"The western omelet, with no ham! You got it? They always put that fucking ham in my omelet!"

"Would you like hash browns with that, sir?" She asked in a low voice.

She was obviously new.

"No! Just make sure they don't put any ham in my fucking omelet, okay!"

He shoved his menu at the waitress. She nodded and turned to me, her face was flushed and she looked as if she were about to cry.

"I'm sorry for my rude friend," I said, hoping to undo the emotional damage Karl had done to the poor girl. "I'll have the strawberry crepe and a side of pancakes."

I handed my menu to her and smiled. She nodded and turned, pressing the menus close to her chest. I could see tears welling up in her eyes as she walked away.

"She'd better get my order right. These dumb waitresses always fuck up my order." Karl muttered before she was out of earshot.

Her head and shoulders dropped and she hurried her pace then disappeared around the corner.

Too late, damage done.

"Karl, why do you have to be so obnoxious? This is probably that girl's first job and she has to deal with arrogant assholes like you at 10 o'clock in the morning. You don't know what she's going through, you just can't be so rude to people."

"Whatever," he grunted, slumping back in his chair. "She needs to have someone like me point out the problem with her profession, or any profession for that matter. What did Sartre say about the waiter in the café? How he has escaped his own freedom as a conscious being and is acting out some social role, trying to be this perfect proponent of society, the perfect waiter, but he has no essence. He is in bad faith, because he has escaped from his freedom as a person, and has become a mechanism from which he'll gain social approval for the performance of his role."

"What does that have to do with anything?" I asked, throwing my hands in the air.

"I'm just saying. Even Marx agreed that in this capitalistic society, workers are alienated from their true selves. They are estranged from their very being. That waitress was trying to be a good waitress for who, us, herself, society? She probably doesn't even want to be a waitress, she probably loves to play the piano and it is her dream to be a concert pianist, but she won't pursue that because it's not "ideal", and her parents want her to fit into society like a good little drone, just like them. Go to work, go home, go to work, go home. That bullshit cycle that drives sane people to lunacy."

"Okay, so you're a Marxist now?"

"I'm not saying that, but the guy had some good ideas."

"Karl, the girl probably has this job because she needs money. You don't know her situation, she may have to work to pay for things because her parents can't afford them."

He rolled his eyes emphatically.

"What did Marx say? Money is the alienated essence of

man's work and his being, and this alien being rules him and he worships it."

"Ugh! You always have to reference some philosopher to prove your point. I'm just saying, that girl didn't deserve you being so mean to her."

For some reason I felt obligated to stand up for the waitress. I didn't know her, but Karl's remarks were unfair in her absence. And even though I was defending her position, I felt belittled and it was beginning to irritate me.

"Who cares," he snorted. "Maybe my arrogance will give her a backbone. Maybe she'll put on a little makeup and fix her hair so she doesn't look like a girl scout anymore. Hell, maybe she'll actually look people in the eye when she's taking their orders. Or even if we're lucky, maybe she'll learn how to be a woman and not let men push her around. These little girls are so dumb, they think they can just run away from home and try and survive in this world and then they end up as prostitutes in the meatpacking district, getting trains run on them by greedy, self-indulgent corporate bastards who leave their nice offices on Wall Street for a quickie blow job from a sixteen year old on the other side of the city."

"Foul. You're just foul." I said, shaking my head.

It was useless, Karl had taken his stance and he wasn't budging. I turned and faced the window. It was beginning to rain outside. People opened their umbrellas and quickened their paces.

"Tell me I'm wrong, and then I'll drop it."

He wasn't going to end the conversation without making his point.

"You're not wrong, you're just arrogant." I said, officially irritated with his pompousness.

INGRID DARLING

I was about to support my statement with a tirade of my own, but our food came. It was brought out by a stout older woman with greasy brown hair. She put our plates on the table and a greasy curl fell in her face. She smelled like freesia and bacon. She was breathing heavily. I don't think she had climbed a staircase in ten years. I looked around for the waitress, but didn't see her. Clearly she was in the bathroom crying.

"Did you need anything else?" The woman asked.

She had a thick southern accent.

"No thank you, we're good." I said picking up my fork and eyeing my crepe.

Karl nodded and gave her a bleak expression. She turned and waddled away.

"All I'm saying is that people are deceiving themselves."

He leaned over and pulled out a thin book from the messenger bag that was sitting on the floor. He flipped through a few pages and stopped, folding it back.

"Listen here, Sartre says that these so called experienced professionals "drag their lives out in stupor and semi-sleep, they've married hastily, out of impatience, and made children at random. They have met other people in cafés, weddings and funerals, and sometimes caught in the tide they've struggled against it without understanding what was happening to them. All that has happened to them has eluded them, and then around forty, they christen their small obstinacies and a few proverbs with the name of experience and they begin to simulate slot machines: put a coin in the right slot and you get tales wrapped in silver paper, put a coin in the left slot and you get precious bits of advice that stick to your teeth like caramels"."

I took a bite of my crepe.

"What book is that?"

"Nausea. It's pretty grim, ineffably Sartre." He said, staring at the cover.

"Oh." I said, mouthful of strawberries.

Karl kept flipping through the book and reading excerpts on every other page that he had no doubt highlighted and scribbled comments alongside the edges and corners. He hadn't touched his omelet. I'm sure it was getting cold, but he didn't care. He wanted to prove his point. I kept my head down, trying to tune him out while pretending to be listening. I nodded along hearing only bits and pieces of what he was saying. My crepe was too good not to enjoy. He stopped talking for a few seconds and I heard his fork scrape against the ceramic plate.

Finally, I thought, *I can eat my breakfast without an NPR lecture.*

The silence didn't last long.

"What the fuck!" Karl bellowed.

I looked up, startled. A few people in the restaurant turned toward us again, quizzical expressions on their faces.

"What's wrong with you?" I cried, annoyed and embarrassed that he had just made a scene.

He threw his fork on the table and groaned. There was ham in his omelet.

INGRID DARLING

Twenty-Seven

The subway was crowded and noisy. A baby wouldn't stop crying and five nine year olds were arguing about whether Derek Jeter was a better baseball player than Alex Rodriguez. I wished they'd shut up. I didn't have my iPod today, so listening to mindless banter was inevitable. The train turned a bend and I strained myself from bumping shoulders with the fat sweaty man seated beside me. He smelled like cabbage and onions. He reminded me of the plump woman who'd served our food at breakfast. It turned out that what Karl thought was ham in his omelet was actually a refried egg. I tried to apologize for his outburst and unnecessary ravings about the entire wait staff, but it didn't help. Everyone in the restaurant was staring, aghast at his dogged vulgarity. The manager had to come out and ask us to leave as we were "disturbing the ambiance of the restaurant". It took Karl five more minutes of ranting before he would even get out of his seat. Needless to say it was a fiasco of a morning.

    Sometimes I wondered how it was that Karl was my friend. He could be so obdurate and incapable of seeing anyone else's perspective but his own. Though I realized his stubbornness stemmed from his relationship with his father, much of it developed within the past few months that I'd known him. With starting research for his PhD and fixating on all the political turmoil in the world, the guy had a lot of pent up aggression about Americans and westerners. I wouldn't have been surprised if he said he was moving to Thailand. He needed to get away, sometimes I worried about him. It isn't healthy for a person to get so caught up with all the ills in the world. Obsession of this nature can only drive one to madness.

The subway pulled to a hasty stop. I almost lost my balance even though I was seated. The doors flew open and people squeezed in and out. A man started yelling at a woman after she insisted she was unable to move out of the way for him to pass her. He tried to push between her and another man and broke a sweat in a failed attempt. The doors closed and the train pulled off as fast as it had stopped. He started screaming profanities and pulled out his Blackberry. He must have been late for a meeting because he kept ranting about figures and moving Bill to 3pm to the marketing department. I tuned him out. The nine year olds were now arguing about basketball players. The fat sweaty man beside me was replaced by an even sweatier man with bad acne. He smelled like body odor. I could feel his eyes peeling the skin from my bones. I looked at him and gave a phony smile, trying to lean closer to the old woman on my other side. She smelled like a furnace, I figured she didn't even shower without a cigarette. She yawned and I almost gagged from the latent 2nd hand in her breath.
Oh my god, get me the fuck off of this train!

Twenty minutes later I was in Brooklyn. It wasn't raining anymore so the two block walk from the subway station to Theresa's brownstone wasn't so bad. Early fall in New York was my favorite. The leaves were changing and the air was crisp. I was wearing a knit sweater dress and black motorcycle boots. The wind wrapped around me as I headed down the sidewalk, passing a woman walking her Yorkshire terrier. I stopped at 136 and walked

INGRID DARLING

up the stairs to the large oak door. Theresa's was the only one on the street with a wood door; all the others were wrought iron and glass paneled. Two girls sat giggling on the steps of the next brownstone. I knocked twice and Theresa opened the door, holding her overweight calico cat, Jimi, a gift Darryl had given her several months ago.

"Ingrid!" She exclaimed, motioning for me to come in.

She was wearing an oversized Bob Marley t-shirt and dark skinny jeans, barefoot. Her long hair was flipped to the side and resting on her shoulders, stray hairs fell in her face as she turned. Jimi flinched in her arms.

"The subway was hell! I really hate that you live all the way in Brooklyn." I said, unraveling the scarf from my neck as I followed her through the foyer towards the den.

She laughed and tossed Jimi onto the long linen couch. He started clawing at the tribal print throw she had draped over the back of it. Despite the fact that Theresa lived in Brooklyn, her brownstone was very cool. Since she had moved in several months ago, I hadn't truly paid attention to the décor. I had been too busy talking about Thomas or engaged in some other conversation to notice how ornate her place was. It had an early seventies meets Morocco kind of vibe and was decorated with lanterns and ethnic tapestries from her travels to Asia and Africa. A large oak bookcase took up half of the room and was jammed with books and pictures. There was a picture of her standing dangerously close to a lion on a safari in South Africa. Apparently the lion wouldn't stop sniffing her and even the guide was amazed at how calm it was around her, she'd told me once. I wasn't surprised. Theresa could tame a lion, that's how diplomatic she was.

INGRID DARLING

She plopped down on the linen couch and started playing with Jimi. I put my bag and scarf on a small side table and sat down with her. A long trunk which she used as a coffee table sat in front of us, covered in coasters with pictures of the Eiffel Tower which she'd gotten on our trip to Paris, and a stack of books on fashion and photography and artists. She was very artistic, insisting that the essence in everyone and everything could be captured in art.

I thought about our encounter at the Dali exhibit three summers ago and how we hit it off immediately. She told me that she was drawn to my light, I didn't really understand what she meant, but I too was drawn to her for a reason I couldn't explain.

"So, how was breakfast?" She asked, reaching onto the trunk for the tea cup which was sitting on an Eiffel Tower coaster.

It was most likely black chai tea, her favorite.

"Ugh! I don't even want to think about it. Karl got us thrown out! Can you believe that? That dumbass couldn't even keep his mouth shut long enough for us to finish our food! I'm so pissed at him right now." I said, shaking my head in disgust.

Thinking about how everyone stared at us after his outbursts made my face flush. She took a sip of her tea and put it back on the coaster.

"Wow. Karl must be at a dead end with his research because I was with him two days ago at Fat Cats and the guy was a wreck, calling everyone incapable and useless. I was a little surprised at how obstinate he was being. So I said, "Karl, what's the deal?" And he just grunted, you know how he does, and avoided talking about it."

"Yeah he must be having problems, I don't know. I was really upset at how he was acting at breakfast. I mean, I'm used to his posturing, especially when it comes to politics and stuff, but he was being downright rude to everyone. He made this poor waitress cry. I felt so bad for her."

"Well, what can you do? The guy is gonna say what he wants."

"I guess." I said, shrugging my shoulders.

I looked around the room and noticed a new sculpture in the corner between the bookcase and the window.

"Darryl gave that to me," she said, before I could even ask.

She had a way of knowing what someone was thinking and would answer the question before it was even asked, sometimes it gave me chills, other times I secretly wished I had that ability.

"Oh? What was the occasion?" I laughed.

It was a bronze bird perched on a branch.

"I don't know. He said it reminded him of me because I'm always perched somewhere about to take flight. I think he was trying to find symbolism in our relationship. It's kinda cool, I guess," she said, opening an old fashioned looking book which doubled as a secret box.

That was where she kept her pot. She unraveled a wad of foil and pulled out a nugget and placed it on the trunk. Then she pulled a piece of rolling paper from the pack and proceeded to roll a joint. Jimi jumped from her lap and crawled over to me.

"If you call a four foot bronze bird on a branch cool." I said, un-emphatically.

We looked at each other and burst into laughter.

"Yeah, Darryl does that. He'll buy me the most random shit and call it an artistic expression of our relationship. So bizarre, but hey, I live with the guy so what can I say?" She tucked a strand of hair behind her ear, licking the edge of the joint paper.

I laughed.

"So what about you? What's been up?"

I suddenly thought about James.

"Well" I began, deciding to tell Theresa about my new crush. "I was at the library looking for a book I needed for my Philosophy class and this guy starts talking to me about the Bible. And he was going on about how the Bible is misinterpreted and he started quoting some philosopher. Anyway, he gave me his number, and told me to call him sometime. He was actually pretty cute. I may call him this weekend or something." I said, thumbing the edge of my dress.

I neglected to mention that I was really attracted to him and that my nervousness was preventing me from actually dialing his number. I thought about James and his piercing eyes.

"That's cool. What'd he look like? Uh oh, Ingrid, you have a secret Bible admirer!"

She put her hand to her mouth in exasperated excitement.

"Shut up!" I threw a red pillow at her.

We both laughed. Theresa and I shared similar views on religion. We both agreed that religion was an institution created by man that hindered spiritual growth rather than encouraging it. She always referenced some philosopher when supporting her belief by saying that the idea of God was a product of ignorance, fear, and superstition and that because our primitive ancestors were terrified by natural phenomena such as storms and fires and floods, they attributed those occurrences to unseen spirits whom they tried to appease through rituals, when in reality it was just nature operating as it should. Theresa wasn't an atheist but she could see how people were. She always said that there was more to the divine than what an institution could interpret.

She finished rolling the joint and lit the end, taking a long drag. Jimi started meowing for attention in my lap. She exhaled a cloud of smoke and passed the joint to me. I thought for a moment about not smoking, but realized that I didn't have to worry about Thomas scrutinizing me for my decisions anymore. Relief rushed over my body.

I no longer have to carry on a façade for others anymore, I thought, taking the joint from her.

I inhaled a drag, the aroma of marijuana filling my nostrils in the process.

"Speaking of religious books," she said, swinging her legs onto the couch and tucking her feet under her butt. "I was reading Alice in Wonderland last night, which was actually the first time I've read the book. I saw the movie when I was younger."

"Me too." I said, exhaling.

I took another hit before passing it back to her.

"Well reading it is really different. I never noticed the spiritual undertones in the storyline."

She took the joint from me and hit it before continuing.

"How so?" I asked, slumping back onto the couch.

I could feel myself drifting into a state of delirium. I usually felt this way when I smoked, before my high kicked in. Jimi started clawing my leg.

"Well," she exhaled. "The whole thing really, with the white rabbit and the alternate reality where Alice can eat mushrooms and get bigger and smaller and will anything she chooses. And remember the part with the caterpillar and how he kept asking her who she was?"

"Of course. He kept saying, '*who* are *you*?'" I chimed, exaggerating my imitation of the caterpillar from what I'd remembered from the movie.

"Yes!"

She passed the joint to me. I took a hit, interested in how she was going to parallel Alice in Wonderland with spirituality.

"Think about it, he kept asking her who she was, as if he was trying to see if she knew who she truly was, if she understood the true nature of herself in relation to the world around her. And she kept saying that she didn't know who she was because she had already changed so many sizes and had consequently lost touch with her own reality. But then he tells her she could be whoever she wanted to be because it was all in how she understood herself. It was like he was her guru, you know, sitting there smoking his hookah pipe."

"So how does that tie into spirituality?" I asked, handing the joint back to her.

Jimi dug a nail into my thigh and a sharp pain shot through my leg, making me wince. I pushed him off of my lap and onto the couch.

"Well, we are all searching, right? We all want to know the answer to life, but few of us realize that we are asking this question. Everything we do, everything we strive to achieve is the basis for the question of our very existence on this planet. We want to know who we are and what it is we are here for. The rest of the world has no idea that their everyday existence is ultimately asking the question as well. Even down to the minutest aspect of their life, like doing the dishes, they are asking themselves what the point of doing the dishes is in relation to their significance in the world. They could easily let them pile up in the sink and go about their lives as if it didn't matter, but they don't, because they understand the complications it would present in the future. So they keep doing the dishes, understanding that there is a purpose to something, there is a purpose to life. Yet they fail to see the connection to the question that we are all asking."

"What do you mean? What are we asking?" I asked.

She handed the joint back to me and I took a long drag. The room was beginning to look like the inside of a glass bowl. I kept my focus on Theresa's face.

"We are searching for the truth. That is why we question and study, research and learn. It's because we are all looking for the answer to the most important question: what is life? Every book we read that can get us closer to the answer, we consider it to be the most important book we'll ever read. For Christians it is the Bible, for Jews it is the Torah, for Muslims it is the Qur'an, and so on. We're constantly searching for the truth and we become like Alice living in Wonderland chasing the white rabbit, in hopes that he will reveal something about our world, our wonderland that we didn't quite understand before."

I handed the joint back to her and turned my focus onto Jimi; he was purring and rubbing against my elbow.

"Are you suggesting that the white rabbit is God?"

"Allegorically speaking, I guess I was alluding to some sort of godlike image. So yes, I guess I am suggesting that people are searching for God in their everyday existence. I mean, isn't through God the only way to understand the truth about our reality anyway?"

"I suppose."

"But to most of the world," she continued, "God is detached from humanity. God is a separate entity from us and therefore we have lost all divinity as beings on this planet."

"I don't understand."

Theresa took a drag of the joint then exhaled. I rubbed Jimi's head.

"Many people believe God is distant, meant to be feared. When in truth, God is everything. And to fear everything is to fear your self. Your self is a part of everything on this planet and it is that which governs the universe. Your self is God, but you don't know this because your mind is so consumed with rational ideas and thoughts. In order for you to understand your true nature, your true self, you must first open your eyes and see the connection to you and everything else around you."

"Whoa!"

She handed the joint back to me. I took a drag then exhaled.

"Like in Plato's Allegory of the Cave, you have to understand that you are seeing shadows of reality, a mere falsification to prevent the truth from being exposed. You have to open your eyes and see the light within, the divinity within yourself. Seek the truth and you will be free, haven't you heard that expression? Because once you can free your mind, you can become divine. You can become everything. You can become God."

I thought about her comment for a minute. A cloud of smoke whirled around my head.

"That's a bit much," I said. "People are so twisted these

days. If everyone thought they were God, wouldn't people start taking matters and actions into their own hands? I mean, people are perverse and society would wreck havoc if everyone starting walking around saying that they were God and that they could do whatever they wanted. I see what you're saying, but to a rational person who sees everything separately, this 'God is everything including you' suggestion could really rattle them."

I passed the joint back to her. She took a long drag.

"You're right," she said, exhaling a ring of smoke.

Jimi jumped from the couch to the window ledge, obviously bothered by our disinterest in him.

"Most people would rather deny it than see the truth to their existence. They'll go on searching by going to church and worshipping and praying and doing good deeds in hopes that a place in heaven will be saved for them. It would rattle them to know that what they were told to fear is what they look at in the mirror every day. And yes, the majority of the world, if this message wasn't clear, would use this to manipulate it to their selfish satisfaction. But then they would not truly understand the nature of themselves. Because if you truly understand God and your relation to everything, then you would realize that whatever pain your inflict on someone else, or whatever selfish endeavor you do at someone else's expense, you are ultimately inflicting that pain upon yourself."

She took another long drag and exhaled a cloud of smoke.

"What do you mean?" I asked, feeling the room pulse.

I was very high.

"If you and I are everything because we are God, then we are essential one being. So if I decided that I wanted to hurt you in some way, then I'm only hurting myself because we are the same thing. Only to the naked eye does it look like we are different, because I'm wearing jeans and a Bob Marley t-shirt, and you are wearing a dress and boots. The only thing that separates us is the fact that we are in different bodies, but we are governed by the same thing, the same thing that governs the universe. The same God is in both of us. We are essentially the same being."

She handed the joint back to me but I waved her off. I was too high to smoke anymore.

"When'd you get so in touch with yourself?" I chuckled.

She laughed.

"I don't know. It just came to me the other day when Darryl and I were watching Lost."

We sat in silence for a few minutes. I glanced over to the hookah pipe sitting under the window next to the bronze bird. She'd gotten it in Turkey the summer before we met. I turned back towards her. She was lounging on the couch smoking the joint. A faint white cloud circled around her head as she exhaled a ring smoke. She blew out an 'O' and laughed.

Theresa is definitely my caterpillar, definitely my guru.

We turned our attention to the TV that was mounted on the wall next to the bookcase. I hadn't even noticed it was on. That's what happened at Theresa's, it was so easy to get caught up in conversation and forget about the real world. I loved being with her because she took the ease off your back about work or school or anything else that seemed important in your life that really wasn't . She was right, it was so easy to forget the nature of reality as it truly is while trying to make A's and perform well for your boss. It's so easy to forget about God in the everyday, in everything, when you're so busy mulling about, trying to find significance in the stock market.

I drifted off into thought, thinking about God's role in my life, especially within the past ten months. Perhaps I had lost touch with my own reality, preventing me from understanding the nature of the universe, the nature of myself. We sat there for another ten minutes in silence, not paying attention to the TV anymore. Theresa got up and refilled her tea in the kitchen and returned with a mug for me. I took a sip, letting my high absorb the spicy flavors and the ethnic surroundings of the room. I was about to say something but was startled and I lost my train of thought.

"Jimi Hendrix!" Theresa shrieked.

Her cat was now unraveling a yellow silk scarf that had fallen off the chair in the corner of the room. She threw the red pillow at her cat. He yelped and ran out of the room.

A door bell rang, startling me. It was my phone. I had fallen asleep. I sat up and looked around the room for Theresa, she was nowhere in sight. Jimi was perched on the window ledge, staring outside. I grabbed my bag off the side table and reached for my phone. A text message from Jada.

Hey girl, running late. I'll meet you on the corner next to Sullivan's at 9.

I had already forgotten that I was supposed to meet her at Sullivan's tonight.

What time is it?

I closed the text: 8:06.

How long have I been sleeping?

"Theresa?" I called out, standing up from the couch and

stretching.

"Yes?" I heard her call from upstairs.

I walked towards the front door, steadying myself with each step. I wasn't high anymore but I was still lightheaded from my nap. I rounded the corner and looked up the stairs. Theresa appeared at the top with a towel around her head. She was now wearing a black form fitting dress that came just above her knees. She had a mascara wand in her hand.

"I have to go to an exhibit at my mom's gallery in a few. You're welcome to stay and hang out. Darryl should be home in an hour or so." She said, unraveling the towel from her head.

Her wet hair fell to her shoulders.

"No, I actually have to go. I didn't mean to fall asleep. I have to meet Jada at nine uptown."

"Okay. Also, I'm throwing a Halloween party, so you have to come. A lot of people are going to be there so make sure you find a really good costume."

She fluffed her hair, it dripped onto the steps.

"I think I found one." I said, remembering the Harry Potter costume I saw in the window of the Halloween store the night before.

"Great! It's going to be a night to remember," Theresa said, smiling.

"I'm sure," I said.

I walked back to the den and grabbed my bag from the couch. Jimi jumped from the window to the floor and dashed into the kitchen. I quickly texted Jada back, telling her I'd meet her there, that I may be a little after nine. I took another sip of my chai tea, now cold, and hurried to the door.

INGRID DARLING

"Bye." I called.

"See ya." I heard her yell from the upstairs bathroom.

I opened the door and pulled it shut behind me. A blast of cold air shot up my dress as I reached into my bag for my umbrella. It was raining again.

I was home thirty minutes later, took a cab this time. I paid the driver and hurried into the front door of my building and up the stairs to my apartment. When I reached my door I noticed a small package sitting on the doormat. I took out my key and unlocked the door, grabbing the package on my way in. It was a book with a note taped on the cover. I folded the note back: The Alchemist.

Huh, is this Karl's way of apologizing? I thought, closing the door behind me and turning on the light.

I threw my keys and bag on the kitchen table and unzipped my boots. Barefoot, I pulled the note from the book and opened it.

I'm sorry for my outburst at breakfast. I hope you're not mad at me for being so obnoxious. Karl.

PS-I really think you'd like this book, tell me what you think when you finish it.

I folded the note and tossed it into the trash.

Well at least he apologized.

I placed the book on top of a stack of old magazines sitting on the counter. I quickly undressed, discovering that my knit dress now looked like a mohair rug with Jimi's hair decorating the entire front. I had to find something else quickly so I could meet Jada on time. It was now 8:52pm. I decided on jeans and a floral print blouse, put on an extra coat of mascara and grabbed my purse, rushing out the door.

On the way, I texted her amidst hailing a cab.

My umbrella was halfway opened over my head, not providing much coverage. I stood in the rain for five minutes before a cab pulled over. As I slid in, my phone rang, Karl. I silenced it and told the driver to take me to 34st and Broadway. I could feel the phone vibrating against my leg.
He'll have to wait, I thought, *he's not ruining my dinner too.*

INGRID DARLING

Twenty-Eight

I opened the door and inhaled a waft of smoke. Sullivan's. It always reeked of cigars but Jada loved meeting there for the drink specials and jazzy ambiance. She was waiting in the lobby, doing something on her phone. She was wearing a leopard print cardigan, skinny jeans and gold pumps. I waved, walked down the steps and gave her a hug.

"Oh my goodness, it took forever to get a cab! Why the hell are there so many people out on tonight?" I cried, fixing my hair and folding my umbrella.

I stuffed it in my purse and slung the purse over my shoulder.

"I know! I bet we won't be able to find a seat, it's packed in here." She said, turning towards the seating area of the restaurant.

We walked past the two girls at the hostess stand, pushing our way through the crowded bar area towards the back of the restaurant, looking for an empty table. We spotted an open table near the piano and sat down. A young guy with long hair and a beard wearing a felt fedora played the piano while another with curly hair wearing a velvet blazer played the bass next to him. No one paid them attention; too busy discussing their workday and financial successes.

The restaurant was noisy and conversations floated through the air, creating a steady drone of sound to accompany the piano and guitar. There were always business professionals, fresh from a long workday at the office, at Sullivan's. It was obvious which ones were successful and which ones were struggling simply based on overall appearance. The successful ones boasted confidence in their demeanor, faces always smiling and laughing at every comment in the conversation, toasting their comrades with each drink. The men always had their ties loosely dangled around their necks, one hand in pocket, the other holding a beer or glass of wine, chest out. The women were always attempting to exude power and sexuality, obviously desperate for attention and using no discretion in their hopes of making it to bed with one of their male coworkers. Then there were the unsuccessful ones, usually men, consumed with their failing business accounts and stock deficits. They sat slumped at the bar, scotch or brandy for them. I laughed to myself about the scene. It was predictable, ordinary, dull.

I looked over at Jada, she was still on her phone.

"Your hair looks good." I said, breaking her attention away from texting.

"Thanks! I just had my stylist cut and curl it."

She ran a finger through her bangs and put her phone in her bag which was hanging over the back of her chair.

"So what'd you do today?" She asked, picking up the tripod menu sitting in the middle of the table.

"Well, I had a disastrous breakfast with Karl then I went to Brooklyn and hung out with Theresa all day. I got too high and fell asleep. Good thing you texted me or I may not have woken up until Sunday."

She laughed.

"What happened at breakfast?"

"Karl's usual ranting got us thrown out."

"What! You got kicked out? What was he saying?"

"Just bullshit. He gave the wait staff a garish display of pig-headedness. I mean, I don't understand how people can be so rude to the people who are preparing their food."

Jada nodded in agreement, she was a hostess so she understood the point I was making.

"There are too many people who forget that their patience and sincerity would be greatly appreciated by those who are serving them. Obnoxious customers who complain about service and how long they have to wait for their food should just shut the fuck up!" I said.

"Seriously! I have to deal with that all day long. I just want say "take your fat ass to Wendy's if you want your food faster", but I can't because I'll get fired." She said.

I laughed.

"Well, I had an interesting day too. Some guy came into work and complained about my shirt."

"What was wrong with it?" I asked, picking up the tripod menu and glancing at the martini list.

"Well it was low cut and I wasn't wearing a bra. The manager sent me home to change my shirt so it wouldn't offend any of the customers. Can you believe that? Why should it matter what I'm wearing when I'm seating someone? Why is that we have to be 'presentable' in the work place or on an interview? When I go on an interview, I'm trying to sell my abilities to contribute to the company, I'm not trying to sell my outfit or my body so why is my presentation so important?"

"I agree." I said.

"I mean, shouldn't we be more focused on inner

personality? Why does our society judge the peanut by the shell?"

She shook her head despairingly. I shrugged my shoulders.

"Society feeds off looks and appearances, that's what it boils down to."

Just then, a waitress came over and took our drink orders. Jada and I both ordered pomegranate martinis. She nodded and sauntered off. I watched her tuck through the crowd of men by the bar. A man stopped talking and looked her head to toe glance, grinning. She was wearing black fishnet stockings and a black barely there mini dress, no doubt the uniform chosen by the owner to please his male customers. It was unfortunate; she was too pretty to be dressed like a whore.

Two minutes later our martinis came. I took a sip of mine, it was oddly bitter.

"So what are you going be for Halloween?" Jada asked.

"Harry Potter. You?"

She laughed.

"A Treasure Island girl."

I laughed.

"Who's going to be your pirate?"

"I haven't figured that out yet, maybe I'll find one."

She took a sip of her martini.

"This doesn't taste as good as last time." She said, disgruntled.

"Theresa told me she was throwing a Halloween party, are you going?" I asked, taking a sip of my martini.

"Yeah! I'm excited."

"Me too. But I think Thomas will be there. I haven't talked to him in months. I'm kind of worried he's going to bring that girl with him." I said.

I thought about Thomas, imagining that he would show up to the party with his girlfriend and try to act like nothing happened between us. He was probably still in denial.

"What is he up to? I haven't seen or heard anything about him. Is he still on Facebook?" She said.

"I have no idea. You know we're not friends anymore."

"I'm going to check." She said, pulling out her phone.

A nervous knot tied itself in my stomach. Every time I associated Thomas with Facebook it was never good. I sipped my martini hoping she would drop the subject and put her phone away.

"Strange." She said.

I swallowed hard, it was bitter. She faced the phone to me. There was a small abstract picture of squares on the screen.

"*That's* his picture?! What the hell?"

"I guess. It doesn't seem like him at all, right?"

"Not at all. Wait, let me see that again."

I grabbed the phone from her and studied the picture. It was nothing like Thomas. He always had a picture of himself as his profile picture, never abstract art. Thomas wasn't abstract, he was straight and narrow with everything. I was confused and worried and though I hadn't spoken to him in months I knew this wasn't who he was.

"I didn't really know him like that, but it seems like he has changed, a lot." Jada said.

I handed her phone back to her.

"That's what it looks like." I said, still baffled.

"It's crazy how people will change themselves for the person they're dating. I remember dating my ex, and I became a completely different person while I was with him. I cut all of my friends off and when we broke up, I had to apologize to a lot of people. He bought me a ring and everything. Imagine the person I would have been if I had married him." She said, putting her phone back in her purse.

"Wow."

"I would have been married at twenty-one and never had the chance to grow individually. I don't understand these young people who get married before they even know who they are. You are a completely different person in your thirties than who you were in your twenties, and to get married before you know yourself is just stupid. That's why the divorce rate is so high, because people think they know what they want before they know who they truly are."

"Exactly. And then they have babies!" I said, thinking of my friends in North Carolina who were my age, married with children.

"Yes! It works for some people, but the rest is obvious. Look at the statistics. I mean, I'm twenty-eight, single and no kids. People like me are an endangered species!"

I laughed. A memory of Thomas and I crept into my head, we were running through the Louvre in Paris.

I would have been that statistic.

I took another sip of my martini, still bitter.

The waitress came back and took our food orders, I ordered a caesar salad, Jada ordered a cheeseburger. We talked more about Halloween and her job and when our food came we ate in silence, enjoying the music and atmosphere of the restaurant. Conversations still dominated over the pianist and bass player, but the mood was agreeable, I was pleased with our choice in dining. After we finished eating and paid our bill, we each said our goodbyes and parted to our final destinations.

"I'll email you tomorrow," she said, waving as she crossed the street.

She lived a block away. I waved to her and flagged down a cab, telling him where to take me. I was home eight minutes later. The driver paid no mind to traffic lights or stop signs. I paid him and went upstairs to my apartment, looking forward to resting on my couch, exhausted from a long day. Before changing for bed I checked my phone, three missed calls: Karl, my mother, and Karl again.

I'll call them tomorrow, I decided.

I threw the phone back in my purse and spent the rest of the evening relaxing.

The next two days I spent studying for my Statistics of Psychology and French midterms. My classes on Friday morning were dull and uninteresting. A student had a seizure in Philosophy class and the pop quiz was cancelled. Anna sent me an email about a wine tasting for that night, it was being thrown by a mutual friend of ours, but I wasn't in the mood to deal with the people that were going to be there, most likely socialites, gossiping about nonsense. Besides, I needed to ace my French exam; it was, after all, my major.

Saturday morning I woke up earlier than usual, planning to spend the day studying. After about an hour of reading, I decided to shower and run down to Starbucks for some coffee. I dressed, throwing on a tunic, leggings and flats. I grabbed the scarf that was hanging on my bedroom doorknob and wrapped it around my neck, grabbing my keys and purse from the kitchen table. I opened the door and found Karl standing there, hand raised, about to knock.

"I called you ten times!" He cried. "Are you avoiding me or something?"

"Well if I was you wouldn't have let me." I said, frustration creeping into my body.

I turned around and threw my keys back onto the kitchen table, deciding that I no longer wanted coffee. He followed me in and shut the door behind himself. I unraveled my scarf and sat down on the couch. He sat on the ottoman facing me, glancing around at the books strewn all over the coffee table and carpet.

"I'm sorry about my behavior recently," he said in an apologetic tone. "I've been having problems with my research and my professor told me he wasn't going to finance me if I took any longer than six months. Then my brother called the other day, telling me about this fight he got into with my mom about our dad, and shit has hit the fan right now."

He slumped over and put his elbows on his knees and covered his face with his hands. His hair was disheveled, as if he had just woken up. His faded Columbia sweatshirt had a bleach stain on the hood. His jeans were wrinkled and looked like they needed to be washed. I reached over and ran my hand through his hair.

"I'm sorry. I'm sure everything will work itself out." I said, calmly.

I could never stay mad at Karl. Despite his overbearing arrogance at times, he was a nice guy and always meant well.

"I hope so. Did you get the book I left for you?"

"I did, but I haven't started it yet."

"You will enjoy it. So what did you have planned for today?" He asked, a sly look appearing on his face.

I raised an eyebrow, skeptically.

"Nothing much. Why, what were *you* planning to do?"

"Well, my friend Natalie has this spoken word thing in Central Park, and afterwards everyone is going back to her boyfriend's apartment in Soho for beer and pizza. You should come, it'll be a fun day."

I thought about my French midterm and the three chapters I needed to read for Philosophy class by Monday.

I can study on Sunday. Besides, it would be different to get out and hang with people I don't know.

"Okay, I'll go. What time are you going to her performance?"

"In about an hour. I can come back by and pick you up if you want."

"That works." I said.

Karl stood up and ruffled his sweatshirt.

"I'll text you when I'm on the way." He said, turning around and walking over to the door.

"Perfect." I said.

He smiled, opened the door and walked out.

INGRID DARLING

Twenty-Nine

"I'm not ordinary. I'm not supposed to be ordinary. They say we all have a purpose on this planet, a purpose that drives us. Some of us have a purpose to do great things. Some of us have a purpose to fail with a chance at a new beginning. Some of us are ordinary, and some of us are extraordinary. I am not ordinary. I have a purpose in life."

Central Park. The place where people go to create their own worlds amidst the everyday fast paced life of finance, business, trade and politics. Where Wall Street is just a street, instead of a black hole of sovereignty. Where Blackberries and iPhones remain in a car and house instead of permanently attached to a hand or hip. It is a place where one can become a child again. It is a place where freedom is discovered in the trees, in the grass, in the lake, in the tunnels. Forty people sat in the grass, focused on the spoken words.

Natalie stood channeling her energy to all of us listening to her. A friend of Karl's from Columbia, she was getting her master's in literature, and felt that words were a gateway to the soul of man. She spoke emphatically, gesturing every symbol in her speech, very passionate, exuding power and strength through her petite and wispy frame. Her dark brown hair blew wildly in the wind adding more gusto to her already powerful persona. I sat and listened, eyeing the crowd, at ease with my decision to forego studying. She finished her first speech and everyone clapped. She began another and I watched her perform, her words appearing through her, personified by her gestures and stances. She finished two more as I watched, glancing around the park, enjoying the crisp afternoon.

INGRID DARLING

Karl huddled close to me, trying to create body heat. He was no longer disheveled. A quick shower changed his mood as well as his appearance. He now wore a gray and black argyle cardigan, dark jeans and loafers, a gray scarf wrapped around his neck and his hair was neatly messy. After Natalie finished her fourth speech and the clapping settled down, she prefaced her final piece with a quote about love.

"I have yet to meet someone whose greatest need is anything other than real, unconditional love. It is found in a simple act of kindness. There is no mistaking love. You feel it in your heart. It is the common fiber of life, the flame that heats our soul, energizes our spirit and provides passion in our lives. It is our connection to God and to each other," she said, prepping her stance to begin her performance.

"For days now I have felt this powerful sensation throughout my body," she began. "It is not pain and it is not happiness, it is pure love. I have fallen in love. My spirit has been rescued by my other half, by the man who is my other being, my other self, my lost soul"

I glanced at the audience around the park. Hipsters and hippies sat huddled together on their woven blankets in the grass, focused on Natalie's words. Couples were wrapped together, love clearly embracing them. A dog sat with its owner in front of me, panting but quiet, also focused on Natalie's soothing yet powerful voice, her rousing gestures. Karl sat beside me, in his own world of thought, watching. I drifted from Natalie's words and thought about James and his piercing eyes, his familiar smile. The way his jaw clenched after he laughed. He was so handsome. It had been two weeks since I'd met him at the library and I hadn't gone a single day without his face gracing my thoughts.

"Focus on him, focus on what you want, and you'll eventually get it", is what Emerald had told me.

I wanted to see him so badly, to touch him, for him to touch me, for him to kiss me. If only I wasn't so afraid to call him. I had taken the business card he'd given me from the pocket of my jeans and taped it to my refrigerator, hoping that every time I needed a glass of water, it would give me the courage to dial his number. It hadn't worked yet. I wasn't sure what I was waiting for, fate to throw us together, perhaps.

"Love is not automatic, but it is always there, present. It burns from the depths of your soul and shines brightly through you to another. I have love and from love I have romance. Romance is your heart's desire to express that unwritten love that is shared between two people, three people, a hundred people. Love is always there, present, and I have found it."

Natalie's words swept over my thoughts.

James.

A feeling of intense passion swept through my body, warming my chest. I focused on his face, his perfectly masculine bone structure, on his smile.

"The love I share is holy and eternal. The love I share is understood and respected. The love I share is the divine principle and is an intrinsic part of the cosmos. This love pervades all its parts and establishes a universal harmony. This love is shared between us all and it is as sacred as we are divine."

Clapping. Cheering. A whistle. I hadn't realized that Natalie had finished speaking until I looked around at the audience. I had been lost in my own world, thinking about James, desiring for our encounter. I joined the clapping and looked over to Karl. His hand was cupped around his mouth and he was cheering loudly, his scarf flapping behind him in the wind. Scott, Natalie's boyfriend, walked up to her and wrapped her in a huge hug, smothering her with kisses, clearly in love with his girlfriend, clearly proud.

"Scott is planning to propose to her soon." Karl whispered over to me once he'd gotten in a few 'woot's' and fist pumps.

"I bet! I'd propose to her myself! Her words were very powerful. It was so moving. I couldn't stop thinking about--"

I quickly stopped myself, realizing that I was almost about to tell Karl about James. I didn't want him to know that I was lusting after some heartthrob who was way out of my league. Besides, Karl had no idea I'd even met James and I certainly wasn't going to tell him in the middle of the park, with forty people around. Luckily he wasn't listening to me. He had already stood and was walking over towards Natalie. I stood to my feet and brushed the leaves from my backside. A chill shot through my body. I hugged my chest and joined Karl who was standing with Natalie and Scott. A few other audience members rushed to her and gave her hugs and kisses, offering their congratulations on her performance.

"Excellent performance!" Karl applauded then gave Natalie a very generous hug.

She smiled, her bright brown eyes gleaming under thick black eyebrows. I looked over to Scott, standing by her side. His eyes were welled with tears, he was so proud. If it wasn't for the lack of intimacy in the park, he probably would have proposed right there.

"Thanks Karl, I'm so glad you could make it." Natalie

gushed, clearly out of breath from her performance.

She combed her windblown hair behind her ear and smiled, grabbing Scott's hand.

"Did you enjoy it?" She asked, turning to me.

"Oh yes, it was marvelous! You're really a great performer, and your words were so powerful..." I said, trailing off.

I didn't want to sound like an obsessed groupie, especially since I had just met her. I smiled and took a step closer to Karl.

"Marvelous isn't the word, it was brilliant!" Karl exclaimed.

"It truly was, baby." Scott said, kissing Natalie's hand again. "And I think it's about time we all head back to my place to celebrate."

He turned to face us, his dark brown hair falling in his eyes. He combed it back with his hand.

"Sounds like a good plan to me!" Natalie said. "But I have to speak to a few people before I can leave. Will you all wait ten minutes, and then we can catch a cab back to Soho together?" She asked, looking to me and Karl for a response.

"Absolutely!" Karl cried.

She smiled.

"Perfect. I'll be just a few minutes."

She turned around and whisked away, greeting and hugging the other audience members who were waiting to speak to her.

Twenty minutes later, the four of us squeezed into a cab. It took fifteen minutes to get through midtown; the traffic was horrible despite the strange hour. We talked about Natalie's performance and she and Karl discussed an upcoming art exhibit shown by a mutual friend of theirs. Scott and I made small talk, I learned he was from Ontario and had moved to New York to pursue acting. He was currently in acting school at the New York Film Academy and had met Natalie at a performance a year ago. They've been dating ever since. He mentioned his affection for Natalie and how fate played a huge role in how they met. She had just broken up with her ex and he had only been at the Academy for six months when they met at his first performance. She was supposed to go on a blind date that night, but the plans foiled and she ended up going to his show by herself. They met backstage when Natalie was looking for the bathroom and ended up in the hallway where he was rehearsing for the next scene.

He looked over to her, while she was speaking to Karl, gazing lovingly at her face. He turned back to me.

"You know, love can't be found by looking for it or wishing for it, it is a sort of divine accident," he said. "Are you single?"

I nodded.

"Well, love will find you, it always does. Don't go looking for it. Whomever you're supposed to be with, you'll be with, that's what makes living so great. Because it's already mapped out, you just have to make sure you stay on course."

I thought about Scott's words for the rest of the ride, ignoring the conversation the three of them began. I watched out the window at the lights whirring past. It reminded me of life and how the world goes so fast while you try desperately to keep up. Sometimes relaxing into the moment is the best feeling, forgetting about the everyday and just being in the now. I thought about love, about James.

INGRID DARLING

Is he the one for me? How will I know? Was I supposed to call him, did he want me to call?

I had so many questions, too many questions. I took a deep breath and closed my eyes. The cab stopped. I opened my eyes. We were finally in Soho.

The four of us piled out of the car. Karl paid the driver, despite Scott's plea to split the cost.

"No, I got it. You just make sure Natalie and Darling have a good time." Karl said, winking at me.

I raised an eyebrow, sensing something was about to happen that I wasn't prepared for. The cab driver took the cash and sped off. I wrapped my arm in Karl's and leaned into him.

"Um, what's going on? You're acting strange." I whispered.

He chuckled and shrugged his shoulders.

"Nothing out of the ordinary," he said unconvincingly, smiling down to me.

I rolled my eyes and squeezed my arm into his. We followed Scott and Natalie down the sidewalk and up to the brownstone. Scott fished his keys from his pocket and opened the door, gesturing for Natalie, Karl and I to go in before him. The three of us walked up the stairs and into the building, Scott followed.

The hallway was dark and narrow and a pungent aroma of tobacco and marijuana hit me in the face before I took three steps. I could hear loud talking and laughter at the end of the hall, the party had already started. Natalie turned the corner first and an eruption of clapping and cheering filled the room. Karl turned the corner next, with me following. The room was packed with people, few of whom had been in the audience at the park, the rest were obviously friends of Scott's.

The brownstone was ornately decorated with an air of masculinity. Bookcases stuffed with books wrapped around the walls of the den area which spilled into the kitchen. Two oversized recliners sat around a long leather couch, all of which faced an enormous flat paneled TV mounted on the wall between the bookcases. A pool table divided the kitchen and the den, currently covered with bowls of popcorn, chips, beer and several boxes of pizza. Red cups filled every blank space on the kitchen counter as well as the large coffee table in the center of the den. I glanced around at everyone in the room hoping to recognize someone from around campus or class, no luck.

People sat on the couch engaged in conversation, others glued to the TV. A football game was playing. The majority were standing around, talking and laughing. I huddled close to Karl, making sure not to lose him in the crowd of unknown people. I smiled as we squeezed our way through the room and into the kitchen, following Natalie and Scott. As I turned to leave the den, a glimpse of dark hair caught my eye from the corner of the room. I glanced over to the recliner in the far corner and stopped, my breath catching in my throat. Dark eyes, piercing dark eyes turned and met my gaze.

James!

He smiled and winked, flashing a set of perfect white teeth. Then he turned back towards the person he was talking to on the couch.

"Oh my god!" I gasped.

Fortunately Karl was standing in front of me otherwise my

INGRID DARLING

now limp body would have successfully collapsed to the floor.

INGRID DARLING

Thirty

"When you visualize the earth, what do you see? You see white clouds hovering above blue oceans and green lands. You don't see what we see every day: people, animals, and plants, all you see is green, blue and white. Why? Because in relation to the extensive mass of the earth, we humans are like microscopic bacteria, going about our daily lives, growing, building, destroying, and infecting."

Somehow we had gotten into conversation about the world and its inhabitants. Karl, Natalie, Scott and I arrived about two hours ago and the party had finally dwindled to twenty people, eight of whom were stretched out on recliners and lounging on the couch. A group of four guys played pool. Boxes of pizza sat empty beneath the table, along with empty cases of beer. The bowl of popcorn sat on the coffee table, almost empty. The bowl of tortilla chips sat beside the popcorn, with a container of salsa opened next to it. Most of Scott's acting friends had left, leaving the few people remaining James' buddies from NYU.

It turned out that James and Scott were roommates, something Karl knew and neglected to mention to me. Theresa apparently told Karl about my interest in James, and Karl, knowing both James and Scott, chose to christen himself cupid for the evening. He cleverly made sure I accompanied him back to Soho so I would see James again. Karl really was a great guy, and though I was pissed at him for the first hour of the party for not telling me James would be there, I was really glad he hadn't, being surprised was so much better.

I didn't say much to James, we spoke briefly about our

classes, about Dr. Bernstein. I was too nervous to create small talk so I let him do most of the talking, though a skinny redhead with perky breasts kept interrupting our conversation. She was very pretty and I didn't like that she was there, flirting with my James! Now she sat next to him on the couch, too close for my liking, but clearly inept in keeping up with the conversation. The look on her face screamed idiot, making me feel better about the situation. The guy sitting on her other side continued talking.

"What do you see when you visualize a human being? You see a head, torso, legs, hair, and skin. You don't see all the microscopic bacteria that are infecting us daily, growing, building, destroying, as we go about our lives. You don't realize that you are infected with bacteria until you wash yourself, and then you see it stream down your legs and arms and chest. Humans are like bacteria to the earth. We believe ourselves to be so significant, yet we can't even be seen from space."

He grabbed a handful of popcorn from the bowl and crammed it in his mouth, adjusting the glasses on his face. He seemed to be full of pure intellect. The guy on the recliner chimed in.

"Very true. We think we're meant to live on this earth and populate and grow into huge colonies but one day we're all going to get washed away in some ridiculous flood, just like the bacteria on our bodies when we bathe."

His long legs dangled over the end of the recliner. He was wearing a white long sleeve shirt, showing the gut sitting on his abdomen. His tangled hair was in stark contrast to his other features, giving him an air of construction worker meets science teacher. He pulled a small bag full of marijuana from his pocket and threw it over to James, who immediately stood up and crossed the room to the bookcase. For a moment it looked as if he were trying to get away from the pretty dumb redhead, I hoped that was the case.

He pulled an elaborate water bong from the bottom shelf of the bookcase. It was blown glass and colored with green, blue, orange, and red swirls. I watched him pack the bong on the edge of the pool table. He must have sensed my gaze because he turned and met my eyes with his and winked. Flapping began in my stomach again.

Damn butterflies, I've had them all night.

I smiled and turned back to the conversation, inching closer to Karl who was sitting on the recliner with me.

"Why do humans populate and expand? It seems like when we populate, we don't just occupy the area, we destroy it," Natalie sighed.

She sat on the floor with Scott, between his legs. He was stroking her hair.

"It's like an infection," the guy with the glasses said. "If you watch what happens to your skin when you get an infection, you can see your skin deteriorate in the infected area, then begin to turn colors and grow boils, until it's painful, and finally you treat it with a cream or pill that fights the infection and heals your skin. Human beings do the same thing to the earth. We don't do it intentionally, but it still happens. When we move to a new land, we tear up the soil, we build tall buildings and roads and highways, we dig tunnels for sewage and industrial plants, and we mix different elements of the earth and create pollutants that eventually cause smog in our atmosphere."

"Then we cry when it doesn't rain on our beautiful crops and yards." Pretty dumb redhead interrupted, adjusting her low cut blouse even lower on her chest.

The construction worker science teacher stared at her breasts, ogling, but very aware of her lack of intellect. The guy in the glasses nodded and continued, obviously annoyed that he was interrupted by a less than profound statement.

"It's disgusting, and I'm sure if the earth could take a bath to wash away its destructive bacteria, it would," he said.

"Human beings are very interesting," James added, resuming his spot on the couch with the large bong.

"Not only are we one of the most complex organisms on this planet, but we have the ability to reason, which makes us truly unique. We create laws to end the suffering we inflict upon ourselves, and to maintain order and control, yet we fail to control what we are doing to the very planet on which we live." He said, reaching for the lighter on the coffee table and positioning the bong between his legs.

"Yeah, like I said." The guy with glasses added. "We are highly intelligent beings yet we operate like a virus. People keep having children in an overly populated world. That's what a virus does. It copies itself so it can keep spreading all while it endangers every ecosystem around it."

"And you know why that is," Karl said. "It's because we have all lost touch with ourselves. That's why no matter how much we have, our satisfaction is never filled."

"It's temptation that is slowly destroying our lives." Natalie added, crawling over to the coffee table.

She took a tortilla chip from the bowl and dipped it in the

salsa, stuffed it in her mouth and crawled back over to Scott.

"We build houses on top of one another and drive our cars and pollute our earth and we are killing our planet which is home to our bodies. Yet we do nothing." The guy in the glasses said, leaning forward on the couch, looking over to James who lit the marijuana and inhaled deeply into the bong.

He exhaled a long breath, smoke clouding the air in front of his face. He looked at me and smiled, his eyes slightly glazed.

"Yeah, then we sit back and wait for someone to come and rescue us from this hell. We must live in hell because what kind of heaven perpetuates struggle and oppression?" The science teacher said.

The room filled with a faint haze of smoke. Karl stretched his arms over his head.

"This is why our children are dependent on prescription pills for problems like ADD. Fuck, your kid just needs to be a kid. Take him to the playground, that'll cure his attention disorder!" He said.

James passed the bong to Natalie who lit the end and inhaled then handed it to Scott, exhaling.

"Likewise, our older generation is dependent on prescription pills for arthritis and heart problems, when proper diet and clean air would most likely solve the problem." James said.

He was reclined back on the couch, leaning away from the pretty redhead who was still trying to capture his attention with her breasts. She looked pathetic. I wished I was in her seat.

"And then there's us, the middle generation." The guy with the glasses said. "We're all dependent on pills for depression and sexual stimulation and anxiety. I mean, what the hell is going on?

Why do we need these things to cure us? Is it because deep down we are all truly depressed and have neglected to confront the issue, so we develop drugs to do it for us? We keep working and stressing our bodies and drinking alcohol and doing drugs, because it is the only way for us to escape the world that we have created."

"Agreed." James added. "We can be our own saviors if we realize how much potential we have as beings on this planet. We weren't born onto this earth to invent ways to do the things we can already do. We don't need anything we create because the earth has already provided us with everything."

I remembered the conversation I'd had with James in the library. I thought he was kidding when he mentioned the "tête-à-têtes" he and his friends had. But it seemed he was serious. They actually had the desire to sit around and talk about matters like these, all while they were getting high. It was ironic that the topic of conversation was about finding fulfillment in oneself rather than in other things, when they sat here finding fulfillment in other things rather than themselves. I chuckled to myself at the irony in my own life. It seemed there were always things that drew me to the fire. Karl handed me the lighter then the bong.

My stomach tensed, I was suddenly apprehensive about smoking from the bong in front of people I didn't know, especially with James sitting there, watching me. The air in the room was thick and heavy and I felt like all eyes were on me. I glanced around the room only to realize that no one was paying me any attention, they were still in the middle of their conversation. Yet, as I my gaze continued around the room, my eye caught on a familiar plaque above the door to the kitchen:

INGRID DARLING

KNOW THYSELF

I instantly remembered being in Jonah's house several years ago seeing the same sign, but I disregarded it and indulged in my desires. I didn't want to go down that path again. I shook my head to Karl, who then passed the bong back to James. He took a hit then placed it on the floor behind the couch.

"You okay?" James asked.

I nodded.

"I'm fine. I just don't want to smoke tonight." I said, flashing him a smile.

"I respect that. Can I ask why?" He said in a hushed voice, trying to avoid bringing attention to our conversation.

"I really shouldn't smoke. Sometimes indulgence doesn't lead you in the right direction." I said, more to myself than to him.

He smiled.

"Don't worry, I'm against everything other than marijuana. I've been down other paths and they weren't good for me."

I tilted my head, interested in what he was going to say next, curious as to how similar our pasts may have been. But he didn't elaborate.

"I think marijuana is a good thing. The main reason why it was outlawed in the first place is because the government couldn't figure out a way to make a profit on something that grew in America's backyard. If there were a way to control the marijuana market, it could greatly impact society in a positive way. Profits from that market could lead to improvements in the criminal justice system, education systems, healthcare industry, and it would even boost the economy. It's so odd that cigarettes, something that actually causes cancer are available in stores, but marijuana, something that has been scientifically proven to cure cancer, is illegal! This world is so twisted. Besides, they smoked in ancient societies, so why can't we?" He said emphatically.

I chuckled. It seemed we were more alike than I would have imagined.

"This woman in my Ethics class said that humanity is similar to cattle, a herd that follows a herd-like mentality. Most people don't actually know that marijuana can cure cancer because they've been told that it's a "drug" for so long. It's the same as how children in Darfur are brainwashed into becoming genocide soldiers. They just do what they are told. I hope one day people can decide for themselves instead of doing and acting on the words of others," I said.

James smiled as his dark eyes pierced into mine. His smile seemed too familiar, as if I had seen him somewhere before, and perhaps even had a conversation with him. I studied his face, trying to remember, but I couldn't. We continued talking quietly with each other and I felt very close to him, like our conversation was secret, intimate.

Natalie talked and everyone in the room was focused on her, leaving James and I to continue our own dialogue. The pretty redhead sensed his interest in me and huffed, standing up from the couch and crossing over to the guys at the pool table. She was clearly on a mission to find someone to shower her with attention. A wave of relief washed over me. James patted the empty seat beside him.

"Come sit here," he said.

The butterflies started flapping in my stomach again.

INGRID DARLING

"Okay." I said, squeezing from between Karl and the recliner and crossing over James to the seat next to him.

The redhead flashed me an evil expression then flipped her hair and turned her attention to the guys at the pool table who were now ogling her. I smiled to myself, happy to have her out of the picture.

"I was hoping you would have called me." He said.

I smiled shyly.

"I lost your number." I lied, too embarrassed to tell him that my nervousness had prevented me from calling.

"That's understandable. I tried to find you on Facebook, but I didn't know your last name. I don't even know your first name, come to think of it." He said.

"Ingrid. Ingrid Darling." I said, taking a deep breath, suddenly feeling very confident.

"It's nice to finally know your name, Ingrid Darling."

I watched his lips, lips that I wanted to kiss. I turned my head away from him and focused on the conversation within the group, hoping to distract myself from wanting to jump on James. Karl was talking now.

"So what's the point then?" He asked, stuffing a handful of popcorn into his mouth. "I mean, what's the purpose of it all if there's only death at the end. I mean, I spent my time in the Peace Corps only to leave feeling more depressed than before I enrolled into the program. There is so much pain and suffering going on in the world with war and political turmoil and we just turn the other cheek, let it happen. It's disgusting." He said, talking and chewing simultaneously.

"There is a point to life, and especially to keeping mankind from extinguishing itself. That's ultimately the reason as to why you joined the Corps. Isn't that right?" Scott said.

"I guess." Karl sighed, reclining back in the big chair.

"Who was it that said "man can find a justification of his own existence only in the existence of other men"?" Scott asked.

"Simone de Beauvoir, she was an existentialist like Jean Paul Sartre." Karl said.

The guy in the glasses nodded.

"That's right. Her work constantly forces the reader to face the absurdity of the human condition. I just finished reading The Ethics of Ambiguity, intense stuff." He said.

"Totally intense! I mean, existentialism itself is some deep shit." Karl added.

"What is existence anyway?" Natalie sighed, relaxing back into Scott's body.

His legs were curled around her, holding her tightly.

"Existence is a state of being." James said.

He ran his hand over his head, eyes sparkling, mysterious. Everyone in the room turned to focus on him as he continued. He clenched his jaw. I stared at his lips, feeling myself being pulled by his energy. He was so sexy, I just wanted to kiss him. He kept talking.

"By spontaneously existing in the moment, it is possible to tap into that universal essence that flows and exists within all things and beings. We, and all in this world, are manifestations of that energy, bundles of potentialities that have come into being."

The guy with the glasses slumped back onto the couch. His movement shifted my body closer to James. I could feel his warmth. My arm brushed his and a tingling sensation shot through my body.

INGRID DARLING

He looked at me and smiled.

"The universal energy is limitless, only the physical body is bound to the earth, thanks to gravity, but that energy is also space and space is infinite," James said, looking back towards the center of the room.

"That's neat." Natalie said.

"It's a philosophy that's been around for ages," James added.

"Intense." Karl said, rubbing his eyes.

"Yeah, pretty dope." Scott said.

Everyone nodded. I brushed against James again, the connection of our bodies was strong. He must have felt a similar sensation because he lifted his arm and placed it over my shoulder, pulling me closer to him. I nuzzled deep into his body.

The discussion reminded me of both the conversation I'd had with Theresa the other week in Brooklyn, and the conversation about language that took place in Paris. I suddenly realized how every stage of my life lately seemed like a perfectly written paragraph in a thesis, or a book.

If my life were a novel, would James be the conclusion? I wondered.

Just then, the pretty redhead decided that she wasn't satisfied with the attention she was getting from the guys at the pool table. She sauntered over to the couch and took her seat on the arm, right next to James, shifting her hips to draw attention to her butt.

What a sneaky bitch!

James ignored her and continued talking.

The conversation carried on for another twenty minutes. The redhead was now desperately trying to get attention from James but he wasn't having it. I chuckled to myself and nuzzled in deeper, closer to him, happy that his arm was around me and not her. After a while Karl insisted he needed to go home and go to bed. He stood up, wobbling and rubbing his head and asked me if I was ready to go. My stomach gripped, I didn't want to leave yet. I hoped James would tell me not to go as I prepared to get up from the couch. As if he heard my plea, James turned towards me and asked if I wanted to stay longer, that he would accompany me back to my place if he had to. I agreed and Karl left, giving me a sly look before disappearing around the corner and down the hall. The front door thumped shut.

Another fifteen minutes passed and Scott and Natalie decided to call it a night, standing up from the floor and stretching. Scott made his way into the kitchen, grabbing the empty pizza boxes from under the pool table and throwing them in the trash next to the refrigerator. Natalie waved goodnight to everyone, and told me she was glad I came to her performance.

"Sure thing, it was great." I said.

She smiled then gave James and the redhead hugs before turning and disappearing down the hall. I heard her footsteps on the stairs. Scott appeared from the kitchen, waved goodnight to everyone and hurried down the hall and up the stairs after his girlfriend.

The redhead grabbed James' arm and leaned over to whisper something in his ear. He chuckled. My stomach knotted and squeezed. I tried not to show my jealousy. I glanced around the room, hoping to find someone to talk to, it was a lost cause. The guy with the glasses beside me was fixated on the TV, watching some show on the Discovery channel. The science teacher guy was laid out on the recliner, gut out, snoring. The four guys playing pool were now sitting on the floor in front of the coffee table, smoking what was left in the bong, also watching the TV. A feeling of panic gripped me.

Is James going to leave me here and sleep with the redheaded bimbo? What if he wants me to leave? What if I'm ruining his plans of fucking her? Shit, shit, shit!

Thoughts whirred in my head, and made me flush. I needed some air. I pulled away from him and leaned forward on the couch, about to stand and make a bee-line for the door.

Hail a cab and high-tail it uptown to my safe apartment, that way I won't have to think about James and the redheaded slut anymore.

But before I could stand, a strong hand grabbed my waist, sending a burst of sensation through my body, it was James. He pulled me back towards him and brought his face to my ear.

"You're not going anywhere," he whispered, sending chills down my spine.

I glanced over to the redhead who shot me another evil expression and stood up from the couch. She grabbed her coat from the back of the recliner Karl was previously sitting on and slung it over her shoulder. She walked haughtily past the four guys on the floor and disappeared down the hall, a second later the front door slammed. I smiled to myself, relieved she was gone.

"Oh? What if I needed to get some air?" I asked, dropping my voice to sound sexier.

He grinned and tickled my neck with his nose.

"I can give you all the air you need." He said, firming his grip on my waist.

I bit my lip. His touch sent fire through my body, heating my chest, arms, legs, insides. A feeling of desire exploded through me, I wanted him to hold me closer, to kiss me.

"That'd be nice, because I'm feeling kind of flushed right now." I said, flashing him a shy smile.

"Well, maybe if we found a different room, one where the air isn't so thick, you'll feel better." He said in my ear.

His breath tickled.

"Where'd you have in mind?" I asked, turning to face him.

He pulled back and gazed into my eyes. His eyes looked lighter now that I was so close to his face, more hazel. He seemed even more familiar now, and I was almost certain I had seen him before. I returned his gaze.

"My room is upstairs, we can chill out there for a little while. What do you think?" He said, trying to gauge what my reaction would be.

I hesitated and bit my lip. He opened his mouth to say something but didn't, his eyes focused on my lips.

God I want him to kiss me!

"Okay. That's cool." I said, trying not to sound too eager.

"Good." He said quickly, pulling away from me and standing from the couch.

The movement jolted me into the guy sitting next to me. His eyes tore away from the TV and up to James.

"You out, man?" He asked with a raspy voice, his eyes were glazed over.

James shook his head.

"We're just going upstairs. Feel free to hang out until whenever." He said, stretching his hands above his head.

His body looked so big, so masculine, from where I was sitting. The long sleeved shirt was fitted and pulling against the muscles in his back, showing their definition. He was so attractive. He turned around and gave me a questioning expression, as if he had been reading my thoughts.

"Are you ready to go upstairs?" He asked, grinning at the fact that he had just caught me ogling him from behind.

"Um, yeah," I said, tearing my eyes away from him, embarrassed.

I brushed my hair behind my ear, inching forward on the couch. He held his hand out, I received it and he pulled me up towards him. He walked over to the kitchen, putting the empty red cup from his other hand on the counter. I grabbed my coat and bag from the recliner and followed him down the hall and up the stairs to his room.

The upstairs hallway was narrow and dark. His room was at the end. I walked in after him and glanced around the room. A big poster of Gandhi was mounted on the wall over a narrow desk in the corner of the room. Beside the desk was a large window that came almost down to the floor, a plant sat in front of it. Stacks of books lined a small bookcase next to the door along with photographs of him in front of the Eiffel Tower, the Pyramids in Egypt, and in a gondola in Venice. I chuckled to myself at the irony of the places he had been, thinking about where I'd traveled to in the past. The walls were painted a deep red, almost brown. I felt connected to his room, comfortable in it.

"You can put your stuff on the chair over there." James said, pointing to the chair in front of his desk.

I walked over and threw my bag and coat on its' seat. Still

flushed, I decided to take my sweater off, which I also put on my pile of belongings on the chair. I turned around in time to see him close the door and take off his long sleeve shirt. His body bent with the movement, lifting the shirt he wore beneath it up slightly, revealing a perfect row of abs and a dark happy trail to his jeans. Excitement lit through my body. He threw the long sleeve shirt into a basket in the closet and sat on the edge of his bed.

"Feel cooler?" He asked, his eyes piercing into mine.

I took a deep breath, suddenly overwhelmed with a desire to run and jump on him.

"Yes." I said, lowering my eyes to my feet.

I slipped out of my boots and placed my bare feet on the cold hardwood floor. I only wore leggings and a tank top at this point, no longer feeling flushed. "Good. Come over here." He said, gesturing for me to come to him.

I stood for a second, gazing at him. He looked so good sitting at the edge of the bed, his jeans fitted against his legs, the black t-shirt tight against his muscular torso. His face darkened by the dim lights. I walked towards his arms. He wrapped them around my body.

"I'm glad you showed up tonight," he said. "I was beginning to think I would never see you again."

"Really?" I said, suddenly angry at myself for having been too embarrassed to call him.

"Yeah. I thought you were so cute that day I met you in the library. You were talking to Dr. Bernstein and were really engaged in your conversation. Most girls aren't interested in topics like that, but you were really into it. I really liked that about you." He said, looking into my eyes.

"Oh." I said, not knowing what else to say.

"I should've gotten your number then, but I couldn't tell if you were interested in me or not, so I didn't." He said.

His eyes lowered, revealing a hidden shyness.

He did want to see me!

I instantly felt relieved. He looked back up to me, focusing on my lips. I opened my mouth, hoping he would follow my lead and kiss me. He did. His lips felt so good, so soft. We kissed softly first, then more passionately, his hands gripping my waist, feeling up my shirt, pulling it up and over my head. My tank top was now off and lying on the floor. I stood in front of him with my lacy black bra and leggings, barefoot, and kissed him on his shoulders and biceps as he kissed down my neck and the tops of my breasts. Without warning, he stood and hoisted me onto his hips. I gasped, wrapping my legs around his waist. He sat back down with me now sitting on top of him, kissing me and pulling at my pants.

"I want these off." He said.

"Me too!" I cried, practically begging for him to peel them off of me.

I wanted him so much, so intensely. I had never felt such passion for someone before.

This is crazy, why am I acting like this? I thought, but suddenly realized that Thomas was the last person I'd had sex with, which was more than a year ago.

I pushed James back onto the bed and straddled his hips, kissing his lips intensely.

"Then let's get them off." He said, pulling his face away from mine and turning his attention towards relieving me of my pants.

INGRID DARLING

In one movement, my pants joined my shirt on the floor, leaving me straddling James in my lacy underwear.

"Whoa." He gasped, glancing at my panties and bra.

His eyes landed on mine and I smiled and leaned down to kiss him again. His hands felt down my waist and pulled me onto him. The movement created a blast of electricity through my body. He hoisted himself up and flipped me onto the bed.

"You are beautiful." He said, pausing to look down at me.

I blushed and dropped my hands to the bed. His eyes locked into mine, holding his gaze longer than I expected. I stared back at him, feeling more connected to him than I had with anyone else, like I was a part of him, like I touched his soul. He bent over and ran his hand through my hair, kissing me softly on the forehead.

In one motion his pants were laying on the floor with the rest of my clothes. He reached over to the small bedside table, pulling a condom out of the drawer. I looked over my head at the table, which had a framed picture of James and an older woman, I assumed it was his mom. He was grinning proudly in the photograph, his arm wrapped around the woman. She smiled gently, in a very ladylike poise.

"That's my aunt," he said following my gaze to the photograph.

"Oh." I said, returning my eyes to his which were now focused on opening the condom and pulling his boxers off.

"She was my favorite aunt. Breast cancer took her." He said, throwing his boxers to the growing garment pile on the floor.

"I'm sorry." I said, suddenly aware of his compassion.

Heat rose in my body again. I felt so close to him, closer than I had with any other person, like we were the same soul, in two different bodies.

"It's alright. She's in a good place now." He said, smiling to me.

He ran his fingers through my hair again and kissed my lips. I pulled his body close to mine until he was lying on top of me, his body was warm and strong, his erection pressing hard against my inner thigh. The butterflies flapped hard and fast inside of me, anticipating the arrival of James to take them to ecstasy.

We had sex, incredible sex, for an hour and a half. My body twisted and contorted in ways and positions it never had before, accommodating his size and sexual appetite. By the end, my mouth felt like cotton and I was drenched in sweat. He too was dripping, worn out from our exhausting performance. We laid on the bed, huddled close, staring into each other's eyes. He kissed me on my forehead, my nose, my cheeks, tasting the perspiration on my face.

"You're incredible," he said, running his hand down my waist and wrapping it around my body, pulling me closer to him.

"You're not so bad yourself." I said, smiling, feeling more secure about being naked and sweaty in front of him.

I kissed his shoulder and bicep and snuggled closer to his chest. I felt a twitch between my legs from him.

"I want to go again." He said.

I smiled and bit my lip, looking into his eyes.

"I'm too tired, how about another time?" I said, hoping it was the right thing to say.

In truth I wanted to jump on him again, to ride him until the sun came up, to make love until we were too tired to move, but I didn't want him to think I was too easy. Refusing sex was the only way for him to realize that he had to gain my trust, to pursue me, if he wanted me in his bed again. He raised his eyebrows, showing a look of confusion, as if he had never been refused a round of great sex before, but he smiled.

"Okay," he said. "At least I know I gave you a good ride."

He winked and hugged me tight.

"Oh, trust me, you definitely did!" I giggled, inhaling the scent from his body, sweat and pheromones.

I smiled and closed my eyes, feeling myself drift away. I thought about the conversation we had just had downstairs.

What is existence? What does it mean to be an experienced being, and how were these experiences important in our lives?

I thought about my experiences. How each one felt like a different world, like a dream, and I was finally waking up. My thoughts drifted to the past, to Thomas, and how I'd never felt this way with him.

What does James mean to me? I asked myself, but before I could hear the answer, sleep took over.

INGRID DARLING

Thirty-One

Halloween

I carefully applied the lip gloss to my lips and smiled into the mirror. I stood back, glancing at my entire outfit: the dress, the cape, the glasses, the wand. I chuckled to myself thinking it was appropriate for me to go to the party as Harry Potter especially since I'd spent the past year warding off demons and getting scarred in the process. Just then, I heard my phone buzzing from the kitchen. I ran out of the bathroom and grabbed it before it could go to voicemail. It was Jada, she would be at my apartment in ten minutes. I told her I was ready and to text me when she arrived so we could get on the road immediately to avoid any traffic between here and Brooklyn. Tonight was Theresa and Darryl's costume party, a party I had been excited yet anxious about since Theresa had told me Thomas would be there.

"I don't know if he's bringing his girlfriend, but I just wanted to warn you." She'd said.

I told her it had been almost a year since I'd seen Thomas and that I no longer had emotional feelings for him. She told me she was proud of me for being so strong and that I deserved to have good things in my life. She was a great friend.

I ran back into the bathroom, making sure my hair was in place and the rest of my makeup looked good. If I was to see Thomas tonight, I wanted to look amazing, I wanted him to regret leaving me for some girl who lived four states away, I wanted him to desire me so I could smile in his face and tell him that I was happy without him. I was happy without him. I'd met new people, learned new things, and understood myself more than I had when I was with him. Sometimes it takes stepping out of your comfort zone to truly understand who you are and what you want in life.

I thought about James, about how he made me feel when we were together, how different it was with him than it had been when I was with Thomas. But I hadn't seen James since the night I went to Soho with Karl, three weeks ago. I'd woken up the next morning with a headache and no toothbrush. I didn't want James to see me with messy hair and smeared makeup so I left before he'd woken up. I left a note on the nightstand with my number, telling him I had a great time with him, but he never called. I'd lost the business card with his number and was too embarrassed to search for him on Facebook. I figured I was just another one night stand for him, but it didn't bother me because I had changed that night. Being with him gave me hope that there was someone wonderful for me somewhere in the world, that I could find love with, whether it was with him, or someone else. I had hope now, something that was taken from me when Thomas broke my heart. But my wounds were healed now, I didn't need Thomas anymore, I was over him. I was now ready for the next stage in my life, open to new people and experiences. My phone buzzed again, a text from Jada.

I'm downstairs, it read.

A nervous knot tied itself in my stomach as I grabbed my purse from the couch and hurried out the door.

We arrived in Brooklyn at 10:30pm. The party had been

going on for an hour, which meant most of the guests were already there. Theresa answered the door wearing a blond wig with a bow, a blue dress and a white apron.

Jada and I laughed.

"Who are you?" I asked.

She smiled.

"Alice. *Whooo are youuu?*" She cooed.

"Harry Potter!" I exclaimed, twirling the wand in my hand. "So where's your white rabbit?"

"He's in the kitchen making more bourbon apple cider. You guys look great, come in!" Theresa said, ushering us inside her brownstone.

As I walked by her, something sparkled from her finger. I immediately grabbed her hand and noticed a beautiful emerald cut engagement ring on her ring finger. I gasped.

"Oh my gosh! When did this happen?" I cried.

Theresa smiled.

"This morning. We were going to make an announcement about it later on tonight." She said.

"Wow, that is beautiful." Jada said, leaning in to look at the ring.

"Thanks."

"I'm so happy for you." I said, pulling her into a tight hug.

"I was finally ready," she said. "But we'll talk about this later. Let's get some drinks."

The three of us made our way through the crowded hallway to the kitchen where we found Darryl in a full rabbit costume with the head sitting on the counter. I laughed and hugged him, telling him congratulations. He smiled and poured me a cup of apple cider.

INGRID DARLING

The bourbon was strong and took me by surprise. Jada, Theresa, Darryl and I stood talking for a few minutes. Jada asked about when they were planning to get married and Theresa said they hadn't discussed anything yet. She looked at Darryl lovingly, I was happy for them, they were meant for each other. I asked Theresa if Karl was coming to the party, she said that he hadn't responded to her invite so she'd assumed he wasn't. I looked around the room, hoping to see other people I recognized. Everyone was in full costume and it was hard to know who was who. One thing I did notice, Thomas wasn't there, not yet at least. I took another sip of my apple cider, hoping it would settle my nerves.

Music blared through the speakers as I danced with a knight in the middle of the room. It had been two hours since Jada and I had arrived and the brownstone was now packed with all sorts of characters. I spotted Theresa over by the bookcase and decided to give my feet a break to chat with her for a bit about her engagement. I squeezed through the crowd and met her, panting. She was talking to a girl dressed as a cat and stopped when she saw me.

"Harry!" She cried. "Having fun?"
"Yes. I've been dancing all night. Have you seen Jada?"
Theresa pointed over to the window.
"She's over there, dancing with a pirate."
I followed her direction and saw Jada dancing very close with a handsome guy in a pirate costume. I smiled then turned back to Theresa. The girl in the cat suit disappeared.
"So," I began, but she cut me off.
"Thomas is here." She said bluntly, looking over towards the kitchen.

INGRID DARLING

My stomach tightened and a chill crawled up my spine.

"Do I look okay?" I asked, quickly, not following her gaze.

I ran my hand over my hair, smoothing it behind my ears then adjusted the cape around my neck. Theresa looked me up and down.

"You look great," She said. "He brought that girl. Will you be alright?" She asked, giving me a nervous glance.

A wave of nausea swept over my body. I had never met Yvonne and I never wanted to meet her. I couldn't believe he had the audacity to bring her to my friend's party, especially when he knew I would be here. Betrayal swept over my body, reminding me of when he broke up with me, when he left the country with her and put all of those pictures up for everyone to see. He'd hurt me so badly and it still seemed as if he didn't care. I couldn't look in their direction so I kept my attention on Theresa. She looked me in the eyes, judging my expression. I suddenly felt very dizzy. I wanted to sit down.

"Ingrid, are you okay?" She asked again.

I nodded then felt a hand grip my waist. I jumped, startled. It was Jada.

"Thomas is here." She said promptly.

I nodded again, trying to force the lump in my throat back down.

"I need a drink." I said, steadying myself against the bookcase. I thought I would be ready to see Thomas, it had been almost a year, but I was nervous and I didn't want to get upset. My heart drummed in my chest.

"I'll get it." Jada said, quickly, then turned around and squeezed through the crowd towards the kitchen.

"Listen, Ingrid. If you want him to leave, just tell me and I'll tell Darryl. You're one of my best friends and I don't want you getting upset." Theresa said, grabbing my shoulder.

"I'll be fine. Can I just stay by you for a little while, I feel dizzy and I don't want to faint and make a fool of myself." I said, trying to compose myself.

She nodded. Jada came back a minute later with another cup of apple cider for me.

"I put extra bourbon in there for you." She said. "Are you alright?"

"Yes, thanks. I'll be fine." I said, taking a huge gulp of the cider.

The strong bourbon ignited my chest, dissolving the nausea. I suddenly felt better. I turned and glanced around the room. It felt like I was in dream, with all of the different characters and costumes, nothing seemed real, like I was in wonderland, like *I* was Alice. I spotted Darryl in his rabbit outfit in the corner near the kitchen, he was talking to two people in capes. They had their backs to me but I immediately figured it was Thomas and Yvonne.

I was right. The taller of the two turned to the side and I saw Thomas's profile, it looked as though he were dressed as some kind of sorcerer. Yvonne turned beside him and I noticed she had a witch hat on and was holding a broomstick. I couldn't see her face because she wore a long curved nose with a wart on its end. I wondered if she was pretty. I couldn't remember from the pictures I'd seen on Facebook but I assumed she was since Thomas left me for her. But it didn't matter what she looked like, her costume was appropriate for how I felt about her. She was a witch in my eyes, and she seemed to have cast a spell on my ex-boyfriend.

"I'm gonna go back and dance with that cute pirate." Jada said, breaking my attention away from Thomas and Yvonne.

"Yeah he's hot, and you two look great together in your costumes." I said, forcing a smile on my face.

"I know and he's intelligent. I might even let him see my buried treasure!" She winked. "Come find me if you need me." She said, slipping through the crowd to her pirate.

I nodded and watched her slink up to her new man. I sighed and thought about James, wishing he were here with me.

"So tell me about the engagement." I said, turning back to Theresa and taking another sip of the cider.

The dizziness had faded and I felt myself returning to normal. She and I talked for a few minutes about how Darryl proposed, places she was thinking about having the ceremony, and potential dates. The music was too loud for us to carry on a long conversation so finally we decided to dance and talk about it another time. We danced to a few songs, Darryl came over and danced with us, and I'd almost forgotten that Thomas was there. Almost.

As I squeezed through the crowd towards the kitchen to refill my apple cider, I accidentally walked directly into him. Initially I didn't notice because I held my head down, trying to avoid stepping on anyone's costume, but he said my name as I passed, stopping me in my tracks. I wanted to turn around, to punch him in the face and tell him he was an asshole, but decided that karma would handle that for me and it was only productive for me to be nice. I looked up, meeting his eyes, suddenly afraid that I would have feelings for him again if we spoke, afraid that I would cry and beg him to take me back, but I felt nothing. I stared at him for a few seconds before speaking.

"Hi Thomas." I said, flatly.

"How are you?" He asked.

A drunken Marilyn Monroe bumped into him, spilling her drink down his cape. I smiled to myself.

"I'm good. I hope you're well." I said, studying his face.

He looked different, as if he were not the same person I had dated for two and a half years, as if I were suddenly seeing him in a different light. I remembered how I'd felt about him when we first met, how I thought he was so handsome, so perfect. The difference now was glaring, as if I were an artist examining my work only to discover that I had failed to arrive at perfection. It reminded me of when we were in Italy, and how mesmerized I was by Michelangelo's David. Only now could I see the flaws, only now could I see that his head, hands and feet were disproportionate to the rest of his body. I hadn't read the caption on the base of the statue, but Thomas had, and he told me once we'd left the museum that David's proportions were not quite true to human form, but I hadn't listened. I didn't want to believe that my statue of perfection was indeed imperfect.

"I'm well, just finishing grad school." He said.

I nodded, lowering my eyes. A hand slipped around his waist, I figured it was Yvonne. My heart skipped. I raised my eyes again to his and gave him a half smile then turned towards the kitchen.

"Good for you." I said, whisking through the crowd.

He wasn't perfect, and just as David was the model for the statue of an adolescent boy, the somewhat over defined features rung true in their natural rendition of a boy not quite fully grown. I pushed into the kitchen and walked straight over to the apple cider bowl, thinking how my feelings for Thomas had changed, how he wasn't the person I fell in love with, that he was still just a boy trying to become a man. I poured myself some apple cider, suddenly feeling very compassionate towards Thomas, as if I understood why he made the decisions he made. It was because he was lost, he hadn't found himself yet and I could see it. It took getting my heart stepped on, shrinking sizes, and almost drowning in a sea of tears for me to figure out who I was. Thomas still had a long way to go and I felt bad for him. Theresa appeared next to me.

"I just saw you talking to Thomas." She said, adjusting the wig on her head. "Everything okay?"

I nodded.

"Yeah, but it was weird, I felt nothing for him." I said, taking a sip of my drink.

She smiled.

"You guys had what I call a heartless bureaucracy. Everything looked great on paper, but there was no democracy beneath the surface. It seems like you two are very different people who just looked good together."

"Yeah I think you're right." I said, thinking about how Thomas and I differed on opinion, on belief, and on life in general. I wondered if he had substance with Yvonne then quickly decided that it was none of my business.

"You'll know when you've found the right person. I knew when I did." She said, refilling her cup with cider. "Besides, you're a wizard and we both know that wizards and sorcerers can't agree on anything."

She smiled and winked then disappeared into the crowd.

INGRID DARLING

Jada and I stayed at the party for another hour. She and the pirate exchanged numbers and planned to go on a date sometime the following week, she told me in the car on the way home. I was happy for her. I told her I bumped into Thomas and I no longer had feelings for him. She told me that was how it was, that sometimes time is the best thing for a broken heart. I twirled the wand in my hand. She was right, time had given me the chance to know myself better and learn to forgive Thomas. I was glad he refused to respond to my emails, glad I was given the space to realize that he wasn't the one for me. My dad once told me, "if a door refuses to open, let us accept not opening it and then we are free". Thomas had closed the door on me and freedom was with me on the other side. I chuckled to myself at his costume, at Yvonne's, at mine. We all chose characters that could do magic, but magic couldn't mend a relationship, and it certainly couldn't keep one. I wondered what would happen to them if they lost their wands. I rolled the passenger window down, a blast of cold air swept through the car. I tossed my wand out into the night. I didn't need mine anymore, I didn't need to do magic because I had myself and that was all that mattered.

INGRID DARLING

Thirty-Two

November, 2009

The next day was Sunday. I awoke early and went to breakfast by myself. I sat in the booth at Jive's, thinking about Thomas. I'd held onto his things after we'd broken up as a way of holding onto the time we'd shared with one another. Though I didn't want to be with him anymore, I guessed keeping his belongings was a subconscious attachment I still had to our long extinguished relationship. I had no need for them now, I had no need for him now, I was free. After breakfast, I returned to my apartment, and spent the next two hours rummaging through my closet for anything that belonged to Thomas, reminded me of Thomas, or had been given to me by Thomas.

I filled three large trash bags with clothes, shoes, magazines, DVD's and pictures. Theresa called while I disarranged and asked if I would be the maid of honor in her wedding. I told her I would love to and that I was finally getting rid of Thomas' things so it was best if I talked to her later. I could hear her smile through the phone and she said she would call me tomorrow with the wedding details. I hung up with her and tied off the trash bags, leaving them at the front door to take to Goodwill in the morning. I wandered through my apartment, which suddenly felt full, despite the blank spaces on the walls and bookshelves. It was clear that I had been filling my life with things and people rather than replacing the void with self knowledge and inner peace. I had found my peace now and it was satisfying. My phone rang again, it was Emerald. I silenced it, deciding to call her in a few hours, after I'd rearranged my apartment.

    I began with the bedroom, moving my bed from one wall to the other and replacing the empty spaces on the dresser with pictures of myself and trinkets from my travels. I sorted through my drawers and found the leather journal Thomas had given to me for my birthday two years ago. My first thought was to toss it along with the rest of what he had given me, but I hesitated, opening the cover and glancing through the pages. I read through the poems I'd written and dreams I had recorded several months ago. I sat at the edge of my bed, thinking of the transition I had been through in the past few years, how I had grown into myself and that it felt like I had been born again.

    I sat for twenty minutes, thinking, meditating in my thoughts. Then I suddenly felt compelled to write. I always had a problem getting my thoughts out, always had a block on my mind, but for some reason my thoughts were momentarily clear, on the tip of my tongue, ready to be recorded. I rummaged through my dresser for a pen and tossed the cap onto the bed, ignoring where it landed. I positioned the journal on my lap, prepared to write. I didn't know who I was writing to or what I was going to write about. It was as though my hand just moved and my soul did all the writing for it. They call it automatic writing, when you let your thoughts do the talking for you. So I let my inner voice speak as I scribbled into the leather journal. This is what I wrote:

    I don't know what is going to happen in the future. It's not meant for me to know. If I knew everything before it happened then it would defeat the point to life, which is to grow and understand and learn about myself as a part of this universe. I believe that everything in life is meant to happen exactly as it does. People walk in and out of your life at the moment they are supposed to, as a guidepost towards your own self-discovery. We all experience life differently and if we are astute enough to see the signs, then we will see that our experiences together are what make each of our lives connected. Bonded with the purpose of preserving humanity, of protecting ourselves against our weaknesses, and strengthened by our unity, our compassion, and our universal love towards one another. We are all manifestations of that love, of that energy. We are bundles of potentialities that have come into being, here on earth. That is why every moment is sacred and we are divine. Our divine self does not judge experiences; it just sees them for what they are, moments in time when we get to play at being human.

I have discovered who I am. My metamorphosis happened in North Carolina, in Manhattan, in Paris, London, and Italy, but mostly in my heart. No longer a slave to my passions, I have found myself within myself. Through the ups and downs, the highs and the lows, I have come out on top, free and complete. I have discovered my identity and no one can take that away from me, because I am me. I am Ingrid Darling.

I sat back onto the bed and held the pen in my hand, shaking, staring at what I had just written. I had no idea where the words came from, why I suddenly had the urge to write all of what I wrote, but I didn't question it. Stunned, I closed the journal, whose pages were covered on both sides with my small, neat handwriting, and placed it on the surface of the dresser.

I'll have to read that later, I thought, still confused by my compulsivity.

It was as if my inner voice was telling me everything I had neglected to pay attention to during the past few years of my life. I'd had so many ups and downs, met good people and not so good people, and it was all a lesson for me, to teach me more about myself. Every experience taught me what I needed to know to be a stronger person, and every person taught me what I needed to know to understand who I was. I thought about a quote that I had heard once that said, "if you know how to listen, everybody is the guru", and it was absolutely true because everyone I had encountered was a reflection of myself.

I thought about Karl and Jada, about Theresa and Darryl, about Anna and Lark, Thomas and James, about Emerald and my family. Every one of them impacted my life in a way for me to learn, whether it was forcing me to grow intellectually, or pushing me to develop spiritually. I loved all of them for that, despite whatever selfishness or selflessness was behind their actions. I sat and thought for a few more minutes, thinking about my friends and how little they knew of the impact they'd had on my life. I wanted to tell them, to let them know how much I cared for each of them, how much they'd shown me who I was. I walked back into the kitchen and found my phone, two more missed calls: Jada and Karl. I smiled to myself at their sagacity, then I called Emerald.

The next week went by fast. We discussed our final exam essay in Ethics. Dr. Bernstein, who'd shortened the paper from

INGRID DARLING

3,000 to 2,500 words, claimed proper reasoning rather than word count would provide the best results. I decided to start drafting for the essay, and by Sunday I'd already written 600 words. I included what I had said in class a few months ago in response to the discussion on free will and the ambiguity of the human condition, how people were constantly searching for freedom in the everyday as a result of understanding the uncertainty of their circumstance. How man learns from his own experiences that it is best to trust himself than allow outward impressions and influences to direct the course of his own actions. That the problem with humanity was that it was easiest to be a mere sheep in the herd, to follow one another like cattle than it was to exercise one's own free will. It is fear that prevents man from becoming aware of his own truths and abilities.

I thought about my fears. I was afraid of vulnerability, which was why I closed myself off to happiness once Thomas walked out of my life. I was afraid of rejection, which was why I hadn't called James. I was afraid of myself, which was why I had masked my fears with cocaine and other drugs. I remembered what Karl had told me, how man fashions a truth for himself that his material goods will provide him with the ultimate comfort, the ultimate freedom, but in actuality he becomes a slave to his passions and ignorantly perpetuates its dominion over his life. I had been a slave to my passions. I knew those material things, even the satisfaction I found in another would not provide me with the ultimate comfort. I knew it was only a substitute for that true inner peace. I had forgotten what inner peace was, I allowed my soul to escape my body, I had gotten lost. Careful observation of my life over the past four years helped me understand my own ambiguous nature, helped me with my own grasp on reality, on life, on happiness. I wouldn't find happiness in things; I wouldn't find happiness in another, unless I found it first in myself.

On Monday I scheduled a meeting with Dr. Bernstein to discuss my draft thus far. He smiled at my comprehension of the material as well as my ability to produce an accurate essay based on real life experiences. He said that it was Plato's idea to create a school where people could learn what they inherently knew but had somehow forgotten, and that it was rare for a student to display such wisdom. I told him that I only learned from my experiences and that in truth, we can only learn from what others help us see within ourselves. Before I left his office he asked me if I had understood the quote he'd mentioned to me in the library at the beginning of the semester. I responded, saying I'd learned that ignorance is slavery, self knowledge is the truth, and only the truth can set you free. He sat quietly for a moment studying my face. Then with the slightest admiration, he smiled and nodded. I gathered my belongings from the desk opposite his, nodded in response, turned and walked out.

I returned to my apartment after the rest of my classes, feeling good about myself. I set my tote on the kitchen table, slipped out of my boots, and unraveled the scarf from my neck. It was late in the afternoon and I had skipped lunch, so I was hungry. I walked into the kitchen and stood staring at the refrigerator, debating on whether to make a sandwich or order take out. I lifted a magnet from the door and my class schedule fell to the floor, revealing a taped business card beneath it:

INGRID DARLING

James Frederick Blake, Asset Manager.

I gasped, suddenly remembering that it had been there since the day we met, but having started school, I'd completely forgotten about it. And since the refrigerator door was now covered with schedules and papers and pictures of my friends, I hadn't even noticed it was there, right in front of my face. I tore the card from the door and walked over to the kitchen table. I pulled the laptop from my tote and flipped it open.
It's time to face your fears, Ingrid.
I figured a phone call was too direct, and since it'd been a several weeks since I'd seen him, I didn't want him to answer and forget who I was, so I decided to write him an email. I sat in the chair, arms crossed, staring at the screen. I didn't want to sound too forward, but I didn't want to be vague either.
Honesty is probably best, I concluded, and then proceeded to write.
I wrote that he had been on my mind since the day we met, that I had been afraid to contact him but my feelings towards him were stronger than they had ever been for a person. I told him how he had been in my dreams, how his face graced my thoughts every day, how I wanted to see him again and if he felt the same, would he want to see me again. I told him that the only reason why I was writing him this email was because I felt it was best to be honest with him, that I wanted to see him again, and I hoped to see him again. I concluded by asking him to respond if he felt the same, but if he didn't, it would be alright. I added my signature, read it once, read it again then finally pressed send. Being so open in the email was slightly embarrassing, but I was glad I had done it. And in truth,

if he didn't respond, I would be alright, because I was comfortable with myself now. I knew who I was, and that was most important. I closed the laptop and threw out the business card, deciding that if I were meant to be with James I would, whether I had his information or not. Then my stomach grumbled, so I made a sandwich.

INGRID DARLING

Thirty-Three

Thanksgiving

I helped my mom set the table for dinner. We were having our entire extended family over to dine at our house for the evening, so my parents were rushing around; making sure everything was in place. Content to help, I took the liberty of decorating the living room, dining room, and den while my mom and aunts cooked in the kitchen. As my cousins and grandparents arrived, I greeted them at the door, taking their coats and welcoming them for the evening.

My uncle who'd given me the makeup kit told me I looked beautiful, that I was glowing and there was no need for anything God hadn't already given me. I smiled and apologized for being so rude the last time we spoke. He accepted, saying that some people just get lost on their way to the light and act out, out of helplessness, but it seemed I had found my map again. Then he winked and disappeared into the den.

After dinner I sat in the living room with my mom. I told her that I was happy and that I now understood what my dream meant. She smiled and told me that she'd had faith in me and that she knew I would eventually hear what my inner voice was trying to tell me. She said that God works in mysterious ways, and the only path towards understanding those ways is to first understand your self.

"You are the only one who gets to be you," she said, "So make sure you know who you are."

INGRID DARLING

I told her that I knew who I was now and how grateful I was for every person and every situation that helped along the way. She responded by saying that every moment in life is meant to guide us to a newer, better stage, and I was now ready for everything great that would soon come for me.

I returned to New York two days later. Despite the turbulence, the flight in was the calmest flight I'd ever had. The woman who sat next to me on the plane stayed on my mind for the rest of the day. Her curiosity about my book became my biggest lesson because I had always known the path, I had just gotten lost. My journey could continue now that I found the way again.

After unpacking my bags, I opened my laptop to check my school email, of which I'd received an approval letter from my French professor agreeing to advise my research course next semester. I breathed a sigh of relief, thinking how difficult it would have been to find another professor willing to undergo such extensive research, in French no less. Then I opened my personal email once I'd responded to my professor and gasped. The first email in bold was from James. My stomach fluttered, butterflies. I hesitated before clicking on his response.

What if he says he isn't interested, that I was just a one night stand, that I didn't mean anything to him? I thought, embarrassment flushing my cheeks.

Part of me wanted to delete the email, to pretend as if he'd never responded. I couldn't get hurt again, I refused to be hurt again. But then the self-conscious feeling subsided and I took a deep breath, clicking on his email. Regardless of his response, I wouldn't let myself be upset. I had already had the most painful emotional experience I could have and now I was strong. Now I was healed. Now I was free. So I read the message.

>Ingrid,
>
>I'm sorry for responding to your email so late. I have been so busy with my research that I never made the time to check my other email accounts. I'm flattered that you've been thinking about me and I hope you know that I've been thinking about you. I wanted to tell you this but I first met you a few years ago at a New Year's party. I thought you were so pretty, but I was afraid to say something because you were with your boyfriend. I'm guessing that isn't the case anymore. You are such an interesting girl and I really want the chance to get to know you better. I had a great time with you the night you stayed with me and I think you are absolutely beautiful. I'd love to see you again soon. Let me know if you'd like that.
>
>James
>
>PS- If you're free, let's do something next week, we can talk about eternity and write stories without words.

I smiled as my heart raced wildly in my chest. There was no doubt about it: *James is definitely my conclusion.*

INGRID DARLING

Epilogue

November, 2010

I'm going home for Thanksgiving.
And this time, James was coming with me.
He and I have been together for almost a year now. After several successful dates, he asked me if I would be his girlfriend, which I agreed to with vigor. Soon after, I introduced James to Theresa and Darryl, who were married in late September at Theresa's grandfather's estate in England. I was the maid of honor, Jada was a bridesmaid. Jada brought her pirate from the Halloween party whose name I later learned was George. George owned a restaurant in Hoboken, New Jersey, so Jada quit her job as a hostess and moved across the water to be with her man. James and I moved in together, to a two-bedroom condominium in Tribeca. James' father owned several Real Estate companies and was generous enough to sell us one of his condominiums at a decent price. He even offered to hire me once I finished my studies at NYU.

Anna finally called me and revealed that she had gone on a spiritual quest to India by herself following her breakup with her boyfriend. She said she was tired of chasing men for their money and realized that wealth doesn't solve every problem. She told me she'd apologized to Karl and the two of them had been spending a lot of time lately. He even convinced her to join the Peace Corps. They would be going to Sudan in January.

After their honeymoon, James and I visited Darryl and

INGRID DARLING

Theresa in Brooklyn. After the four of us ate and talked for a while, Theresa pulled me to the side and asked if I'd heard about what happened to Thomas. I shook my head and asked her to tell me, sparing no details. As fate would have it, Thomas learned that Yvonne had been cheating on him for several months with his cousin, Martin. Once he'd learned about her unfaithfulness, he sold the engagement ring he prepared to give her and bought a one-way ticket to Buenos Aires. I laughed in disbelief while Theresa told me of his misfortune, remembering what I'd told him at his house on the night of the blizzard.

I told Emerald of Thomas' misfortune several days later over the phone. She told me it was inevitable that Thomas was going to learn what happened when he broke the Golden Rule.

"Karma has a way of paying off the deeds that are put forth," she'd said.

Once our conversation about Thomas ended Emerald told me that she was pregnant and expecting a girl in the spring. I scolded her for not telling me sooner, but was nonetheless happy for my friend. She and her boyfriend were going to get married after their daughter was born and she wanted me to be in the wedding. I agreed and told her I would see her while James and I were in town for Thanksgiving. Before we hung up, she asked if I'd heard from Lark.

"No, why do you ask?" I said, curiously.

"Someone told me they saw her outside of a homeless shelter one day. She apparently looked strung out on heroin or crack or something of the sort," Emerald said.

A lump raised in my throat.

"That's terrible. I hope she's alright," I said, realizing that it'd been four years since I'd last seen Lark.

"I hope so too," Emerald said before we said goodbye to each other.

I spent the following few weeks thinking about Lark, about our past friendship, and how perhaps by forgiving her we would be able to rekindle the relationship we used to have. I realized that while I was angry at Lark for her actions against me, I was not mad at her, I was mad at myself for allowing another person to upset the peace within me. And now that I'd restored my peace, I could finally forgive Lark.

Since it was almost Thanksgiving and I would be returning home to North Carolina, I decided that I would call Lark while I was in town. I told James of my decision and he told me he was proud of my ability to forgive others' past mistakes.

Everything was in order for our departure the morning of our flight, the cab would arrive in a half hour to take us to the airport. James made some coffee while I sat at the kitchen counter and quickly checked my email. I opened my inbox, read through a message from my research professor then saw two emails from familiar names. The first one was from Jonah.

I haven't heard from him in years!

I smiled and opened the message. The subject line read: Forever 27.

Hey Ingrid, I heard you were in school at NYU and traveling all over the world these days. That's really cool. I'm still bartending, not really sure what I'm gonna do next, thought about going back to school for business so I can own my own bar someday. Anyway, I'm guessing you heard the news. It's really unfortunate, Lark had a good heart. I guess she was our forever 27. Hopefully I'll see you soon.   Jon

Huh? What news?
I closed the message as confusion clouded my mind. I rolled the mouse over the second email, which was from Lark's sister Gabrielle.
I haven't heard from Gabby in almost 7 years! I thought, puzzled and worried.
I read the subject line before clicking on the message.

To those who have loved, is how it began.
As you all know, Lark was my very dear, very brave older sister. She passed yesterday morning in the home of her boyfriend. She was found in the bathroom slumped over the tub with a syringe in her hand and a bottle of pills at her feet. The pills were the medication she was taking for her depression and the syringe I need not explain. My sister, unfortunately had a disease, and that disease ultimately killed her. I am horrified and saddened to discover that my beloved Lark was a heroin addict, supplied to her by the very person she lived with. And though Lark was as much at fault for her mistakes, her life should never have been taken at such a young age. I ask for your prayers to my family for our loss and I ask that you take heed the lesson her death has brought forth. I loved my sister very much and she will be sorely missed.
Peace and Love,
Gabrielle Johnson

I stared at the screen, unmoving. A deafening silence echoed through the room as I read the message again.
What!? Lark is dead?
My mind raced and my heart quickened its' pace.
James poured some coffee in a mug and slid it along the counter to me, but suddenly noticed my blank expression and stopped. His mouth moved to say something, but I couldn't hear him. I could only hear the drum of my heartbeat in my throat and between my temples. I could feel the color draining from my face. James placed the coffee pot on the counter, sat down next to me and touched my shoulder.

"What happened?" he said, but the sound was distorted.

The only thing I heard was my thoughts.

Lark is dead? Lark is dead! Lark is dead.

I shook my head in disbelief, ignoring James plea to tell me what had happened.

"What is going on?" He finally demanded, jolting me from thought.

I quickly skimmed the message again, hoping I'd read something wrong, hoping it was a joke and everything was really alright.

"L-Lark died," I stammered once I realized I'd read the email correctly.

"Oh no!" James said in a distressed tone. "I'm sorry to hear that. How did she die?"

"Heroin overdose."

My voice quivered. I covered my cheeks with my hands and closed my eyes. I felt James' arms wrap around my body, he hugged me tightly.

INGRID DARLING

"I-I need to call my mom," I stammered, opening my eyes and reaching for my phone.

I called my mom and told her of the news. She said she just heard as well and wanted to wait until I was in North Carolina before she told me.

"The wake is in a few days, so you will be able to attend while you're in town," she said.

Her voice quivered as well.

"Okay, James and I will go," I said.

She told me she loved me and wished me a safe flight, then we hung up. I placed the phone on the counter and closed the laptop. James stood and began moving our luggage to the door.

"I'm so sorry to hear about Lark, Ingrid. If you'd like, we can visit her family while we're in North Carolina," he said.

I nodded and thanked him, still in awe of the tragic news. I sat at the counter for several more minutes, unmoving. Tears welled in my eyes and rolled down my cheek. I was sad for Lark, sad that she and I never had the chance to rekindle our friendship, sad she was taken in such a terrible way.

She deserved better.

A few moments later, James alerted me of the taxi's arrival.

"I'll bring the luggage down, take your time sweetie," he said, shuffling our bags out the door.

I wiped the tears from my face and put my phone in my purse. I glanced over the counter for anything else I may need before we departed and noticed the coffee mug sitting next to the laptop. I picked up the mug and studied the caption around its' base.

Fortune sides with one who dares, it said.

INGRID DARLING

Lark dared too much, I thought, crossing the room and grabbing my coat from the couch.

I slung the purse over my shoulder and walked towards the door. I glanced around the condominium once more, opened the door and walked out. I thought about Lark as I took the elevator to the first floor and exited the building. James was helping the driver load our luggage into the trunk of the taxi. I crawled into the backseat as her face flashed through my mind.

Lark was fortunate to live as long as she did, succumbing to her addictions and desires and never learning from her mistakes. I had learned once before, slumped over the tub in my own bathroom that you have to be careful, because as it turns out, fortune only smiles once.

INGRID DARLING

A Note from the Author

I began writing this novel in October of 2009, in hopes of capturing the essence of what I thought was important in all of the religious works, the philosophical ideas, and the contemporary theories of mankind throughout history. I hope my dream of a writing a novel that expresses everything I've learned has come to fruition.

Just as I have learned from my studies, I feel that it is essential for people to understand the history of humanity as a whole to realize our significance to each other. The future hopefully brings the world to a place where we have no need to harm one another because we have realized how special we are as humans. We need not be careless with our lives and the lives of others as it upsets the balance of nature. Cruelty should never be tolerated, even cruelty to ourselves. I hope we can come together as a species and disregard the cultural, racial, and sexual differences between each other because we are truly a collective spirit and we can only thrive as a whole.

About the Author

Nicole Burgess is the founder of NBM Publishing. She is author of *The Awakened Soul's Field Manual* and *Vérité*. An entrepreneur based in Chapel Hill, North Carolina, she creates stories that explore consciousness, transformation, and authentic living across books, film, theater, and podcasts.

Learn more at **www.nbmbooks.com**

www.ingramcontent.com/pod-product-compliance
Lightning Source LLC
LaVergne TN
LVHW091541070526
838199LV00002B/158